12/07

Hot Lunch

Alex Bradley

DUTTON CHILDREN'S BOOKS

DUTTON CHILDREN'S BOOKS
A division of Penguin Young Readers Group

Published by the Penguin Group
Penguin Group (USA) Inc., 375 Hudson Street, New York, New York 10014, U.S.A. | Penguin
Group (Canada), 90 Eglinton Avenue East, Suite 700, Toronto, Ontario, Canada M4P 2Y3 (a
division of Pearson Penguin Canada Inc.) | Penguin Books Ltd, 80 Strand, London WC2R
0RL, England | Penguin Ireland, 25 St Stephen's Green, Dublin 2, Ireland (a division of Penguin
Books Ltd) | Penguin Group (Australia), 250 Camberwell Road, Camberwell, Victoria 3124,
Australia (a division of Pearson Australia Group Pty Ltd) | Penguin Books India Pvt Ltd,
11 Community Centre, Panchsheel Park, New Delhi – 110 017, India | Penguin Group (NZ),
67 Apollo Drive, Rosedale, North Shore 0745, Auckland, New Zealand (a division of Pearson
New Zealand Ltd.) | Penguin Books (South Africa) (Pty) Ltd, 24 Sturdee Avenue, Rosebank,
Johannesburg 2196, South Africa | Penguin Books Ltd, Registered Offices:
80 Strand, London WC2R 0RL, England

CIP Data is available.

Published in the United States by Dutton Children's Books,
a division of Penguin Young Readers Group
345 Hudson Street, New York, New York 10014
www.penguin.com/youngreaders

DESIGNED BY IRENE VANDERVOORT

Printed in USA   First Edition

1 3 5 7 9 10 8 6 4 2

ISBN 978-0-525-47830-0

for Sarah Shumway and me
I mean Sarah Shumway and I
no, Sarah Shumway and me
wait—Sarah Shumway and he?
she and he?
them?
us?
ok, ok, ok
just for:
Sarah Shumway

Hot Lunch

1

Some Cans of Beans

rue, there was a moment, right after Ms. Valeri had explained the assignment and announced that everyone should select a writing partner, when I knew I should pay attention and at least try to find a partner who I didn't hate. But it was, after all, the first hour of school on Monday, and I was awake only marginally, and my stomach was knotted up in a distracting way that seemed to communicate that maybe *two* Twix would have constituted a decent breakfast, but one Twix most certainly did not. If I just sat tight, maybe I wouldn't have to choose a partner. I could be my own partner. Molly, meet Molly. So I just sat there, doodling a vine up the margin of my notebook while my classmates moved about the room, choosing partners.

Seth Lawson crouched next to me. He was wearing his tuxedo T-shirt again. "Molly," he said, "wanna pair up?"

"No," I said. "I most certainly do not."

"Fine," he said. He left.

When everyone else had found a partner, Ms. Valeri stood at the front of the room with Cassie Birchmeyer and asked who else remained unattached. I sighed loudly.

"Molly?" Ms. Valeri said.

"Bring it on," I said. "I am so ready for my partner."

Cassie eagerly pulled her desk over to mine. The desk made a tremendously loud screeching noise as she moved it.

"Hey there!" Cassie said, sitting down. "I'm glad we're partners!"

"Why?" I asked.

"Well, I've always liked your hair," said Cassie. "It's so . . . blue. Did you dye it yourself?"

"My cat helped," I said.

"Your cat . . . ," Cassie said, confused. Then she laughed. "That's a joke."

"No it's not," I said. "My cat is a certified hair colorist."

What I knew about Cassie was almost nothing, and I liked it that way. But the things I did know were unappealing. First, I knew that Cassie was relatively new to Sunshine Day High School, having arrived near the end of last semester—April, I think—and that she still didn't quite fit in—not because she was odd (Sunshine Day was peopled with an astonishing collection of freaks), but because she was *normal*. Therefore, on the one hand I liked that Cassie was different *(normal)* from most of Sunshine Day, but on the other hand I didn't like it because normal, in my opinion, is just a polite way to say completely loathsome. Plus, Cassie was too tall and too blond and too athletic. And she was the only member of the girls' golf team, which struck me as obviously perverse in just so many ways.

We looked at the handout Ms. Valeri had given us.

Survive It or Not!

You and your partner are standing on opposite sides of an ice-cold river in the middle of a vast wilderness. You each have a limited number of supplies (listed below). Your task is to pool your resources, cross the river, and survive for a week. *Only together can you prevail!*

Together, write two pages describing how you will succeed. As with all Flash Assignments, this response must be e-mailed to me by midnight tonight.

Good luck!

I looked at my list of supplies: some cans of beans, a camping cookstove, a rope, four ski poles, a bag of sand, a magnifying glass, scissors, swimming goggles, two toothpicks, and a large beach ball with a pea-size hole in it. Great. What the frick, bro? How could that worthless collection of crap be any use to anybody anywhere at any time? I, for one, felt uninspired. I wasn't so sure I really *needed* to cross the river.

"I'll read you my list," Cassie said, "then you can read me yours."

"Awesome."

"First, I've got a corkscrew, two toothpicks, thirty meters of dental floss—"

"Is it waxed?" I asked.

"Is it wa— . . . I don't know," said Cassie.

"Is it mint flavored?"

"It doesn't say."

"Then we should probably ask Ms. Valeri," I said.

"Really? Okay?" Cassie raised her hand. This was excellent. Cassie was gullible.

"We're wondering if this dental floss is waxed," Cassie asked Ms. Valeri when she came over.

Ms. Valeri leveled a look at me through her vintage granny glasses—her I'm-thirty-but-still-under-the-illusion-I'm-cool glasses. "No," Ms. Valeri said. "It's plain floss." She left to help other students.

The remaining items on Cassie's list were two sleeping bags, a box of granola bars, a canister of propane, a can opener, a poncho, a knife, and a bow with no arrows.

"Look," I said, "we've both got toothpicks. So I propose we just sit across the river from each other picking our teeth and enjoying the sunshine."

Cassie looked at the assignment, confused. "But it doesn't say anything about sunshine . . ."

Later that night, Cassie and I were IMing. After school, Cassie had invited me to her house to work on the assignment—ha!—but that sounded like the worst idea possible, and she lived on the far side of Hillsdale, so I proposed an IM-a-thon instead. I liked the idea because it meant I didn't have to see Cassie, hear Cassie, or smell Cassie's fruity shampoo. I was distressed, however, to discover that Cassie's IM name was !Cas!sie!.

We'd been IMing for at least fifteen minutes, and getting absolutely nowhere.

!Cas!sie!: What about the beach ball? Maybe you could float on it?

bLaRg: do i haf 2? why don't u just swim across?

!Cas!sie!:   But how would I bring the propane and other stuff?

bLaRg: don't forget da floss

!Cas!sie!:   Ha ha!

!Cas!sie!:   :)

bLaRg: u did not just :) me

!Cas!sie!:   ;)

bLaRg: buh bye

!Cas!sie!:   Hey, what does blarg mean anyway?

bLaRg: it's an expression of boredom and contempt

!Cas!sie!:   Neat!

bLaRg: like this: oh uh, here comes cassie. blarg.

The phone rang. I didn't recognize the number.

"Hey there!" said a girl. "It's Cassie."

"Oh. How'd you get my number?"

"It's in the student directory."

"We have a student directory?"

"I just thought we could figure out this assignment faster if we talked," she said.

I didn't like this. This was the kind of assignment, like most, that I normally would do half-assedly, or even quarter-assedly, and yet still manage to get a B+. I didn't like someone else, especially this perky and earnest Barbie, pushing me to do the assignment whole-assedly.

"Lookit," I said, "here's the dealio. Put the floss and the can opener in your pocket and swim the damn river."

"But we need the fuel and sleeping bags. Plus, it says the water is ice-cold."

"Well I'm not going to cross the river."

"But you've got a beach ball."

"With a hole in it!"

"You could plug the hole with your finger."

"And hold on with my other arm, and swim with *what*? My third arm? My prehensile tail?"

"We could figure out a way to patch the beach ball," Cassie said. "And you could dump the sand out of the bag and put the beans and the cookstove in the bag and tie the bag to you with the rope and then swim over."

"You're trying to drown me," I said.

"No, I—"

"Look," I said, "I'm not much of a swimmer."

"Then I'll teach you."

"I happen to think you won't," I said.

"Sure I will. I'm a lifeguard. I'll teach you to swim."

"From across the river?"

"Sure!"

"That's just dumb," I said. "Profoundly dumb. Like a black hole of dumbness."

"I didn't mean to—"

"Look, why don't you just swim the river and we'll be done with this stupid assignment."

"But I don't think—"

"New idea," I said. "I'm hanging up."

I hung up, but within a few seconds the phone rang. I answered by barking "Swim the river!" and then hung up again.

The phone rang yet again and I answered and this time Cassie started talking immediately. She said, "I really think that if we work together we can figure out—"

I hung up. See, this is why I hated group assignments: they meant trouble. It's like the teachers thought that in addition to heaping homework on us, they had to find a way to make the process of doing the homework as annoying as possible. Make us work with each other. It was a demented practice.

I looked at the phone on the bed beside me. It had been at least a minute since I'd hung up on Cassie the third time. That was good. I willed the phone to continue not to ring.

It rang.

I looked at it, thought about throwing it across the room, but went ahead and answered. "No!" I screamed. "Just swim the river before I come over to the other side and choke you!"

There was silence on the line for a moment.

"Molly?"

It wasn't Cassie.

"Yeah . . . ?" I said.

"It's Pappy."

My grandpa.

"Oh, hi, Grampa."

"Good night for yelling, eh?" he said.

"Sorry about that. Thought you were someone else."

"It's okay. I didn't understand it anyway."

He was calling me from downstairs. He'd lived in the guest suite behind the kitchen since last winter. My room, which had been my brother's before he went to college, was over the garage, and the distance between my room and Grampa's room was large, and therefore Grampa often called me on the phone instead of trying to yell up the stairs for me.

"Now," he said, "I see that it's eight in the P.M., and I seem to recall that we had an understanding that the two of us would engage in a certain game of wit and wordplay called Boggle at this precise hour."

"Sorry, sorry," I said. "I'll be down approximately immediately."

"Perfect!" Grampa said, and hung up.

I turned off my phone, put my laptop to sleep, pulled on a sweatshirt, and went downstairs. In his room, Grampa had already set up the game.

"So what are we playing for tonight?" I asked. We usually had some wager.

"How about if I win you have to call me Pappy?"

"We've been over that. I am not going to call you Pappy."

"How about Poppy?"

"Poppy makes you sound like a girl with freckles."

"What's so bad about that? Make an old man happy."

"No way," I said. "How about whoever wins makes the other person a deluxe root beer float?"

"Game on," he said.

I got back to my room about ten, my stomach full of root beer and ice cream (I'd lost, but that didn't mean I couldn't have a float, too). I turned on my phone. I had one voice mail. It was from Cassie's phone number. Great. I almost erased it without listening to it, but then I decided that I wanted to know how upset she was. I wondered if anyone had ever stood up to her before. But the message she left turned out to be about ten seconds of silence. What did that mean? What was *that*?

I checked my e-mail, but there was nothing. So I'd shaken off Cassie. So. Well. That was good. That was fine. Mission accomplished. I'd just write my own version of the assignment. It wasn't due for an hour and a half, which was plenty of time. Who needed Cassie Birchmeyer? I didn't. The *world* didn't. And who needed, for that matter, to cross the stupid fake river in the stupid made-up assignment? I knew for a fact that all Ms. Valeri cared about anyway was if the writing was any good, and I knew I was a good writer, and therefore I could do the assignment brilliantly on my own. That was fine. Everything had worked out for the best. Everything was great.

2

Wild Strawberries

Molly Ollinger
Sophomore Lit.

I tried to warn her. I tried to warn my partner. There I was, standing on the other side of the raging river, watching the huge saber-toothed tiger sneak up on Cassie Birchmeyer. Now, we all know that those saber-toothed tigers are terrific hunters. They know how to stalk their prey. Cassie was distracted, fussing with her poncho, her floss, and her can opener, and she just didn't see the huge tiger. I yelled and yelled, but Cassie didn't seem to understand the warning. The river was too loud. Then, unfortunately, Cassie was no more.

Wow! Who knew there were saber-toothed tigers in this place?

Sure I was sad. Then I got on with life. That's what you have to do. You have to focus on being alive. I looked at what I had. I had all those cans of beans. I had a magnifying glass. I had toothpicks. I also had scissors, which were a truly useful thing to have. Most of all I had myself. As far as I could tell, there were no saber-toothed tigers on my side of the river. In fact, when I started looking around, I realized that I was standing in the middle of a paradise. I was in a broad valley, with tall grasses waving in the breeze, and yellow flowers bobbing here and there. Fat bumblebees buzzed hither and thither. The weather was perfect! The sun was warm, the sky was deep blue, and there were bitty puffy clouds meandering about like so many wayward sheep.

I walked into the wilderness, away from the raging river. I walked, I breathed, I listened to the songbirds. In the distance, dark mountains rose, their snowcapped tops shining like diamonds. So I would venture there, I decided, to the mountains.

It was the kind of day that made you say, "Now, this I could get used to." I found a patch of wild strawberries in a meadow beside a lake. I ate strawberries, I drank from the lake. I clambered along the lakeshore and found a nice flat boulder where I stretched out and slept, warmed by the sun. I woke, ate more strawberries, then headed back out onto the green plain and toward the mountains. It was late afternoon, and my shadow was growing long. All around me, the emptiness was so full. I didn't know exactly where I was going, but I knew that I was in a great place and that I was headed to an even greater place, and that that's what mattered. I continued on, alone, into the wilderness. . . .

3

Floating, Individually Wrapped,
Chocolate-Dipped Caramels

To me, the fact that Ms. Valeri's so-called flash assignments were due at midnight, and that she graded them and handed them back the very next morning during first period, was depraved. It meant that Ms. Valeri had to either stay up late or get up very early to do the grading—she wouldn't admit which it was—and that kind of industry and commitment to the students was typical of the faculty at Sunshine Day High School, and something that I didn't really think was entirely necessary. I preferred that the teachers think about me less, care about me less, and leave me alone more. But usually they didn't. Such was life in a private day school founded by hippies.

Anyway, we got our papers back the next morning. I can't say that I was thrilled by my grade, but on the other hand, it was a passing grade. It would do.

I noticed that Ms. Valeri handed a paper back to Cassie, which meant that Cassie must have turned in her own version of the assignment, just like me.

Cassie hadn't tried to talk to me before class, and she didn't try to talk to me after class. I figured the whole episode was over. I could get on with the important business of passing the time.

When fourth period came, I happily settled into my normal chair in study hall. I always sat at a table in the corner of the room and had the whole table to myself. Study hall was my favorite hour at school, and I sat there with my headphones on, the collar of my puffy black vest turned up, and my textbooks tucked safely away in my messenger bag under my chair. I was waiting out the hour, per usual.

I had a rather enjoyable study hall until, with about ten minutes left to go, I heard someone sit down across from me. I looked up. It was Cassie.

"No," I whispered.

"No, what?" she asked.

"Whatever it is, the answer's no."

"But," she whispered, "I've decided that I'm sorry, and I wish we had a chance to do it all over so we could do it right."

I watched Cassie talk, then motioned to my headphones and shook my head.

"Can you take those off for a second?" Cassie asked.

I sighed and removed my headphones. They were huge headphones—I had found them behind my parents' *record* player—and I liked to wear them basically anytime I wasn't in class.

"Did you hear what I said?" Cassie asked, still whispering.

"You said off with the headphones," I answered, whispering, too.

"But before that."

"Possibly," I whispered.

Cassie's brow furrowed. She looked at my notebook. I'd filled one page with sketches of tiny butterflies, and the facing page with oodles of floating, individually wrapped, chocolate-dipped caramels. Oodles upon oodles. I could tell that Cassie didn't like them. Her brow furrowed. Then she closed her eyes and put her palms flat on the table. She opened her eyes and started again.

"I wanted to . . . ," she said. She paused. "I came over because I've decided I'm sorry and I wish we could do it over again."

I kept on sketching.

"*The team project*," Cassie clarified.

"Oh," I said. "That."

"I thought maybe," Cassie explained, "we could ask Ms. Valeri if we could try the assignment again."

Across the room, Mr. Fedder looked up from his desk. "Significantly quieter, girls," he said. He scratched his mustache. The man had more hair on his lip than he had on his head.

"We're sorry," Cassie said to him.

"I get it," I whispered. "You got a bad grade and you can't stand it."

"No, that's not—"

"So what did you get?" I asked.

"I'm not going to tell you."

"Because I got a D," I said. "And I'm okay with that. I'm just hunky-dory with that if it's the price I have to pay for not working with you."

"But . . . but couldn't we just ask if we could do it over?" Cassie asked.

"Why would I want to do it over again? It was horrible! You'd have to *pay* me to work with you again. Pay me a lot!"

Suddenly, Seth Lawson was crouching there beside us. Today he had on his "Superpoodle" T-shirt.

"Please!" he whispered. "You know the rules. Nothing above a whisper."

"We are whispering," Cassie whispered.

"Well, sort of," Seth said. "But really it's more like hissing. Really *loud* hissing."

"Why is it," I said to him, "that every time I turn around you're crouching beside me saying something that is exceedingly bothersome?"

"I'm just trying to remind you of directives agreed upon by the Students for Study Hall Interest Group," he said. "You know, SSHIG."

There was a whole thing going on about study hall this year. The teachers wanted to eliminate study hall because they said that American kids were now competing against Chinese kids and therefore there was just no time for slacking off. The students had been split on the issue: most of them truly did use study hall to complete homework, but they also *really liked classes and learning*, and thus the prospect of new classes (one of which was rumored to be a computer hacking class) was a thrilling one. Eventually, though, after much debate in the underground student newspaper, *When It's Noon Here, It's Midnight Somewhere Else*, this consensus was reached: study hall needed to be preserved as a sacred hour of homework time, and one of the most effective ways to demonstrate to the faculty that study hall must be kept was for the students to use their time there in visibly vigorous academic toil.

"You guys know how important it is that we show that study hall is not broken and doesn't need to be cut," Seth said.

I rolled my eyes. I turned a page and continued sketching.

"We're sorry," Cassie whispered to Seth.

"It's okay," he whispered back.

"We're both sorry," Cassie said.

This wouldn't do. This wouldn't do at all.

"Look: *I'm* not sorry," I said in a normal voice. "Not in the least." Then I got pretty loud. "So you can suck on it, Lawson!"

4

Oh God: The Hams

fter the bell for lunch rang, I headed upstairs to my locker. Sunshine Day was housed in what had once been an elementary school—right on the edge of downtown Minerva, Minnesota—which meant the whole building was basically just an upstairs and a downstairs, plus the cafeteria and gym sticking out the back.

Cassie bounded up the stairs beside me.

"Why'd you do that?" Cassie said. "That wasn't cool, getting us both in trouble by yelling."

"I personally thought it was supercool," I said, "so we're going to have to agree to disagree on that point."

"You're difficult, you know that?" Cassie said.

"I have been duly informed."

"You're almost impossible!"

"If you're trying to insult me, you need to put more into it than that."

"I'm sorry for *caring* or whatever," said Cassie, "but I just thought we could do the assignment right and fix this whole thing."

"There's nothing broken that I can see," I said, putting my stuff in my locker.

Cassie was looking at my locker.

"What are you looking at?" I asked.

"I've never seen a locker that messy," she said.

Of course it was the messiest locker Cassie had ever seen. Hers was probably tidy, decorated with teddy bear stickers, and scented with potpourri. My locker, which had been mine last year, too, was full of layers of old paper and lots of candy wrappers. So I said, "But I'm saving all this paper for this year's Recyclebration."

"Recyclebration?" Cassie said. "When's that? That sounds exciting."

"It isn't," I said. Then I remembered what I was here for. "Criminy," I said. "I forgot to bring my lunch." I had made it, I packed it, I put it on the kitchen counter, and then I left it there. Oh, my lovely little bag with my mustard sandwich, my candy bar, and my Capri Sun. "Now I have to eat the hot lunch. Blarg." I closed my locker—which Cassie was still staring at—and headed back down the hall. I looked back and saw Cassie standing there, arms crossed, chewing her bottom lip.

"Okay!" she finally called out. "I got a D, too!"

"D stands for *dang*," I said, disappearing down the stairs.

Then I heard Cassie scrambling down the stairs after me. She was like an evil puppy that followed me wherever I went.

"But I've never had a D," Cassie said. "And I don't deserve a D. Why should I get a grade that I don't deserve? Group assignments are stupid because smart people get lower grades than they deserve and dumb people get higher grades than they deserve and so who's that fair to? Nobody. That's what I'm saying."

"I think you just called me dumb," I said.

"No! No, I didn't!"

I put my headphones on.

"Stop that! Take those off! Can't you see that I'm trying to talk to you!"

"So talk," I said.

We walked along the lower hallway, and to my relief, Cassie seemed to be out of arguments. Silent Cassie was much more bearable than talking Cassie.

Why would I want to help Cassie? Honestly, no reason seemed evident. Sure, I wouldn't be totally distressed if I could somehow transform my D into a B, but I didn't really see any need to go out of my way to do that. And the fact that Cassie *wanted* to improve her grade so badly just made me more certain that there really was no way I was going to assist her in that endeavor. What about what *I* wanted? I wanted to be left alone, and she wasn't doing that for me, so why in the heck should I help her in her little grade-grubbing miniquest? Maybe a D would do her good.

We entered the lunchroom—sometimes called "the village green" because of its ugly, leaf green carpet and because we had our Before School Meetings and abominable Community Heart Searchings here. The lunchroom was already full, and in one corner that SSHIG group—Seth Lawson's little project—had its usual lunchtime protest going on. Today the protest consisted of six students lying prone under a huge cardboard tombstone that read: STUDY TIME—RIP. In the opposite corner, Brad

Berrington was getting out his acoustic guitar. Anybody could sign up for Noontime Expression, talent or no talent. Usually, the latter. You got a microphone and half an hour to do anything except incite violence.

The good news was that Dr. John, our principal, had propped open the door at the back of the lunchroom, which meant we had permission to eat outside if we wanted to. Thank goodness. I always ate outside if I could, because it meant I could get the maximum amount of separation between myself and everybody else.

"Molly!" Brad Berrington called as I passed near him. He was tuning his guitar. He was under the mistaken impression that since I had once told him he sounded like a "significantly sadder" version of Bob Dylan that I actually thought he was a good musician. "Any requests today?"

"Yes," I said. "Keep it quiet."

"I know a lot of quiet songs," he said.

I gave him a thumbs-up.

I got in the lunch line. Cassie was still right beside me.

"I have to tell you something," Cassie said.

"Still?"

"I already talked to Ms. Valeri, and she said the only way we can raise our grades is to do the assignment again the right way."

I paid the kid at the cash box—a freshman pip-squeak named Clyde Brewell. I took a lunch tray.

"Enjoy your lunch!" Clyde said cheerily.

"I'll try," I said.

"See, it's obvious you can hear what I'm saying, even with your headphones," Cassie said, "so I'm going to just keep talking. I don't see what's so wrong about me asking to do the assignment the right way. I don't know why you're not interested in accepting my apology and everything, and I don't—"

"You didn't apologize," I interrupted. "You told me that you'd decided you were sorry. That's not an apology."

I slid my tray across the stainless steel counter. The two lunch ladies ladled food—or something resembling food—onto it.

"No ham, please," I said to Marta Zetz, the head cook, but it was too late, and the oval of ham was already on my tray. "Okay, I'll take the ham," I said.

Cassie was gnawing her bottom lip again. "I'm not through talking about this," she said.

"I am," I said, and I reached into my vest pocket. "This is me turning up my music to drown out all further communication."

"No!" Cassie yelled. "Listen to me!" A few kids looked at her, but mostly the outburst was lost in the din of voices and Brad Berrington's pitiful guitar plinkings.

"Sorry, no can hear," I said. I picked up my tray—now loaded with dry-looking ham, wrinkled peas, unnaturally orange scalloped potatoes, pale applesauce, and a lopsided corn muffin. I walked to the big cooler and reached in for a pint of milk. Cassie followed me, silent.

This had gone too far. It was time for her to go. I would ignore her.

"I like milk," I said, shaking the little carton. Then I addressed the milk directly: "Boy, I sure like ya."

I noticed that Cassie, who was standing just a bit too close to me, was red in the face. It was possible that she was holding her breath. Her eyes were bright and fiery, and after watching me talk to my milk, she reached out, slowly—so slowly that I had a lot of time to think about what was about to happen—and gripped my huge headphones and then yanked them off. They clattered to the floor. No one in the lunchroom seemed to notice.

I stood there, my hair messed from the inappropriate removal of my headphones. I felt my skin flush. I could hear my heartbeat get louder and faster. I set my tray down on top of the milk cooler. I pushed my hair out of my face. I looked down at my headphones. I bent and picked them up, put them around my neck. Then I shook my carton of milk some more, opened it, took a drink, said "Ah!" and then reached out and poured just the tiniest bit of milk on Cassie's shoulder.

"Whoops!" I said. "Oh my gosh!" I said. "I *spilled* some." Then I poured the rest of the milk down the front of her shirt.

For several seconds, both of us stood motionless. There was a backup of four or five students who were waiting to get to the milk cooler.

Then, simultaneously, we were both in motion. I reached for another milk while Cassie simply lifted my tray of food and upended it over my head. It stunned me momentarily, but then I got the milk open and reached to pour it on Cassie again, but Cassie ducked away and the milk just roped through the air and splatted on the floor.

Cassie had already grabbed another student's tray of food before I even knew what to do next. I was then confronted with an airborne lunch—the hot flap of ham, the peas pelting my neck, the cold applesauce, the thunk of the muffin hitting my forehead. I realized that though the supply of milk at my side was sizable and accessible, it was essentially useless because I couldn't waste time opening lots of little cartons of milk. Still, I grabbed two cartons and lobbed them, unopened, at Cassie. They both missed, but that was okay—it provided a necessary distraction, and it gave me time to dash for a place of safety and endless ammunition. That is, I ducked behind the lunch counter.

Marta Zetz yelled, "Now I do not think dat we will be doing dat now!"

"Shut up!" I yelled, and I soon had handfuls of peas in the air, and Cassie was using a tray as both a shield and a baseball bat—hitting the peas back toward me—and looking around for something to throw.

Marta Zetz screamed again, "You will be stopping dis here!"

And then I was into the potatoes with both hands, and they were good because they threw easily and also flung a cheesy sauce, and I scored a direct hit on Cassie's face.

"Cheese!" she yelled.

"In your face!" I screamed.

Marta Zetz screamed, "I-do-not-know-what-you-think-dis-is-but-it-is-my-kitchen-I-am-here-dis-is-not-to-be-had-I-am-not-standing-for-it-and-you-will-stop!"

I thought I had this thing wrapped up. I thought I had things under control. After all, I had access to all the food I needed, and Cassie had nowhere to go for cover. But just as I lobbed a large portion of potatoes at her, she made a move, dodged the potatoes, and leaped over the lunch counter—quite spectacularly—and reached for the hams. Oh god: the hams.

"No!" I screamed. "I'm a vegetarian!"

"Tell that to these hams!" she yelled back.

Six hams hit me.

Marta Zetz cried: "I am lost!"

Cassie yelled: "I did *too* apologize!!!"

Then came chaos.

5

Peas Will Come Out of Ears

The last time I'd been sent to the principal's office was a long time ago, in another world altogether, really—a better world—and I'd gotten in trouble for an act that I perceived as honorable and which I'd planned and performed with my best friend, Patty Cable. Patty Cable! We were best friends from fourth grade until ... I guess until she went to Minerva-Hillsdale High School and I went to Sunshine Day.

Anyway, in fifth grade Patty and I conspired to liberate our classroom's gerbil, Barry, because we were pretty sure that he was longing for a life in the wild and felt listless and hopeless in his little cage with just himself, a wheel, and his own poops for company. We executed our plan almost perfectly, getting Barry into the side pocket of Patty's cargo shorts without being noticed, then smuggling him outside to the playground for recess, only to have him scramble out of Patty's pocket as Mrs. Cassanaugh was asking us if we'd like to be recess monitors next week—because we were such good kids. Barry ran to a weedy ditch and was never seen again. Patty and I were sent to the principal, and we both cried, but we didn't get any real punishment.

Now here I was, five years later, sitting outside Dr. John's office because of a stupid food fight that wasn't my fault, a fight with someone who was about as far from my best friend as possible. To top it off, I smelled strongly of ham, *very* strongly of ham. Ham juice was in my hair. And on my shirt. There was even, I noticed, a small piece of ham in one of the cups of my earphones. I looked at it. Stupid ham. I asked Ivy Franklin—the secretary—if I could have a tissue. Ivy said yes—though in a disapproving tone—and I got up, got a tissue, used it to remove the ham from my earphones, then dropped it in the trash.

"I'm a vegetarian," I explained.

Ivy just kept watering the dozen or so houseplants that sat on her desk.

My stomach grumbled. I hadn't actually eaten anything for lunch.

Dr. John walked into the outer office from the hallway. He looked at me. He pointed to the open door of his office. I followed him in. Inside, Cassie was already sitting in one of the chairs in front of Dr. John's desk. They hadn't let us wait within sight of each other. As I sat down, I saw that Cassie had been crying, and I wished I'd been able to hear her crying from where I'd been waiting in the outer office. It might have made me feel better. It would have helped pass the time.

Dr. John sat down behind his desk, then he pushed himself backward, in his wheeled office chair, rolled his way around the desk, and stopped behind us. He asked us to turn our chairs to face him.

"Now we have a little triangle of communication," he said. "The three of us can have a chat. We can calm down and connect."

"Dr. John," Cassie said—and I noticed that she was still crying—"we're really so sorry that this all—"

But Dr. John held up his hand, stopping her, and said, "Let's take these things in order. It's a fell wind that blows, and the first thing we have to do is take shelter."

This was typical of Dr. John, talking in muddled riddles.

"Besides," he continued, "I'm not sure you owe *me* an apology, per se. Except for the pea that is lodged in my ear."

"I think that's my fault," I said.

"Well, I suppose I'm lucky I didn't get anything worse than that," he said. "There were a few moments there when it seemed like we wouldn't be able to stop you girls. It was like you girls were two oceans fighting over which one is the wateriest."

Wateriest?

"We're sorry!" Cassie said, still crying.

Dr. John nodded. "And I'm very curious to know who pulled my ponytail."

We both shrugged.

"Well, no matter," he said. "Ponytails can be pulled pretty hard without actually hurting. Applesauce will come out in the laundry. And peas will come out of ears. I hope.

"But the first thing I want to tell you girls is that Mrs. Zetz is okay. She just fainted, that's all, and now she's just fine, though I had to calm her down a bit. Actually, I had to calm her down a lot. But I think that's understandable."

He paused. He rubbed his beard. He looked up, looked out the window at the sky. He got a faraway look, like he did whenever he was thinking of the 1970s.

"Can you tell her that we're so, so sorry?" Cassie said.

"We'll get to that," he said, snapping back to the present. "But right now I need to tell you that I have talked with

Ms. Valeri, and so I have an idea of where things went wrong with you two. Now, I haven't read the papers you turned in, but Ms. Valeri described them to me. So, help me out here, let me see if I follow.

"You guys are paired up for this assignment about cooperating to survive in the wilderness. Do I have it right so far?"

We nodded.

"Good. And tell me, do you think survival is a good thing?"

Cassie nodded.

"Molly?" Dr. John asked.

"Okay, I'll agree to that."

"Ah, good," he said. "So we're on the same page. Well, or—no, wait, actually we're not, right? Because you two couldn't get along well enough to work on an assignment about working together for your very survival . . .

"Molly, Ms. Valeri says that your paper describing your trek through the strange countryside was beautiful. But perhaps the part where a saber-toothed tiger eats Cassie was a bit mean."

Cassie inhaled in surprise. She looked at me. "You had a tiger eat me?"

"I tried to warn you . . ."

"See, these things hurt," Dr. John said. "You can't swing a stick in the dark and not be surprised when you hit someone. And, Cassie, I hear that your paper contained a lot of effort and determination, although the idea of hunting rabbits with a pocketknife is a bit difficult to accept. But you see, you both got Ds because you both didn't do the actual *assignment*, which was to work together."

"We worked together *apart*," I said.

"Yes," Dr. John said, "that's clever, Molly. But it's like a beautiful bowl that's cracked and won't hold water."

"Dr. John," Cassie said, "we're so, so sorry about everything!"

"I want to point out that that's the fourth time she's apologized on my behalf," I said. "And I want to be clear that she doesn't speak for me."

My stomach growled audibly.

"Is it the pea in my ear making me hear things incorrectly, or are you guys still bickering?" Dr. John asked.

I opened my mouth, but Dr. John held up his hand again.

"Now," he continued, "you know I'm a big believer in sitting down and talking things through. We gotta calm down and connect, right? And part of me wants to sit in here until we untangle this mess. But I find myself uncertain that talking will dispel the cloud of dark energy between you two.

"You two also know that one of the core beliefs of our school community is that the standard crime-slash-punishment paradigm of student discipline is flawed and self-defeating. We believe in building up each other with respect and consideration, not belittling each other with a system of penalties and shame.

"But here's the rub," he said. "The things that you two have done run counter to that very system of beliefs. You've failed to communicate, you've disrespected each other, the school, the employees—namely the lunchroom staff—and our principles of conduct. So I find myself concluding that the very thing needed in your case is a solution—and I use that word because it's better than the word *punishment*—that addresses—and I use that word because it's more accurate than *fits*—the conflict—and I use that word because it's more precise than *crime*."

"What?" Cassie asked.

"Punishment that fits the crime," I paraphrased.

Cassie sobbed.

"Yes, well—solution that addresses the conflict," Dr. John said. "Because conflict is natural. Conflict is all around us. It blocks us if we let it. So we have to be smarter than it. We have to go to the roots of it. And therefore, the first thing I'm telling you to do, *individually*"—he looked at me—"is to apologize to Marta Zetz and the kitchen staff for the disrespect you showed them. Does that sound reasonable and intuitive?"

We nodded.

"And second," he said, "in order to bring you two together, and to instill in you a sense of respect for the kitchen staff and their work—and *food* after all, which we should never take for granted—I've decided that for the next two weeks, you will both spend your fourth-hour study hall and lunch hour working in the kitchen under the supervision of Mrs. Zetz."

He slapped his palms on his thighs. "That's it," he said. "That's what you're going to do."

Cassie dabbed her eyes. "You're not going to suspend us?" she asked.

"No."

"Oh thank God," she said, then started crying harder than before. Dr. John handed her a new tissue.

"I have a question," I said.

"What is it?" Dr. John asked.

"Do I have to wear a hairnet?"

6

Pounds and Pounds
of Half-Eaten Goulash

To apologize to the lunch staff, Dr. John ordered us to show up at school superearly the next morning. I had to get up a whole hour earlier than usual. I shuffled downstairs and found Grampa at the kitchen table eating a ginormous bowl of oatmeal.

"What are you doing up?" he asked.

"The universe hates me. Per usual."

"Well, you're not supposed to be up. Nobody's supposed to be up. This is Pappy's time to have the kitchen to himself."

"And that's a pasta bowl, not a bowl for oatmeal," I said. "I need some sugar."

I had a Pop-Tart and a root beer.

It was a misty morning, and as I walked to school my hair started to get damp, and by the time I reached school I looked like my whole head had been steamed. I went to Dr. John's office, and they were all waiting for me there: Dr. John, Mrs. Zetz, the three women who worked for her, and the much younger, black-haired guy named Edmund who also worked in the kitchen but was more of a janitor than a cook.

So I did what I had to do. I apologized.

Afterward I left the principal's office and wandered down the hall and up the stairs. It was still a good half hour before most of the students would show up, and I was sort of pleased to have the school to myself. Then I saw Cassie sitting on the window ledge in the stairwell, looking out the window dreamily. I knew she'd apologized to the kitchen staff just before me, but for some reason I wasn't expecting to run into her here.

"Good morning!" she said.

"Okay," I said.

"Isn't it a pretty morning out there?" she said. "With the mist and the way the leaves are starting to change color?"

"Maybe."

"Is autumn your favorite season or what? 'Cause I know it's mine."

"Autumn is one of the top four seasons."

It was like she didn't even hear me. Jokes had no effect on her.

"So how was it?" Cassie asked.

"How was what?" I asked. Why was she pretending to be my friend?

"How do you feel about your apology to the kitchen staff?" she clarified.

"Like it's over."

"I was nervous," she continued, "but I knew it was the right thing, and now I feel good."

"That's what matters most."

"And now," Cassie said, "I'm excited about learning to cook. I think it's going to be fun."

"Fun?" I said. *"Fun?"*

"Yeah, fun," she said.

"You're serious?"

"What? What's wrong with fun?"

"Hey, fun is fun," I said. "Nothing wrong with fun." I continued up the stairs.

"Bye!" Cassie said.

At the top of the stairs, I muttered "Fun?" and shuffled toward my locker. I mean, who talked like that?

Later, in art class, even though Cassie was sitting twenty feet away, she sent me a text message.

See ya in the lun
chroom! Gonna
have a blast!

I texted back:

fun city
signed
blarg

After we reported to the kitchen for fourth period, the first thing we did was put on aprons and hairnets.

"This feels like Halloween!" Cassie said. "Getting to wear these costumes."

Then Mrs. Zetz told us to set the napkin dispensers and salt and pepper shakers out on the lunchroom tables. Cassie seemed to enjoy this task and chatted merrily as we worked, even though I didn't really respond. Then, as we were finishing that task, I said, "Is this *fun* yet? Are you having *fun*?" Later, as we stood in the serving line serving up the slop, I would talk to the kids I knew and say things like, "Hey look at me, Brad, I'm having so much *fun* serving these canned green beans to you," and "Check it out: I'm having *fun* learning to cook!" and so on and so forth.

It was, to be honest, too easy. I could tell it was getting to Cassie, because as our time in the kitchen went on she became less chatty and more sour-looking. And the fact that we didn't actually get to do any cooking at all, and that Mrs. Zetz complained about every task we did, and that our final duty of the day was to scrape the half-eaten food off of the returned lunch trays—well, it all just added up to such a resounding unfun experience that I could see Cassie was disappointed. "This is a hot, steaming load of *fun*," I said, plopping a big blob of goulash into the industrial-size trash can that stood between us. "If I'd known I was going to have this much *fun* I would have brought my camera." She didn't say a thing, but her jaw was set in anger.

The only fun thing about the day was sticking it to Cassie. It was the purest kind of pleasure I'd experienced in months. On the other hand, it was clearly unfair, since she obviously lacked any defense against sarcasm. It was like playing Ping-Pong against an opponent without a paddle. So I felt a wee bit guilty about it, and it did get old pretty fast, and when we were released from our duty and told we could have the last eight minutes of the lunch period to eat our own lunch, we stood together and looked skeptically at the remnants of the lunch still steaming in the warming trays behind the serving counter. I could tell Cassie wasn't going to say anything. And in my mind, there were two things I wanted to say. The first was, "Eating this food will be like ingesting pure *fun.*" The second thing was: "Well, I *am* hungry." And that's what I did say. I was done with the fun campaign.

I got a tray and put a roll on it and then went and sat at the work counter in the middle of the kitchen. I pulled a packet of mustard and a candy bar out of my pocket. I put the mustard on the roll. Cassie was still standing in the middle of the floor, looking at the horrible leftovers.

"At least sit with me if you're not going to eat," I said. I wasn't sure why I said that. It had come out of me without any planning on my part.

Cassie filled her tray with food and sat down across from me. She took small bites of her food. She eyed my mustard roll suspiciously.

So we ate in silence, and when I finished I was looking at my hands, and I said, "I've got goulash under my fingernails," which was true, and Cassie looked at me for the first time in several minutes and said, "Me, too," and then the warning bell for fifth period rang.

As I was walking to class, I passed Seth Lawson, who was carrying the big fake SSHIG tombstone.

"Thanks for the fantastic goulash!" he said.

"Are you crazy?" I said. "That goulash came out of huge cans and smelled like old shoes."

He pointed to my head. "Are you guys supposed to wear those things all day?"

"What things?"

I touched my head. I still had my hairnet on.

After school, in the computer lab, I e-mailed my brother, Les, at college. I gave him a rundown of how the kitchen duty had gone, then I got philosophic:

It wasn't the worst day in the kitchen, but I'm sure it'll get worse. Why is it that things always get worse? Think about it, the first piece of a pizza you eat is better than the fifth one. The first time you go swimming each summer is a lot better than the tenth time you go swimming. And just look at life. You start off with childhood and games and the excitement of being alive and discovering new things all the time, and by the time you're in high school, nothing's as good or as interesting as it used to be. And what comes after that? Adulthood? Work? Stressing out about mortgages and how your lawn should be greener? Commuting? Raising kids? Wiping their puke off your clothes? Then you get old, and your body slowly fails you, and sooner or later you die. So even life gets worse over time.

Blarg, I guess.

Double blarg.

I gotta motor. Why am I still at school?

So I headed home, cutting right through downtown Minerva. It wasn't much as downtowns go—little storefronts around a town square. And I'd just crossed Spring Street when I saw Cassie right in front of me, sitting at the bus stop, reading.

I crossed the street so I wouldn't have to walk right past her. I put on my headphones and walked faster. I avoided looking in her direction, and I also made a point of pretending that I was invisible. That would do the trick, I figured. Why would Cassie want to talk to me anyway?

I walked faster.

I was almost safe, I figured.

Then I heard someone running up behind me.

Please not her, please not her . . .

"Hey!" said Cassie, beside me.

I stopped. I took off my headphones. "Hi," I said.

"Of all the people to run into after school!" she said.

"Tell me about it," I said.

"I was waiting for my bus. I saw you walking by."

"I saw you, too."

"I've never seen you around here."

"Really?" I said. "Never?" I saw her here at least three times a week, probably. "You've *never* seen me walking past here?"

"Nope," she said. "Where you going?"

"Home." Why had I noticed her every time she'd been at that bus stop, yet she'd never noticed me?

"You live near here?" she asked.

"More or less."

"Wasn't that goulash the worst?" Cassie said.

I shrugged.

"I like your barrettes!" she said. "Did you make those?"

"What is your obsession with my hair?" I asked.

She shook her head.

"And why is it," I said, "that you have such a perverse impulse to *fix* everything?"

"I . . . I don't . . . I—"

"Because it's really not appealing. It's really revolting."

"I don't understand. I'm just trying to be nice."

"Trying to be nice is different than actually *being* nice," I said. "You need to understand that we are not friends."

She stood there looking stunned.

I put on my headphones and walked away.

At home the back door was locked, so I went around to the front door, since that was the only key I had.

"Is that a burglar?" Grampa called from in the house.

"Yes," I said, heading upstairs. "I'm stealing my own stuff."

He popped into the foyer below me. "Steal away, just be quiet about it."

"Will do."

"Oh, I was at the Community Center this morning and I saw Glenda Bauer."

"Who?"

"Patty Cable's grandma," he said.

"Oh. Yeah."

"She says you and Patty don't come around to see her anymore."

"No. I guess not."

"She says Patty's a cheerleader at the high school."

This was news to me. "I know," I lied.

"Remember that time you and Patty Cable decided to go caroling on your own?" Grampa asked. "And you came by our house and you sang about twelve songs for Grandma and me?"

"Yeah. I remember."

I mumbled something about homework and went to my room. As if the day hadn't been dark enough, what with having to get up at the butt crack of dawn to apologize to the neo-Nazi Mrs. Zetz for a food fight that wasn't my fault, then having to work in the kitchen with Cassie, having to wear hairnets, having to scoop pounds and pounds of lukewarm, half-eaten goulash into the trash, having been accosted by Cassie on the walk home—and realizing that after all the times I'd walked by the bus stop and noticed her there, she hadn't noticed me even once. Now I ended the afternoon by hearing, from my grandpa of all people, the bleak and depressing news that my once-best-friend, Patty Cable, who I hadn't talked to since we had a fight almost a year ago, had gone over to the dark side completely and was a cheerleader at Minerva-Hillsdale High. As if it wasn't enough that our friendship had dissolved? Now I had to wrestle with the knowledge that her character had eroded to such a point that she no longer resembled the friend I had once loved. It was a final betrayal.

7

Dern Salt!

The next day, Thursday, Cassie and I were in the lunch-room, topping off the saltshakers a few minutes before lunch, when Clyde Brewell came in, went into the kitchen, returned carrying the little metal cash box, climbed onto his stool near the lunch counter, readied his hole puncher, and pinned his LUNCHROOM ATTENDANT badge to his shirt pocket. Then he checked his watch.

"Ask him how long till the bell," I said to Cassie. "I bet you his watch is synchronized with the bell."

Clyde was a lost cause, even as freshmen went. His hair was wet from showering at the end of P.E., and it was combed neatly. His button-down shirt was tucked in, and his leather shoes were polished. All in all, it was a sad display of boy.

"Ask him . . . ," I prompted.

Instead of asking Clyde what time it was, though, she waved. "I'm Cassie," she said.

"Hello," Clyde said. "I am Clyde."

"And this is Molly," Cassie said.

"My name is not Molly," I said to Clyde. "My name is nothing. You don't know my name. Okay?"

"Okay," Clyde said. He was just went on smiling.

"Got a question for you, though," I said. "How long until the bell?"

He looked at his watch. "Exactly two minutes right . . . now!"

"Amazing!" I said. "So precise!"

Suddenly, Mrs. Zetz was standing in the doorway to the kitchen, and she yelled, "Girrells! With the salt and to fill them up! They don't do it on dare own!"

So we went back to work. I held the funnel while Cassie poured the salt from a big ten-pound bag.

We were on the last shaker when Cassie's grip slipped and the salt spilled over the edge of the funnel and onto my hand. Unfortunately, earlier in our shift we had been asked to cut dozens of pieces of toast on a diagonal (we weren't trusted with the actual toasting), and I had managed to cut my finger. And so now, as Cassie said, "Whoops! Dern salt!" I felt the salt slip under my bandage and start to burn. It hurt bad, so I started shaking my hand, and that made it hurt worse and so I cussed incredibly loudly, which brought Mrs. Zetz out of the kitchen.

"I hear filthy!" she said. "You!" She pointed at me.

"Cassie spilled salt on my cut," I explained.

"It was a total accident," claimed Cassie.

"*You* make mess with salt," Mrs. Zetz said, still pointing at me, "*you* get salt in cut, *your* fault. Then you curse, filthy!"

"But she spilled the salt!" I argued.

"You make mess! Your fault!"

"But I—"

"Your fault!" she yelled.

A couple minutes later, we were in the serving line—me on toast duty, Cassie on meatball duty—and *somehow*, Cassie *just happened* to drop a meatball on my feet.

"Ick!" I said. "That's gross."

"So sorry," said Cassie, singsongy.

In the next ten minutes, she dropped two more meatballs on my feet, and of course I was wearing flip-flops and therefore I got meatball juice all up between my toes. I was pretty sure that meat juice was being absorbed through my skin. Finally, when a fourth meatball fell, I complained to Mrs. Zetz.

"You drop meatballs for purpose?" she asked Cassie.

"No," Cassie claimed. "It's just that they're so slippery. I'm really sorry."

"Yes," Mrs. Zetz said sympathetically, "sometime the meatballs, dey get away from you, dey tumble down, slippery . . ." She laughed a little.

Near the end of the shift I was told to take a bag of trash to the Dumpster. I knew it was punishment for the trouble I'd caused with my cut and my cussing and the salt mess. Cassie, after all, had been allowed to sit down and eat already. It was obvious that Mrs. Zetz liked Cassie better than me. So what? If anything, Mrs. Zetz's affection for Cassie was an affirmation that Cassie's character was highly suspect.

But I couldn't believe how heavy the trash bag was. Were there a couple of bodies in there? I hefted the bag and waddled out of the kitchen, but as I reached the back door of the kitchen,

I realized the bag was dripping something—right on my non-meatball foot. And the dripping was something meaty, too.

I opened the back door and saw that it was raining. I'd have to dash through the rain to reach the Dumpster. Fine. Maybe it would wash the meat juice off. I ran for the Dumpster, dragging the bag behind me and then heaving it into the Dumpster. But when I turned back toward the school I saw a trail of trash. The bag had torn open as I dragged it, and now there were dirty napkins and the leftovers from dozens of meatball lunches all over the asphalt. Meanwhile, I was getting soaked. So I just did what I had to do. I ignored my gag reflex and gathered up the trash.

And something about being out in that cold rain, with my arms dirty up to the elbows with other people's trash, made me realize how clear it was that Cassie was after me. She had poured the salt like that on purpose, knowing it would get into my cut. And she had clearly dropped the meatballs intentionally. Cassie sticking it to me every chance she got. Fair enough, I figured. Let's do this thing.

Heading back inside—finally—I was opening the kitchen's back door when I saw something in the shadows between the school and the walk-in freezer. The freezer stood like a little garage right outside the kitchen's back door, and there was a narrow alley between the school and the freezer, and back in there was Edmund Mundis—the kitchen janitor or whatever—smoking a cigarette. He was looking right at me.

"You're wet," he said.

He couldn't be much older than my brother. His hair was glossy black, and he had a dumb little black goatee, too.

"Did you see me there, with all that trash all over the place?"

"Yeah."

"Why didn't you help me?"

"You didn't ask."

"That's lovely," I said. "Really lovely."

He smoked. The overhang of the school kept him dry. I reached for the door.

"I want to tell you something," he said.

"What." I stood there with the door half open.

"I didn't buy your apology yesterday," he said. "I could tell you didn't mean it."

"So what?" I said.

"So nothing," he said. "I just thought you should know."

"This is a nonsmoking campus," I said, then I went inside and told Mrs. Zetz that Edmund was smoking behind the freezer. Mrs. Zetz marched out the back door. I got a piece of toast and sat at the counter and ate it. Cassie was nowhere to be seen. Soon, Mrs. Zetz reappeared.

"Edmund not smoking," she reported. "He closing lid on Dumpster so rain not get in. You sloppy, leave lid open. Edmund not smoking, Edmund working! Good worker, not like Molly! Molly sloppy! Molly liar!"

8

Dese Beans, Dese Weenies

When Dr. John had doled out our "solution" for the food fight, he had included the requirement that Cassie and I were responsible for telling our parents about what had happened. Now, I have no doubt that Cassie marched home and told her parents just like a good Girl Scout. I, on the other hand, approached that particular part of the "solution" as optional.

That night, Mom called me from downstairs. Even she had started to phone me from downstairs instead of walking all the way up here.

Mom had just gotten home from work—it was eight o'clock—and asked if I wanted to go down to the fabric store with her.

"Probably not," I said.

"But you used to love going to the fabric store."

"You can't prove that."

She was quiet for a little bit. Then she said, "I'm coming up there."

"That's entirely unnecessary!" I argued.

She hung up. I sat there on my bed and waited. After a bit, she knocked on the door and came in. She looked at my room, which wasn't perfectly clean, and at my books and papers spread out on my bed.

"Do you do all your homework on the bed like that?" she asked. "That can't be good for your posture. You have a perfectly nice desk over there."

"And?"

"Look, come to the fabric store. Remember how I used to make a quilt every winter? Well, I'm going to do it again this year. And you're so good with colors, helping me pick the right combinations."

"You don't have time to quilt. Not at home at least. What are you going to do, quilt at work?"

She nodded. She said, "Things are going to change soon. I'm going to work less. Just come to the fabric store with me."

"But I'm busy," I said. "Homework."

"Okay, okay," she said. She sniffed. "Do I smell meat?"

My flip-flops were right by the door. She probably smelled the meatball juice, which persisted even after a thorough washing.

"Why would I have meat in my room?" I asked.

The next day, we got to help cook. Sort of. I got to open can after can of pork and beans and do a little bit of stirring. Cassie, on the other hand, got to make instant mashed potatoes. Then Mrs. Zetz let Cassie help bake the peanut butter cookies—which were cut from a huge log of dough from some cookie-dough factory—while I was assigned to put out the napkins and salt-shakers by myself. I pushed the napkin cart into the lunchroom, scuffing my feet, and went about my task—putting the napkin dispensers *exactly* in the middle of the tables like Mrs. Zetz required. Then I realized that Clyde Brewell was over sitting on his little Lunchroom Attendant stool, wearing his little Lunchroom Attendant badge, and a ridiculous smile.

"You don't have to smile, you know," I said to him. "There's no one here."

"You're here," he said. "And I'm here."

"True, but I don't want to see your smile and you *can't* see your smile, so save yourself the effort and stop it."

He laughed. "You're witty."

"No, I'm mean," I said.

I continued with the job. When I checked again Clyde was still smiling.

"It must be interesting to work in the kitchen," he said. "Do you like to cook?"

"*Cooking* is not the best term for what goes on in this kitchen."

"I like to cook," he said. "It's a life skill."

"A what?"

The lunch bell rang.

"A life skill," he repeated. "Something I'll use for the rest of my life."

"I'm going to have to leave you now, and none too soon."

"Okay, Molly. See ya later!"

"No!" I said. "We went over this. You don't know my name."

"Okay!" he said, grinning broadly.

"I don't want to hear you saying my name."

"Okay!"

Behind the serving counter, I was put on coleslaw duty. Today, Mrs. Zetz was smart enough to keep me separated from Cassie so we wouldn't slow down the lunch line with bickering or dropped meat products. My serving tool was an ice cream scoop, and as I portioned out a round scoop of slaw on each tray it made a little suction sound and then it made a sort of splatting sound on the tray. I'd started the lunch hour by saying, "Here is some slaw for you!" each time I plopped slaw on a tray, but Mrs. Zetz told me to be quiet.

At the other end of the line, Cassie was portioning out the instant mashed potatoes, also with an ice cream scoop, and between us were two of the lunch ladies, one manning the beans and weenies, one spooning a canned peach half onto each tray. At the end of the counter was a basket of peanut butter cookies, above which hung a hand-lettered sign of Mrs. Zetz's own making—yellowed around the edges it was so old—that read ONE TRAY, ONE DESSERT. The students were allowed to pick their own dessert, but anyone caught breaking the ONE TRAY, ONE DESSERT rule was dealt with by Mrs. Zetz herself. In other words, no one ever took more than one dessert.

The lunch rush was on, and beans and weenies being a favorite, the line was long today. The Noontime Expression gig was a quiet senior named Beatrix Taylor. A poet. I listened to her for a little bit to take my mind off the horrible food I was serving.

> I spoke . . . sequestered . . .
> and ranged.
> Overrelaxed.
> My tights are loose!
> So soft
> your
> nose

in tandem.
How long . . . till someday?

Holy smokes that was bad poetry!

We had served three big trays of beans and weenies and the fourth one was halfway gone when Nicole Boll-Weicher, a junior best known for wearing three pigtails, leaned toward the glass and tapped it, pointing at the bean and weenie tray.

"What's that?" she asked.

"Beans with weenies," the lunch lady Dina said, not even looking up.

"No, I mean what is *that*?" Nicole Boll-Weicher said, pointing at something specific in the tray of beans and weenies.

At this point, because Nicole had paused long enough to slow down the lunch line, Mrs. Zetz arrived, standing between Dina and me. I was sure Mrs. Zetz would say something to get the lunch line moving again, but instead, Mrs. Zetz looked at the beans and weenies and immediately shouted, "Time for fresh tray!" and she pulled the half-full tray of beans and weenies off of the serving table and placed it out of sight on a side counter and then swooped in with another tray of beans and weenies.

"Is fresh tray the beans the weenies!" Mrs. Zetz said, loud enough for everyone to hear. "Is favorite of students, dese beans dese weenies!"

Nicole Boll-Weicher stood there, looking at the new tray of food, then said, "I'm not hungry," and wandered away.

It was puzzling. Why would Mrs. Zetz remove a good tray of beans and weenies? What had Nicole seen? I glanced to my right and caught Cassie's eye. Cassie shrugged, but there was something about the shrug that I didn't like. The shrug was not spontaneous. It was not innocent.

Still, I felt pretty good. It was Friday, after all, and in another ten minutes I'd be done with kitchen duty until Monday. Cassie and I took up our positions at the tray-return window, and because most people liked beans and weenies, the trays mostly came back clean. That meant we didn't have to scrape off much food before piling the trays to the side so that Edmund could run them through the dishwasher later.

As we worked, Mrs. Zetz pulled down the partition that separated the lunchroom from the serving counter. Then she sat at the counter in the middle of the kitchen and asked me to come over.

"Just me?" I asked.

Mrs. Zetz nodded.

I looked at Cassie, and Cassie gave that fake shrug again. Something was up.

After I sat at the counter, Mrs. Zetz said, "You help Dina cook the beans and the weenies, did you?"

"I opened the cans of beans. I poured the cans of beans."

"Take off your gloves," Mrs. Zetz said.

"Okay." I took off my latex gloves.

I didn't like how calm Mrs. Zetz was.

Mrs. Zetz held up her hands. "Me see your hands."

I held up my hands. Mrs. Zetz nodded.

"What is your cut hurt like?" Mrs. Zetz asked.

"My cut? It's fine." I was still wearing a bandage around my left index finger, from where I'd nicked it yesterday.

"Mm . . . ," Mrs. Zetz said. She got up and walked to the side counter. There, she picked up the tray of beans and weenies that she'd removed from the counter in the middle of the lunch rush. She brought it over and sat it down in front of me.

"What you see dare?" she asked.

At first, I saw only the obvious: beans, weenies, and a ruddy sauce. But then I saw something else, nestled in the beans. It was paler, and curved, and . . . and . . . It was a bandage, a bandage that was in the shape of a cylinder, as if it had slipped off of someone's finger. That's what Nicole Boll-Weicher had seen. That's why Mrs. Zetz had pulled the tray from the serving table.

I looked at Mrs. Zetz. "It's not . . . not mine," I said. Mrs. Zetz's face was like stone. "Look," I protested, "I've had this bandage on since this morning. It's my own Scooby-Doo! bandage, see? It's . . ."

But I could see that Mrs. Zetz had already judged me guilty.

The kitchen was quiet, even though everyone else was still working. I looked at Cassie, but Cassie ignored me. She had done this, of course: planted the bandage, knowing I would get the blame. And it was such a devious, mean, and vile thing to do, that it was sort of cool. For a moment there, I wondered if there was more to Cassie than I'd thought.

9

Junior Mints in the Brainpan

Saturday come midnight I was not sleepy. I e-mailed my brother.

Dearest Les—

Yo! Not sleeping! Gotta write bro. It was warm here today and I decided to take advantage of it so I stayed outside, reading on the patio. But I fell asleep after lunch and only woke up when a ladybug crawled up my nostril. Ladybug okay. Three-hour nap = not sleepy now. Plus, had a Frappuccino and some Junior Mints an hour ago.

Haven't talked to you since, what, my birthday? Blarg. Grampa went fishing today and came home and made me smell his hands and they stank like fish even though he'd washed them.

Yeah, so this stupid hot lunch thing is getting worse. You remember Mrs. Zetz, don't you? Her and her "dirty dozen" menus that she just repeats over and over. All the food's prefab crap that they just heat up and slap onto the trays. And Mrs. Z doesn't like me. And the girl I'm working with is out to get me.

It all makes me wonder, when did I get so skilled at losing friends, but bad at gaining them? Wasn't like that in grade school. Kids were nice to me and I was nice to them. But then came junior high, when being nice was suddenly a cardinal sin. Thank goodness I still had Patty as a pal. Remember how Patty and I kept constantly updated lists of the most horrible kids in school? Also, remember her backyard with the two trampolines? That was crazy fun.

Tell you what: third grade, now that was a good year. Fifth grade. Fantastic! But seventh grade? Eighth grade? And my freshman year? They were all just blocks of time to be endured.

Maybe I'm just contrary because it gives me something to do. Blarg.

Eh, don't listen to me. Late-night ramblings. Junior Mints in the brainpan.

xoxo/Moe

Then I realized I hadn't checked my e-mail since morning. I had a message from Cassie. Why should I even open it? The subject line was blank. I opened it.

Hope your cut hurts.

Nice. I wrote back:

Dear Cassie,

Thank you so much for your concern for my wound!
I do appreciate it. How nice it is to be thought of.
Indeed, my cut does hurt just a little bit, but it's getting
better! I'm taking good care of it and washing it and
keeping it covered by fresh bandages and I'm sure that
in no time my finger will be as good as new and when
that day comes, and come it will, I will take my healed
finger and I will do a one-finger karate chop to your
jugular. So that's how my finger's doing.
M.

She e-mailed me right back:

*You know, don't you, that they call you Molly
"O'Linger" because you're always lurking and
sulking and lingering around.*

So I e-mailed her:

Hey, ever notice how there's an ass in the middle of
Cassie?

Then I shut my notebook.
O'Linger? Who called me O'Linger? Who even knew my last
name . . . ?

On Monday, Mrs. Zetz told me to scrub the floor of the stockroom. Clearly, this was part of the penalty for the bandage incident. The stockroom floor was sticky and smelled like a drawer

full of old rubber bands. The shelves were lined with huge cans of things like lima beans, sauerkraut, and gravy. A person could starve in there, even with a can opener.

As I was scrubbing, Edmund the kitchen janitor dude walked by and said, "Ha!"

Still, I had time to think. I was also unsupervised. So when no one was around I put the salt in the sugar container, and the sugar in the salt bag.

Soon after that, Cassie came to the doorway. She was helping Dina bake the pineapple upside-down cake, which was clearly the reward for being such a good kitchen helper. The cake was one of the few desserts that was made from scratch.

"I need the sugar," Cassie said.

"You can't walk on the floor until it dries," I said.

"But I need the sugar."

I got the "sugar" and passed it to Cassie.

"How come you can walk on the wet floor, but I can't?" Cassie asked.

"Because my soul is pure," I said.

Next, I was asked to top off the saltshakers. Okeydoke! So I filled them with sugar. While I was doing this, Clyde came into the lunchroom.

"Hi!" he said.

I didn't answer.

Clyde went into the kitchen and got his cash box and came back out and put it on his stool. Then he came over and stood near me.

"I was wondering," he said.

"Wondering what?" I said. I looked at him. He was more

neat and tidy than usual. He was actually wearing a sport coat. It was horrible.

"I would like to request the pleasure of your company at the Autumn Fete."

I spilled some sugar when I heard this. Clyde just kept standing there, grinning.

"I don't believe this," I said.

"I'm really happy you want to go with me."

"Hold up, bucko. You haven't even given me time to say 'hell, no.' "

His smile faded. "To say what?" he asked.

"To tell you, Clyde, that there's absolutely no way that this little delusion of yours has any relation to reality. To tell you, *Clyde*, that if you think I would even consider going anywhere at all with you then you clearly have not been party to our earlier interactions. To tell you, *Clyde!*, that I think you're a miserable, small-boned, freakish, bland, striving, pale, awkward, sexless, short, and confused boy!"

He stood there, listening. Then he stood there some more. It looked like he had frozen in place. He wasn't blinking.

Finally, he said, "But I thought— But Cassie told me—"

"Cassie!?" I yelled. Of course she had put him up to this.

"I'm departing now," Clyde said, and I could see tears rimming his eyes, and then he walked across the lunchroom and back into the school.

"Where does Clyde go?" Mrs. Zetz barked from the doorway to the kitchen.

"I have no idea," I said.

"What did you do to our Clyde?!"

"I didn't touch him, I swear!"

"You yelled him. I heard you yell him! Clyde come back!"

Mrs. Zetz called. "Now who will sit with the stool to take the money? And also, the cake is ruined! It is salt, with salt! Now have to change dis sign."

Mrs. Zetz reached for the ONE TRAY, ONE DESSERT sign and taped an index card onto it so that it now read ONE TRAY, ZERO DESSERT.

"Never has dessert been zero!" Mrs. Zetz said. "Zero!"

Cassie came out of the kitchen. "It was her!" she said, pointing at me. "She made the cakes salty! I went into the stockroom to get the sugar and what she gave me was salt. She swapped the sugar and the salt!"

Mrs. Zetz glared at me. I shook my head. Then Mrs. Zetz walked over to me. There was the spill of sugar on the table. Mrs. Zetz wet her finger and dipped it in the sugar and then tasted. "Is sugar," she said.

I was promptly assigned to take not one but two full bags of trash outside. Of course, it had been raining all morning, and at first I thought about refusing to take the trash out—knowing it was Edmund's job, really—and then I realized that perhaps, if I was lucky, I could catch Edmund smoking again.

As I left the kitchen's back door, I heard a scuffling noise back in the alley between the freezer and the school, so I knew he was there. But I didn't look. I went to the Dumpster, pretending to mind my own business. Then, as I returned to the school, I looked in the little alley. It was empty. On the ground, though, was a smoking match.

Back inside, the lunch bell rang. As I came into the kitchen, I was confronted with Cassie and Mrs. Zetz standing over one of the big trays of cottage cheese. Cassie was holding something in the air. Something invisible?

"Dis is *your* hair, Molly?" Mrs. Zetz said. "Cassie find in cottage cheese. Blue hair!"

"Oh, great," I said.

"Dis not good, not right to leave hair in food, blue hair."

"I must have a defective hairnet," I said.

"Dee-fec-tive . . . ," Mrs. Zetz said. "No, you are sloppy, not dee-fec-tive hairnet."

"But I didn't work on the cottage cheese!" I said. "I didn't even get close to it!"

"Sloppy!" Mrs. Zetz barked.

"Then let me show you something!" I screamed. "Two can play this game!" And I reached for the tray of cottage cheese and pulled it off the counter so that it fell and spilled across the floor.

"No!" Mrs. Zetz screamed. "Lovely cheese!"

Then everyone saw that there was something in the cottage cheese. Lots of somethings . . . Bandages! Lots and lots and lots of bandages!

"Oh my God!" I said, in mock alarm, because of course I'd planted the bandages. "It looks like Cassie—who was in charge of putting the cottage cheese in the tray—must have lost dozens upon dozens of her dirty bandages in the tray! I can't believe it! There must be no other explanation! What a horrible lapse of food safety on her part! What a terrible breach of respect for the food! Now let's punish her! And to think that we didn't even know that she had any cuts, but look, she must have, because look at all these bandages in the cottage cheese!"

There were students at the lunch window now, looking in on this scene with shock. Dina and the other lunch ladies were stunned, too.

Mrs. Zetz's mouth hung open, looking at the cottage cheese, looking at the bandages, then I grabbed her arm and pulled her through the short hallway, past the stockroom, and toward the back door.

"Come with me," I said.

"I . . . I . . . I . . . ," Marta Zetz stammered.

"There's one more thing," I said, and I pulled Mrs. Zetz out the back door of the kitchen and pointed to the alley between the freezer and the school, and there stood Edmund, a cigarette in his mouth. "That!" I said. "I wasn't lying the other day, see?"

"I . . . don't . . . I . . . I . . . ," Marta Zetz blubbered.

"This I need," said Edmund.

"Now, let's go serve lunch," I said. "Or what's left of it. You can have a talk with Cassie later. And Edmund."

I made to go back inside, but Mrs. Zetz just sort of stood there, stunned beyond reason—her lunch lady circuits overloaded—so I had to pull her back through the doorway, and through the hallway, and past the stockroom, and into the kitchen again. And then, at the moment we entered the kitchen, there was some kind of war cry across the room, and I looked just in time to see Cassie charging us with a whole tray of baked spaghetti. Before there was time to react, the spaghetti was airborne.

10

Most of the Airborne Spaghetti

We waited outside Dr. John's office. It was after school, and Ivy Franklin had gone home, and so we were alone in the outer office, and we sat there, at opposite ends of a bench, and listened to the clock tick, and watched the raindrops slide down the windowpanes. Inside the principal's office were Cassie's dad and both of my parents.

"Do you think we should try to listen at the door?" Cassie asked.

It was the first thing either of us had said to each other since the kitchen.

"Wouldn't help us," I pointed out.

The clock ticked—it was almost five o'clock.

"The thing is," Cassie said, "I never told my dad about our first fight and how I have to work in the kitchen. So now I'm going to have to deal with both that and this."

I looked at her. I was surprised that Cassie, who seemed so eager to please, hadn't told her dad about what had happened last week.

"I didn't tell my parents either," I admitted.

"You didn't?"

"It didn't seem newsworthy."

"If that's not newsworthy, what is?" Cassie asked.

I shrugged.

"Well, what about today? Today was at least slightly newsworthy," Cassie said. "I mean, with Mrs. Zetz screaming through the hallways and everything."

Cassie smiled. I smiled, too—couldn't help it.

Suddenly, the door to Dr. John's office opened, and he appeared there frowning, and then Mr. Birchmeyer and my parents came out, all three looking similarly dour.

"Girls," Dr. John said, looking at us, "your parents are going to wait out here while the three of us talk. Okay?"

In his office, with the door closed, we sat in front of Dr. John's desk and he sat behind it. No triangle of communication this time. It was darker in Dr. John's office than the outer office. He had some of the blinds closed. He looked tired.

"I'm not sure I get it," he said. "I don't understand why you two are still at each other's throats. Is there a *reason* for it?"

We shook our heads.

"No reason?" he asked. "You're just mean to each other because you don't have any better things to do? I mean, look, no one's forcing you to be friends. Is it about a boy? Something like that?"

"No," I said.

"Okay, fine," he said. "I'm not going to pry. I'm not going to take that route. But clearly you two have had a failure of connection, a monumental one, and if you don't face that side of your personalities, you'll make your lives hard—not just now, but for years to come. Think about it: each of you is going to have to deal with thousands of different people in your lifetimes—family, coworkers, in-laws, friends, neighbors, dentists, mail carriers—and it'll be a whole lot easier if you figure out how to get along with people you don't like. It's not about *liking* everyone, it's about getting along. It's about the flow of living. That's just a piece of advice really, though I find it sounds pretty feeble, considering present circumstances. But it's all I have right now. So you'll have to forgive me."

"I forgive you," Cassie said.

"I didn't mean that literally."

"Oh," Cassie said.

"Let me ask you this," he said. "Can you two explain what happened today, and last week, too, without resorting to blaming the other person? Because if you can, I'd be happy to listen."

We both just sat there.

"That's what I thought. And so I want to offer up this radical notion: neither one of you is to blame."

"Does that mean we're not going to be punished?" I asked.

"You know," he said, "a clam takes a tiny piece of sand—an irritant—and turns it into a pearl. You two, on the other hand, have taken a tiny piece of sand—and we all know there are plenty of irritants in this world—and turned it into a minor catastrophe. See what I'm saying?"

Cassie, in a little voice, said, "Yes."

Dr. John sighed. "It's been a busy afternoon. You two started an avalanche that rolled all the way down the mountain. There have been developments that you have not been privy to, even though they are the result of your actions. First, Mrs. Zetz has announced her retirement."

This was a shock. Cassie and I looked at each other. Sure, we'd caused a great many muck-ups in the kitchen this morning—and last week, too—and we'd been there when Mrs. Zetz had snapped—the moment after most of the airborne spaghetti landed on her—and we'd listened to her rant, first in English, then in a language that was maybe Polish, and we'd watched her leave the kitchen, ranting all the way to Dr. John's office, where he and she had talked for about ten minutes before she left the school. We knew that much. But that she'd *retired*? That was newsworthy.

"She told me she was retiring," Dr. John continued, "pretty soon after she started speaking English again. I tried to calm her down and get her to wait a few days before making any such decision, but she wouldn't hear of it. She's made her decision.

"The second piece of information is that two of the kitchen staff have resigned, partly in sympathy for Mrs. Zetz and partly, I think, because the public schools can afford to pay them about two dollars an hour more than we can. So, as you can see, our kitchen is suddenly leaderless and short staffed."

Cassie's eyes were welling with tears. "Did Mrs. Zetz say she was quitting because of us?"

"Yes."

"We didn't mean to—" Cassie said.

"Ah," Dr. John interrupted, "but you *did*. That's the thing about being mean: it affects more people than you intend."

Cassie took a tissue and blew her nose like a trumpet.

Dr. John went on. "Your parents and I have been sitting in here trying to figure this thing out. First of all, it turns out that neither of you had told them about the original incident that put you in the kitchen.

"And in the matter of what to do *now*, we went over many possibilities, from reprimands and suspensions, to community service, to apologies, and even expulsion. But the solution we came to is elegant, appropriate, and in line with all of Sunshine Day's core values: you two will be taking over Sunshine Day's hot lunch program."

"What does that mean?" I asked.

"You are in charge of the kitchen. You ruined the kitchen, so now it's yours."

Cassie said, "You're kicking us out as students and now we're just cooks!?"

"Not exactly. We looked at your class schedules and it will work rather well. You two will come in early, before school, to get things going in the kitchen. And you'll both take a break from the kitchen to attend literature class. But other than literature, all your morning classes are electives—let's see, chorus, art—and then your fourth period is study hall. So you'll go to lit. class, but then work the rest of the morning in the kitchen. In exchange for your work there, you'll be given tuition credits, and also academic credit for work study, and if you want to keep up with your chorus and art classes, both Mr. Koehler and Mrs. Dean have said they'll be happy to work with you after school. In the afternoons you'll have your normal class schedule."

I raised my hand. This was all just a bit surreal.

"You don't have to raise your hand, Molly. Speak."

"I don't know how to cook," I said.

"I guess we'll see, won't we?" Dr. John said. "Keep in mind, too, that this is a school, and that learning is our mission."

"And," I said, "I'm not sure this whole thing is fair."

"Fair?" Dr. John said. "I'm not sure simplistic judgments are the best way to assess this situation. It seems, after all, that your judgments about each other are what got you into this mess in the first place. Besides, do you think it was fair what happened to Mrs. Zetz? Do you think it was fair that no one got a full lunch today? Do you think it was fair to yourselves to ruin a sensible solution to your original fight? Do you think it would be more fair if you were expelled?"

"No!" Cassie said. "We'll do it! We'll be the cooks."

"But how long are we going to be in charge of the kitchen?" I asked.

"Ah, yes. You can thank your parents for coming up with the answer to that. You're in charge of the kitchen until the food is better than Mrs. Zetz's."

"And how exactly will you be able to tell that, without using 'simplistic judgments'?" I said.

"Democracy," said Dr. John. "Everyone who eats a hot lunch will get to vote whether the meal was better than Mrs. Zetz's food. When you get a majority vote for five consecutive days, that's it, you're done."

"Okay," I said. "All we have to do is tell the student body that to avoid our horrible food all they have to do is say that our food's great, even if it isn't."

"Nope," said Dr. John. "I would consider that election fraud. Anything like that would result in further punishment."

"Don't you mean 'solution'?" I asked.

"No, I mean punishment."

11

Instant Pudding Is the Devil's Own Invention

I called Les that night.

"Moe!" he said. "What's shakin'?"

"Why aren't you in the bio lab or studying or whatever? I was planning a long, elaborate voice mail."

"You can call back and leave a message if you want."

"Too late now," I said. "I've lost that magic voice-mail feeling."

I told him about what had happened in the kitchen today. He was a good listener, but his reaction to the news was too calm.

"So, you'll learn to cook," he said. "Sounds kinda cool."

"No! Not *cool*. Don't you get it? I'm a *lunch lady* now."

"Lunch girl," he said.

"And I don't have a good feeling about it. It's like when I was six and I wanted to fly my Hello Kitty kite and we went to the park but there was no wind. And you were like, no problem, just hop on the handlebars of my bike—backward—and I'll pedal fast enough to *create* wind to the fly the kite."

Les was laughing.

"And I knew that wouldn't work. But I trusted you and I wanted the kite to fly so badly . . . so I got on the handlebars."

"And we crashed."

"And I still have a scar on my arm, and my kite landed in the street and got run over."

"Your point being?"

"I knew that it was a bad plan. And that's exactly the way I feel about this stupid hot lunch plan."

"Yes, but it's not like you can opt out of this one."

I growled. He was right. "Fine," I said. "But let me just say for the record that it's a blueprint for failure. And I don't even want it to work."

"Okay. Let me write that down: Molly has bad attitude."

In the morning, I was awoken by my alarm clock, my computer, Les's old alarm clock, and my dad's digital watch at the laughably early hour of six o'clock. Not much later, I left the house and walked through the dark streets of Minerva. The sun wasn't up yet, and the town was quiet. There were still a few stars out. I felt a bit like I was walking to my own execution, step by step.

The school was dark, and I walked around its perimeter. There were lights on in the kitchen. I looked at the kitchen door. I reached out and knocked. Then I heard something behind me and looked and saw Edmund wheeling to a stop on his bicycle.

"You don't have to knock," he said. "It's not like you're visiting your aunt."

"I know," I said.

"No you didn't. You just knocked."

"I know that, too," I said.

"You're just brimming with knowledge," he said, and he opened the door, and wheeled his bike inside. I followed.

In the kitchen, Dina—the only remaining kitchen employee other than Edmund—was sitting at the center counter, reading the newspaper and drinking coffee. Edmund poured himself a cup from the old-fashioned percolator on the stove and said good morning to Dina and then disappeared. I stood there, not knowing exactly what to do. Was I the boss? Was I supposed to take charge?

Dina asked me if I drank coffee and I said no and then I yawned.

"This is the best part of the day," Dina said. "The calm before the storm."

We sat there, and Dina asked me a lot of questions about cooking, and if I knew how to do this or that. Essentially, I didn't know anything. I did have a vague idea of how to make English muffin pizzas. Also, I could make brownies from a mix, because Patty Cable and I used to make them all the time.

"I think you'll catch on to cooking pretty quick," said Dina.

I shrugged.

"You're bright and quick and have a love of efficiency," she said.

Love of efficiency? What was Dina talking about? I was about to challenge her on this point when Cassie walked in. She smiled and said a singsongy good morning and took off her backpack.

"What's your problem?" I asked her. "You're late on our first day?"

"I caught the earliest bus I could," she said. "My dad couldn't bring me today."

"It's a bad start."

"It's not like you guys are working yet!" Cassie said. "You're sitting there."

"I just think that if I have to get up early, so should you."

"I probably got up before you. I live a lot farther away than you do."

"Boo hoo," I said.

Dina, turning the page of the newspaper, sighed loudly.

We heard footsteps in the lunchroom and after a bit Dr. John appeared in the tray-return window. He said good morning and then came into the kitchen. He saw the coffeepot and asked Dina if he could have some. She said that was fine.

"Even I don't usually get here this early," he said, pouring a cup.

"Cassie was late," I said.

"I caught the earliest bus!" Cassie countered.

"Off to a good start, I see," Dr. John said.

He didn't punish Cassie for being late. Or commend me for being on time, for that matter. He just laid out the ground rules. Cassie and I were officially in charge of the kitchen and its staff, with the caveat that Dina was in charge of sanitation, food safety, and kitchen safety. Edmund was assigned to his usual jobs, but we could ask him to do additional tasks.

"I don't think this is going to work at all," I said.

"So you're saying you don't think you can do this?" Dr. John said, sipping his coffee nonchalantly.

"I don't think *she* can," I said.

We decided to use Mrs. Zetz's menus for the rest of the week, since the ingredients were already in stock. The first lunch we were in charge of was hamburgers (precooked, frozen), Tater

Tots (precooked, frozen), corn (precooked, canned), pineapple tidbits, and instant chocolate pudding. At Dina's prompting, we called a staff meeting, which really just meant calling Edmund into the kitchen, because the rest of us were already here.

To start the meeting, Cassie read the menu. Then we stood there.

"Now what?" I asked.

"How about we put one person in charge of each item?" Dina said. "So like, Molly, you're in charge of the hamburgers."

"But I'm a vegetarian."

"Okay . . . ," Dina said.

"Why are you a vegetarian?" Edmund asked.

I shrugged. "Meat is gross."

"Meat is gross?" Edmund echoed. "That's it?"

"Yeah," I said. "I just don't like it. I don't know."

"Great," Edmund said. "And I thought maybe you had some scruples, like you'd decided not to eat meat for health reasons or moral reasons or to save the earth or something."

"I just don't like meat, okay?"

"You're probably the type who eats lots of candy and cold cereal."

"No I'm *not*."

"We have a name for that. Candy vegetarian," said Edmund.

"And I have a name for what you are—"

"*I'll* take charge of the hamburgers," Cassie interjected.

"Good," said Dina.

I volunteered to cook the corn. Dina took the Tater Tots.

"We still need someone to make the pudding," Dina said.

"Edmund," I said.

He laughed. "But instant pudding is the devil's own invention."

"We have a mandate from Dr. John," I told him. "So unless you want me to talk to him about your pudding insubordination, I suggest you just do it."

"Fine," he said. "But I'm not going to eat it." He headed down the hallway.

Dina looked at me and smirked. "You're a hard-ass," she said.

Before school every day there was the fifteen-minute Before School Meeting, which I liked to refer to as "A.M. BS." It was a time when the faculty and students could make announcements. It was held in the lunchroom—the village green—and so Cassie and I didn't have to go far to attend it this morning.

Mr. Fedder announced the tryouts for the school's math competition team, the Mathamphetamines. Then a senior named Portia Babbliabali announced a casting call for her new four-act musical, *The Bleepity Bleep Bleep Gang*. Finally, Seth Lawson made a long-winded announcement about a new student-led initiative to get the school to consider using toilet paper that was made with hemp fibers. He was wearing a T-shirt that said MY OTHER CAR IS A BICYCLE.

"Thank you, Seth, for that," Dr. John said after Seth sat down. "I've got one thing to talk about before I turn the floor over to Ms. Valeri and the speech team. Now, a lot of you know we had some activity in the kitchen yesterday."

Oh crap.

"The long and the short of it is that Mrs. Zetz has retired after three decades of loyal service to Sunshine Day."

The room gasped collectively. Somebody, I don't know who, clapped briefly.

"And so now is a time of transition for our hot lunch program," he continued. "And I'm pleased to announce that for the first time ever, students will be taking a leading role in the kitchen. Cassie Birchmeyer and Molly Ollinger, where are you?" He looked around for us. Cassie was near him, and he saw her. "Could you stand up, Cassie?" She stood up. "And where's Molly? Molly?"

He didn't see me. Please let him not see me. Please oh please.

"There you are," he said. "Stand up."

I stood up, and suddenly everybody in the whole school was looking at me.

"Molly and Cassie are our student chefs now, and I hope we can all support them and encourage them to be their best selves.

"In this new phase for our kitchen, we're keenly interested in what you, the students, think of the quality of the food. Therefore, each day you eat a hot lunch, you'll be asked to fill out a ballot asking whether that day's lunch was better or worse than Mrs. Zetz's food. In your opinion. Please be honest. This is your chance to help us change the hot lunch for the better. And please be patient with us as we face the challenges of the current kitchen transition."

Okay, so this is what people would think of me now. They would see me and wonder if I wore support stockings, orthopedic shoes, and had always wanted to be a lunch lady. What kind of life could I build for myself when that was the impression people had of me? To make it worse, my partner was Cassie, so people would associate me with her. I couldn't believe this. This was *me*? This was my life?

"You can sit down now, Molly."

"What?" I said. I'd spaced out.

"You may sit down," Dr. John said.

How long had he been talking? How long had I been standing up? Cassie was already seated. Everyone was still looking at me.

I sat down.

When Cassie and I got back to the kitchen after lit., Dina opened one of the fridges to reveal the huge bowl of pudding, just waiting to be spooned into individual little paper cups. We tasted it, and it was good.

"There's hope for that Edmund," Cassie said.

"I doubt it," I said.

For the next couple of hours, we worked nonstop, following Dina's directions, asking her questions, trying not to burn ourselves or the food, then serving it up to a bunch of students and teachers who kept congratulating us on our role in the kitchen— as if it was something we had chosen to do—and then we manned the tray-return window, and finally sat down and ate a little bit ourselves. As we were eating, Dr. John came in and said that he thought we'd had a pretty good first day. He showed us the Hot Lunch Poll Box and opened it and dumped out a pile of little pieces of paper. He sorted them into two piles.

The final tally was twenty-one "Yes, this lunch is better than Mrs. Zetz's lunches" and sixty-three "No, this lunch is not as good as Mrs. Zetz's lunches." That was only a 33 percent yes vote.

"But not a bad start," Dr. John said.

"But not a good start," I countered.

12

Three Little Piles

Dina sent Cassie and me home with the next day's menu and a list of some of the problems we needed to think about. I read it as I walked home. The menu, meaty as usual, wasn't that hard to do—mostly from cans again. But Dina was asking Cassie and me to do some research and find some actual recipes that we could use next week. Actual cooking, actual recipes. Dina also suggested Cassie and me talk on the phone that night to discuss recipes, the division of labor, and so forth.

At home I poured a bowl of cereal, went to my room, changed into a new shirt—mine smelled like hamburgers—and fed Harley the goldfish. Harley lived on the shelves by my bed. I'd won him at a fair in sixth grade.

"Harley," I said, "you're my only hope. You sustain me."

He ate some flakes. That was his only talent.

I was sitting there eating my Golden Grahams, watching Harley, when the doorbell rang.

Who the heck was that? Our doorbell never rang.

I got up and went to the window. I had a good view of the front door. There, on the stoop, stood Cassie.

"Nuh uh," I said.

She looked eager and happy, as usual. She actually bent down and smelled the roses that were still blooming by the door.

I wasn't going to let her in. It was too much. It was excruciating to have to work with her, but I had to. But no one could make me let her in here. This was my Cassie-free zone. This was my Fortress of Mollitude.

She rang the doorbell again. And then, suddenly, she looked up, directly at my window, and I jumped to the side. I was pretty sure she'd seen me.

I sat on the carpet for ten minutes, finishing my cereal. The doorbell didn't ring again. Finally, I snuck a peek out the window. No Cassie.

In the morning, under the buzzing fluorescent lights of the school kitchen, we sat with Dina and looked at the day's menu. The menu was barbecue pork sandwiches (sprinkle a mix over frozen cooked pork), coleslaw (from a plastic tub), baked beans (from a can), fruit cocktail (another can), and sugar cookies (from a recipe).

"So," Dina asked, "did you find any useful recipes for next week?"

Cassie slid a single piece of paper to Dina.

"Okay," Dina said, reading. "A fancy fruit cocktail recipe."

"Fruit cocktail?" I said. "You looked up a fruit cocktail recipe?"

"Yeah . . . ," said Cassie.

"Unless I'm totally retarded," I said, "that's for *today's* menu, not next week's, and it's an item that *doesn't require a recipe or any heating whatsoever?*"

"It doesn't?"

Dina looked at Cassie over the top of her reading glasses. "It comes out of a can, dear," she said gently.

"Oh," said Cassie.

"You're making me lose my faith in humanity," I said to Cassie.

"You two didn't talk last night, did you?" asked Dina.

We shook our heads.

"Okay. That's your prerogative," said Dina. "Molly, did you bring any recipes?"

"No."

Dina sighed and scratched her nose. "I'm not here to tell you what to do, but if you want to make horrible food, make horrible food. If you want to do better than that, a wee bit of effort would be nice. Even basic food from scratch would be better than the best of Mrs. Zetz's prefab meals. But it's up to you."

I shrugged.

Cassie picked at her fingernails.

Then we went about the day's work, opening cans, defrosting the meat. Dina did all the tasks that even remotely resembled cooking. We'd assigned Edmund to cook the cookies, but with less than fifteen minutes until the noon bell, Edmund crouched by the ovens and looked in at the sugar cookies and whistled.

"The humanity . . . ," he said.

"What's wrong?" Cassie asked.

"I told you I'm not a baker," he said.

We all went over and peeked into the oven. The cookies had spread on the baking sheets to the point where they had all run together. They were still bubbly and gooey-looking, too. They weren't done.

Five minutes later they were burnt.

"One tray, zero dessert," Dina said, surveying the ruined cookies.

"Jeepers," said Cassie.

"Double jeepers!" I said mockingly.

"I'm outta here," Edmund said. He left.

Just after that, I emptied four huge cans of fruit cocktail into a serving tray. I lifted the tray and walked toward the serving table. The tray was heavy, and I could feel my arm muscles trembling, and the next thing I knew, my foot caught on something and I tumbled and the tray was upside down on the floor.

"Oh my God," said Cassie.

"You okay?" asked Dina.

"Yeah."

I looked back and saw that I'd tripped on a kitchen towel.

"Who left that towel there?" I asked.

"You just ruined the easiest thing on the menu!" Cassie said.

"No, *you* did. You left that towel there!"

"But I didn't mean to!"

Something smelled odd. "Wait. What is that *smell*?" I asked.

"What?" Cassie said, sniffing.

"Yeah, I don't like that," Dina said, looking around. "Something burning."

"Can't be from the ovens," Cassie said. "The only thing in there is the buns warming up."

Dina walked over, opened one oven. "Oh for the love of glory," she said, and pulled a baking sheet out. On the sheet were a bunch of sandwich buns *still in their plastic bags*. The bags had melted.

"What is that!?" I said to Cassie. "You didn't take them out of the bags?"

"I thought you could heat them up in the bags!"

"No, you can't. The bags are *plastic*. What universe do you come from where plastic is heat-proof?"

A timer went off.

"Let's just hope the smell didn't get into the beans," said Dina, pulling a big tray of baked beans out of another oven. She put a clean spoon in the beans and blew on it and then tasted.

"Well?" I asked.

"Maybe they're not ruined," said Dina. "Just slightly burned-plasticy."

Edmund poked his head in the kitchen. "What is that stink?"

I explained about the sandwich bags.

"It smells like a baked skunk," he said.

"Shut up!" said Cassie.

At least the coleslaw—straight from the tub—was fine. But the pork somehow came out sweet and very sticky. Even Dina couldn't figure out why—all we'd done was heat the precooked meat and stir in some packets of flavoring.

So each student got a tray with three little piles: decent coleslaw, skunky beans, and cloyingly sweet pork.

"Three piles," said Brad Berrington, surveying the tray I handed to him. "Where's the bun?"

"Just eat it!" barked Cassie.

"Can I write a song about this?" Brad asked me. "About the three piles?"

"Yes," I said. "I would really like to hear that song. The three pile song."

This made Brad happy, and he smiled and wandered to the milk cooler.

Portia Babbliabali was next in line. She was the school's resident musical theater genius, writer-director of last year's hit *Situation Normal, All Funked Up* and the much anticipated *The Bleepity Bleep Bleep Gang*. When I handed her the tray with the three piles she looked at it, took off her sunglasses, and said, "Who *designed* this lunch?"

"It was a group effort," I said.

She was looking at the food like it was a work of art. "I've never seen anything like this. It's strange and haunting."

"It's just bad food," I said.

"No, it's gorgeous . . . ," she said, walking away.

"Something stinks," said Seth Lawson.

"Do you want to explain the smell?" I said to Cassie.

"No."

"Let me put it this way," I said to Seth. "It's the smell of incompetence."

Lots of the students refused to even take the lunch. And many trays came back untouched, or with just the slaw having been eaten. Cassie and I argued as we took the returned trays and dumped the food in the trash.

"This is embarrassing," Cassie said. "Making a lunch no one would touch."

"You're right. Baking plastic bags is embarrassing."

"That's not what I said."

"It's what you did," I said.

"At least I didn't spill the fruit!" said Cassie.

"I tripped on a towel you dropped!"

Dr. John had entered the kitchen and was watching us argue.

"And what was up with the sugar cookie recipe you gave to Edmund?" I asked. "Where did you find such a horrible recipe?"

"I Googled it!"

"Wow, look at you," I said. "Search Engine Sally."

"What does that mean?"

"It means you found a horrible sugar cookie recipe and it's your fault!"

"Aren't you going to stop them?" Dina asked Dr. John.

"No," he said.

All the trays were returned, but we just kept standing there, fighting.

"Maybe if you'd done some research into recipes last night like we'd been asked to," Cassie said, "we wouldn't have had so many problems!"

"Recipes won't help us if we don't know we have to take buns out of plastic bags before heating them!"

"Will too!"

"Not!" I screamed.

"Will!"

I blew a raspberry in her face.

She was stone-faced for a moment. Then she wiped her cheek with her sleeve. "I saw you," she said quietly.

"What?"

"When I came to your house yesterday, I *saw* you."

"Yeah, *and*? Who cares? I've got a suggestion for you," I said, "don't ever come to my house again for any reason. Got that?"

"And I was waiting all night for you to call!"

"So was I!" I said.

"And I'm sorry I didn't call!" she screamed.

"So am I!"

We stood there, looking at each other, breathing through our noses. Had we just apologized to each other?

Then Cassie said calmly, "Maybe if we had more help we could do better."

"But what kind of help?" I asked. "It's not like we can hire someone."

"How about volunteers? Other students."

"Maybe students from study hall . . ."

"A sign-up sheet . . . ," Cassie said.

"A sign-up sheet!" I seconded.

We turned to Dr. John. He was still watching us, his arms crossed.

"Can we put up a sign-up sheet to get volunteers from the study halls?" I asked.

"Yes," he said, then he left.

"More help is a good idea," Dina said, wiping down the serving table. "See, when you two aren't fighting, you're not totally incompetent."

We put the sign-up sheet outside of Dr. John's office. No one signed it that afternoon.

Thursday's lunch was as much of a disaster as Wednesday's. The chili—yes, from cans—tasted like oranges and cinnamon. How? We blamed each other.

No one signed the sign-up sheet on Thursday, even though Dr. John made an announcement about it at the Before School Meeting.

Friday's lunch was burned beyond recognition. The students had to make do with crackers, peanut butter, and raisins.

At the end of Friday, before walking home, I checked the sign-up sheet one last time. I was sure it would be empty.

But it wasn't. It had been signed by Clyde Percival Brewell, our overzealous lunchroom attendant.

13

You'll Eat Your Greens and Like Them!

Brad Berrington e-mailed me that weekend. There was no text, but there was an mp3 attached. It was labeled "thethreepilesong." Surely nothing good could come from the thing. I opened it.

It was a song—just Brad and his guitar. It went like this:

> For lunch I had a lovely tray,
> it had a pile of beans, a pile of meat, a pile of slaw,
> and it was served up by a queen.
>
> Molly O., you pretend to be detached,
> but me I'm hoping you can be catched
> and if my grammar is subpar
> then please forgive me for wanting to . . .
> find your heart . . .
> find your heart . . .
> find your—

That was the point at which I stopped the song. I didn't feel the need to subject myself to more embarrassing cater-wauling about my circulatory muscle. Seriously, the lyrics were frightening. I could feel myself blushing, even in the privacy of my own room. What did Brad think he was doing? Did he think this was an appropriate way to woo me? Not that there was *any* appropriate way for him to woo me, but still, "The Three Pile Song"? Brad had always tried to talk to me, and I had always tried to end our conversations as quickly as possible, but this was the first time he'd written a song for me.

Needless to say, I did not respond to the e-mail.

Moving from one remarkably sad Sunshine Day boy to another: Clyde Brewell marched into the kitchen Monday morning with a pixielike grin on his face and a cookbook under his arm. It was an hour before classes started, and already Cassie, Dina, and I were working.

Clyde said hello and then shook Dina's hand, then Cassie's, then mine.

"Why are you shaking our hands?" I asked.

"It's a sort of 'Hello, I'm pleased to be on the team,' gesture," he said.

"Aw, that's nice," Dina said.

"It's a dork move," I said.

"Are you going to come in early every day?" Cassie asked.

"If you'll let me," he answered. "And I know I'm marching into a tea party that's already under way, but I was wondering if it is at all possible to put me in charge of desserts."

"Tea party?" I said.

"Do you like to make desserts?" Dina asked.

"I don't know," he answered.

"Why don't you know?" Cassie asked.

"Tea party?" I repeated.

"Well, I don't think I've ever made a dessert," he said. "It's just that I've been thinking recently that maybe I would like to be a pastry chef someday and this is the perfect opportunity to test the waters, so to say."

"But you've never made a dessert," I said.

"Nope. But I've got a cookbook!" he said enthusiastically. He held his book out. "It's an original 1950 Betty Crocker. It's a classic."

"Who's Betty Crocker?" Cassie asked.

Dina and I looked at her.

"And I'm not afraid of hard work and sweat!" Clyde said.

"Just don't sweat on the food," I suggested.

Clyde said that he would come in early each day, work for about an hour, then go to classes. He would come back during his third-hour study hall to finish up the dessert, then he'd be in the kitchen during lunchtime to help serve. It sounded fine: if he would take care of dessert, that was one less thing for us to worry about.

That day, we were working with the last menu that Mrs. Zetz had planned and ordered ingredients for. Unfortunately, it was one of her least popular menus: fried chicken, lima beans, cooked greens, half a banana, and raisin cake. Dina heated the frozen prefried chicken, since she didn't trust us with it, but that left us messing about with the lima beans and cooked greens.

Clyde decided to make a caramel cake—from his cookbook—instead of the universally detested raisin cake. Dina let him have a corner of the kitchen all to himself—an area we didn't really use—and he worked steadily before school, and again during third period.

"Where's the melted butter?" he asked us at one point.

"Butter doesn't come melted, honey," Dina said.

"You mean you have to melt it from scratch?" he asked.

"This is our pastry chef?" I said.

After his cake had been in the oven for ten minutes, it bubbled up, overflowed the pan, dribbled onto the floor of the oven, and started to burn there. Thus, it was another ONE TRAY, ZERO DESSERT day.

"Aw, man, no dessert again?" said a junior name Ethan Joskow as we were serving up lunch. "And *greens*?"

"You'll eat your greens and *like* them!" I said. I'd spent a lot of time on the greens—because they came in small cans, I'd had to open lots of them—and if they all came back untouched I thought I would implode at the idea that all that work had been for nothing. So I started saying that little phrase, "You'll eat your greens and *like* them!" each time I plopped a serving down onto a tray. Most of the students didn't say anything but just looked at the soggy, dark greens with veiled disgust.

But when I said it to Seth Lawson, he replied, "I know! Can I have double?"

I gave him triple. Plop, plop, plop.

And that's when I heard something disturbing, something more disturbing than the slappy flop of hot greens hitting the lunch tray: the folk guitar stylings of one Brad Berrington, junior troubadour, starting a song that sounded familiar but which I didn't, for a moment, recognize.

Brad was playing his weekly Noontime Expression gig over in the far corner of the lunchroom, and so far he'd just been singing his usual set of songs, like "Famously Smiling," "Ramblin' Sophomore," and the favorite, "Slow Bus to Hillsdale Mall."

But what was this new song? Why was it familiar and yet frightening? Why did my insides feel like they'd just been gripped by an icy hand?

Brad began singing:

> *"For lunch I had a lovely tray,*
> *it had a pile beans, a pile of meat, a pile of slaw,*
> *and it was served up by a queen."*

At this point, I was out of the kitchen, charging toward Brad.

> *"Molly O., you pretend to be detached,*
> *but me I'm hoping you can be catched*
> *and if my grammar is subpar*
> *then please forgive me for—"*

I yanked the microphone cord out of the amplifier.

"Stop!" I barked.

"But . . . ," Brad said. "It's my new favorite song."

"You can't sing about me in public!" I said. I grabbed the microphone and hit him with it. "You can't sing about me period! It's like stealing my soul."

"Ow!" said Brad.

"You sing, Molly!" screamed someone in the lunchroom. Other kids were whistling and clapping.

"Molly, get back in here!" Cassie yelled across the lunchroom.

I handed the mike to Brad and backed away from him.

"No singing about me," I warned, pointing at him.

"Did Brad write a song for you?" Cassie asked me a few minutes later as we were scraping the little piles of greens off of all the returned trays.

"I swear I never encouraged him in the slightest."

"I think he's cute," said Cassie.

"You're entitled to your opinion."

"Student chefs!" Dr. John barked, entering. "The ballot box *est arrivé*!"

He opened the Hot Lunch Poll Box and dumped out the slips of paper. He counted while we were still taking the returned trays.

We got a 9 percent vote. It was our lowest yet. Lower than the three-pile meal, lower than the cinnamon chili, and lower even than Friday's crackers and peanut butter.

"I've had an idea how to help you," Dr. John said. "Seeing as you're not getting a lot of volunteers."

"Are you going to rehire Marta Zetz?" I asked.

"No."

"Okay, how about hiring a new, non-Zetz head cook?"

"No." He put two pieces of paper on the counter. "These are the rosters from third and fourth period study halls. I've decided to let you pick one or two people from these study halls to help you out."

"Anyone?" Cassie said.

"Anyone who agrees to help," Dr. John said. "Maybe there's a friend who would be helpful, or you know someone who's a good cook, or whatever."

"Jeez," Cassie said. "This could be really good. Thank you!"

"You're welcome," Dr. John said.

"I'm not so sure anyone will want to help . . . ," I said. But I was already busy scanning the third-period roster. I knew darn well who was in the fourth-period study hall—and there wasn't a single person in there I would want in the kitchen. But the third-period roster was new territory, mostly full of juniors, and I went down the list and saw, almost instantly, one name that stopped me. It was like finding a nugget of gold in a sack of pebbles. The name was Devin Harper.

Devin Harper!

But I had to play it cool. "Uh, I don't know . . . ," I said. "Are any of these people gonna be any real help in the kitchen?"

"Surely some of them would be," Dr. John said.

"Hm," Cassie said. "I don't know a lot of these kids." She was going down the list of names with her finger. "Oh!" she said, after a bit.

"Oh what?" I said.

"Nothing."

"What we can do," said Dr. John, "is that you can tell me a name and I'll pull them out of study hall tomorrow and have them come down and talk to you in the kitchen. That way you can kind of interview them, see if they'll be of use to you, see if they're agreeable to giving up their study hall. Is there anyone?"

"I don't know," I said, slumping there, eyes fixed on Devin Harper's name.

"Yeah, oh, I don't know, there's no one really jumping out . . . ," Cassie said. "But, oh . . . um . . . oh . . . how about . . . how about, um, Devin Harper?"

I wasn't sure I'd heard the name right. I thought maybe my own mind had transposed Devin's name for whichever one Cassie had said.

"Sure. Devin Harper," Dr. John said, and he made a check mark by the name. "I will deliver Devin Harper to you tomorrow at ten."

It was the most beautiful sentence I had ever heard.

I know I said earlier that there was no one in Sunshine Day High School worthy of being *liked*. That is true. But there was one person, and only one, who was worthy of being *adored*. Let me put it this way: if Devin Harper had decided to sing a song about me in front of the entire school, I would not have hit him with the microphone. I would have been a willing subject. I would have screamed "Encore! Encore!"

Last semester, the Sunshine Day spring play had been *Ever Since Next Year*, by T. J. Porely. Ms. Valeri required us to attend. So I went by myself and sat in the back corner, ready to endure the night with the aid of the six dollars' worth of candy I had in my coat. But within a minute or two of the curtain going up, I forgot about the candy.

The play was about a man who lived his life backward, starting with his death, and then growing younger and healthier. He retired, weathered the travails of middle age, his children were born, he got married, and so on and so forth until he became a child again, and then an infant, and he could no longer talk or walk, and in the last moment of the play he took a huge breath of air and disappeared between two sheets of fabric that represented the womb.

The character's name was Charles Hunter, and the actor was Devin Harper. For two hours Devin Harper was onstage the whole time. He was alive with the character, and I believed every word he said, and at the end of the play I cried, and then when Devin came out on the stage for the curtain call I had to remind myself that he was an actor, not the character, and I looked at him, and his smile, and thought he was the most gorgeous boy I'd ever seen.

After school, I went home, marched straight to my room, knelt on the floor, looked under my bed, moved some dirty clothes out of the way, and pulled out my old Valentine's Day shoe box from fifth grade. I'd decorated it myself: you know, paper hearts, seashells, and plastic roses, and too much glue. In the box were my sketchbooks going all the way back to seventh grade. I pulled out the book from freshman year and leafed through it. And there, near the end of the volume, were the only words in the whole thing: quotes from Devin Harper's play last semester.

One of the entries was: "And if I clutch thusly, with all my power, all my might, I still cannot hold on to these things. I can only feel more distinctly the sensation of my world retreating."

And: "If I answer yes at last, please do not confuse that with 'I agree, sirs, most wholeheartedly'!"

Yes, I had gone back for the play's second performance. And the next day I checked out a copy of the play and read it in one sitting. I then discovered that the play had been amended. The performance I had seen was *better* than the playscript. Devin Harper's lines were bigger and bolder and more eloquent and raw. Most of the quotations I had loved—the ones I had copied down in my quote book—were not in the playscript.

I understood: Devin Harper had gone beyond the boundaries of the original play, and rewritten his own part.

That's why I fell for him.

14

I Vote for Me Doing the Sausages

I was thinking about Devin as I mixed the biscuit dough the next morning. I checked the kitchen clock—a quarter till ten. I still had time to mix this dough and then clean up before Devin arrived. I checked the recipe at my side, made a note with a stubby pencil, then tucked the pencil behind my ear and kept mixing. I looked at the recipe again. I wanted to check off one of the instructions, but I couldn't find the pencil. It wasn't behind my ear. Where was it? I looked at the huge bowl of dough.

"Oops," I said.

Across the kitchen, Dina heard me. "Oops?" she said. "What oops?"

"Nothing."

"I heard an oops."

"I just . . . just spilled a little baking powder here, that's all."

Suddenly, the bell rang. Fifteen minutes early? Well, the school had had problems with erratic bells last year, and I figured it was happening again.

I dug into the dough—nearly up to my elbows—looking for the pencil. Finally, just as I found the pencil and pulled it out, someone knocked on the door that led into the lunchroom. Clyde, who had just returned from the stockroom, opened the door. There stood Devin Harper.

"Clyde, baby!" said Devin.

These two knew each other?

"A good day to you, Devin," said Clyde.

At that moment, Cassie came back into the kitchen from the hallway that went to the stockroom. Since I had last seen her ten or so minutes ago, she had put on heels, taken off her apron and hairnet, and done something rather clever with her hair. A bun-braid? A *brund*? She was also wearing more makeup than before.

"Devin!" she said. "I'm Cassie. We're really happy you're here."

I looked at the clock on the wall. It still said a quarter till ten, even though it had been at least five minutes since I'd last checked the time. Was the clock broken . . . ? Why was Cassie all gussied up? Did Cassie like Devin, too? Had she sabotaged the clock so I wouldn't be ready when he got here?

We took Devin into the lunchroom and sat at a lunch table. I was trying to pick bits of dough from my arms without looking like I was trying to pick bits of dough from my arms.

"Can I get you anything to drink?" Cassie asked Devin. "Milk or . . . milk?"

"Yeah, okay," Devin said. "Milk sounds superb."

Cassie got up and walked toward the milk cooler. Devin watched her walking away. Then he looked at me, straight at me with his blue eyes. His hair was a little bit shaggy, and I had to resist the impulse to sink my hands into it.

"Woah. What a mess," he said.

He's talking about the *dough*, I told myself, not *me*.

"Biscuit dough," I said. I couldn't think of anything else to say.

Devin touched his cheek. "You've got a little something . . ."

I rubbed my cheek with the back of my hand—a bit of dough came off.

"And in your hair," he said.

Cassie returned with the milk and sat down. Devin opened the milk and took a drink. He said, "Ah . . ."

"Again, we're really happy you're here," Cassie said.

"I'm sure it's neat and everything, working in the kitchen," he said, "but I think I'd rather stay in study hall, get work done, you know? No offense or anything."

"Oh," Cassie said, "Dr. John didn't tell you?"

"Tell me what?"

"It's not really *optional*," she said.

Yes! If her lies and also-crush on Devin would get him into the kitchen, fine!

"But I like study hall," he said. "I use study hall."

"To do what?" I said. I wasn't even sure why I said this.

"To *study*," Devin said.

"The thing is," Cassie said, "we didn't make this decision."

Devin considered this. "So I have to come work in the kitchen?"

We nodded.

"Every day during third period?"

We nodded again.

"But why?" he asked. "Is this punishment for something? Should I go talk to Dr. John and see—"

"No!" Cassie said.

"Your name was chosen at random," I said. "Dr. John knew we could use more help in the kitchen, but he didn't want it to be seen as a punishment, so we drew your name from a hat."

"Fine," he said. He shrugged. "So it goes."

"See!" Cassie said. "It'll be grand!"

I nodded in agreement. "We're going to have so much fun!" I said.

Fun? Had I just said *fun?*

We all three walked into the kitchen. My knees felt a little wobbly. I wasn't quite sure how to act. Being this close to Devin Harper was a bit overwhelming. He was a lot bigger when seen up close. But it was a good kind of big. There was nothing bad about it. There was nothing bad about Devin at all. He had perfect teeth, and his smile was just a little crooked, in the cutest way possible. And he walked with just a bit of a swagger, and his jeans were gorgeous—I don't know quite how else to say it. The boy could wear jeans.

In the kitchen Devin introduced himself to Dina. But Cassie immediately whisked him away to help her get the cans of stewed tomatoes from the stockroom.

"Hey, Clyde," I said. "How do you know Devin?"

"I worked on the spring play with him. I was a lighting technician."

"But you weren't enrolled in Sunshine Day last semester."

"Oh, I got special permission to come and help out with the play."

"Cool," I said. I had to restrain myself from asking things like, so what was it *like* working so close to a god, and did Devin ever mention that he liked blue hair?

"Yeah, Devin's totally cool," said Clyde. "He's righteously awesome and neat."

I stood there watching Clyde cutting pats of butter. We were cooking a breakfast menu for lunch—actually, it had been Clyde's idea. He said breakfast was the easiest meal to cook, so we should do breakfast. But it left Clyde without a dessert to cook today.

"Am I doing this right?" Clyde asked me. I realized I'd been standing there just watching him work.

"Yeah. Hey, do you think Cassie and Devin have been in the stockroom too long?"

Clyde shrugged.

"I better go check on them," I said.

I went down the hallway and into the stockroom. Cassie had sort of cornered Devin and was flirting with him. "Hey!" I said.

"What?" Cassie said, turning on me.

"Devin, I need help with the sausages," I said.

"Dina's doing the sausages," Cassie said.

"I'm taking over."

"But you're vegetarian."

"Yes, but I help out wherever I'm needed."

"No you don't."

"Yes I do."

"Since when?"

"Since forever," I said.

"Are you two sisters or something?" Devin asked.

"What?" I said.

"You kinda argue like sisters, that's all."

Cassie glared at me. Devin dutifully followed me outside to the freezer. I didn't know what to say as we walked, so I didn't say anything. I punched in the lock combination to open the freezer and we went inside and Devin said, "Wow. Cold."

"Yeah," I said. I realized this wasn't very flirty. So I said, "I *know*! So cold!"

"If this door closes, are we locked in here?" Devin asked.

He was standing close to me. On the one hand this might have meant that he was flirting with me. On the other hand, there just wasn't much room in here, so it's not like he had a choice to stand far away. We were so close that I could feel the warmth from his body.

"No," I admitted.

"Your name's . . ."

"Molly."

"Molly," he said.

"Present!" I said.

"What?"

"I mean, you said my name like you were taking roll and I said 'Present!' "

This was the best I could do?

"Oh." He looked around. "Are we going to just stand in here?"

Here he was—the guy who had written all those wonderful lines for the spring play. He was right in front of me. I had to take action. I had to be direct and yet indirect. I had to break through the bonds of cowardice and doubt and step confidently toward the future. *Right now.*

I looked Devin in the eyes and said, "If I answer yes at last, please do not confuse that with 'I agree, sirs, most wholeheartedly'!"

"What the—hey, that's from the spring play."

"Oh, yeah," I said casually. "That play was good. Hey, weren't you in it?"

"I'm doing my best to forget the lines from that thing. But seriously, how long are we going to be in here?"

"It's just that I think it was the best play I've ever seen. And the extra writing you did was awesome."

"Extra writing . . . ?"

"Yeah, how you expanded your character's dialogue."

"Oh, yeah. Thanks. Yeah."

"You're a really good writer."

He said, "I can't feel my face, it's so cold."

A minute later, we were counting out boxes of sausages when the door of the freezer opened and Cassie was there and she said, "Dina said I'm doing the sausages and Devin's helping me."

"Dina doesn't have the authority to say that," I said.

Devin was standing between me and the doorway, so to talk to Cassie I had to look around him.

"Well, I'm the meat expert," Cassie said, "so I say I get to do the sausages."

"What kind of sense does that make?"

"Total sense."

"No it doesn't."

"It's ridiculous."

"So says you."

"That's right. *One* of us is sane at least."

"I don't even know how to answer that."

"Ha!" barked Cassie.

Devin sighed.

"You can't just have your way," I said to Cassie. "This kitchen is run by both of us. It's not a dictatorship."

"All right, then it's a democracy, so let's vote on this."

"Fine," I said. "I vote for me doing the sausages and Devin helping me."

"And I vote," said Cassie, "for me doing the sausages and Devin helping me."

"Okay, a tie," I said. "Big whoop. Democracy can bite my butt."

Cassie said, "Why don't we let Devin be the tiebreaker?"

"Okay," I said. "Devin, what do you say? Do you want to make the sausages with me, or do you want to work with her and get pulled into her sick little world of anger and delusion?"

"You didn't have to put it like that," said Cassie.

"Me or Molly," I said to Devin. "How do you vote?"

Devin stood there, arms crossed over his chest, shivering. He furrowed his brow, thought about it, then he said, "Uh, what's Clyde doing? Can I help Clyde?"

It all led to more bad food. With the wrangling over Devin we did a poor job focusing on the tasks at hand. We cooked the sausages too early and on too low a heat, and Dina decided to throw them all out in the name of food safety. And when I got Devin and Clyde to help me with the biscuits, we were too energetic and overhandled the dough, so that the biscuits came out tough and dry. The bickering while we cracked the eggs resulted in a dozen eggs falling off the counter, and we caused Devin to spill the honey by both trying to help him.

Devin left at the end of third period and we salvaged as much of the lunch as we could. Luckily, the number of students and faculty eating hot lunch every day had dropped from about eighty to less than thirty since Mrs. Zetz quit, so we did end up having almost enough food for everyone.

At the end of the lunch hour, as we were cleaning off the returned trays, we saw Devin talking to Dr. John in the lunchroom. After a moment, Dr. John looked over toward the kitchen.

"Uh-oh," I said.

"Should we go over there?" Cassie asked.

"Definitely not," I said.

But then Devin and Dr. John were done talking and Dr. John came into the kitchen.

"Great day in the morning!" he said. "Breakfast for lunch was a good idea. Like seeing a butterfly in the middle of January. Or having an old friend knock on your office door and say, hey, brother, ditch this job and let's drive out to the woods and watch the stars all night long. Yeah? Yeah?"

Disturbing stuff. But seeing as Sunshine Day was founded by a bunch of hippies—including Dr. John—it was understandable that sometimes they got a little carried away with the trippy imagery.

"This guy," Dr. John said, pointing across the room at Clyde, who was in his corner reading his cookbook. "I heard it was his idea to have breakfast in the morning. Don't let this guy go."

"Thanks," said Clyde.

"Hey, what was the Hot Lunch Poll result today?" Cassie asked.

"Aha! Good news. Twenty percent."

Twenty percent was only good news in the sense that it was an improvement over the past few days. Still, it wasn't even half of what we needed.

"Just out of curiosity," I said, "exactly how many yes votes did we get?"

"Six."

"Six?" I said. "Six people in the whole school?"

"Including a very enthusiastic vote from me. I vote yes every day because I know how hard you're working. Oh, and Seth Lawson told me he votes yes every day because he thinks a student-led kitchen is a progressive movement worth supporting, even if the food isn't progressive."

"Nice," I said. What it meant, though, is that there were four people in the whole school who were voting yes on the basis of the food.

"I've got a bit of a downer to deliver to you, though. Devin Harper has asked if he could be excused from the kitchen. He's so busy with rehearsals for *The Bleepity Bleep Bleep Gang*, and he really needs his study hall time."

"Oh, sure," Cassie said, "we totally understand."

"Coolness," said Dr. John. "Catch you chefs later."

He left.

"I think," I said, "Devin can bleepity bleep bleep his bleeping bleeper if working in the bleeping kitchen isn't bleeping cool enough for him."

"Yeah . . . ," Cassie said. I could tell she was upset.

We finished cleaning the rest of the trays, then Cassie washed up and left the kitchen. I sat at the counter, with a few minutes until the bell, eating a dense biscuit. The disappointment of the morning—of having Devin right there in front of me, and then having him whisked away—made me glum. I didn't even feel like blaming Cassie. Maybe if I were a better person or a better communicator or funnier or cuter or smarter, Devin wouldn't have wanted to leave.

Clyde came over and sat near me.

I looked at him. I continued gnawing on my biscuit.

"Can I just say something?" he said.

"Don't know."

"I just wanted to . . . well, I heard Brad's song yesterday. And, plus, someone forwarded it to me and so I heard it again, and—"

"Wait. Someone forwarded *what* to you?"

"The mp3."

I stared at him. I wasn't hearing this. This was *not* happening.

"The mp3 of 'The Three Pile Song,' " he clarified.

I put my head down on the counter.

"And I just wanted to tell you that I don't think you're detached. I think you're the opposite. You're attached. You're so attached that maybe sometimes it hurts."

I still had my head on the counter. Maybe I would just stay like this.

"Anyway," said Clyde, "that's what I wanted to say."

He paused a moment, then I heard him stand up and leave.

The news that the mp3 was being circulated was bad news on top of bad news (the fact the song existed in the first place) on top of bad news (the fact that Brad had performed the song in front of the entire school) on top of bad news (the Devin Harper fiasco) on top of bad news (the fact that two weeks after the food fight we were still in the damn kitchen, with little hope of escaping) on top of the general bad news of my life. So I had a big bad news sandwich. Worst of all, I couldn't do anything about the damn song. True, I could punch Brad Berrington in the ear the next time I saw him. I could destroy his guitar. I could maybe poison his lunch. But it wouldn't erase the song from people's memories or hard drives. Honestly, what was I supposed to do? What else could go wrong? Or, to put it more accurately, what else *would* go wrong? In my experience, wrongness just created more wrongness—a whole storm of wrongness—and right now it was thundering awfully loudly.

15

It Would Be Wrong of Us Not to Have a Second Piece

The rest of that week we tried and failed to recruit good help from the study halls. On Wednesday, we got Justin Porter to come. We thought he would be handy in the kitchen because he was a Boy Scout and always bragged about all the things he could cook on a campout.

"Let's rock and roll!" he said. He clapped his hands together and looked around the kitchen. "What can I do?"

"Hm," I said, "do you know how to bake potatoes?"

He pointed at me. "Yes! Yes I do!"

We brought him the bag of potatoes. He looked at them. He adjusted his glasses.

"But," he said, "it occurs to me that the way I cook potatoes is to wrap them in foil and put them in the coals of a hot campfire."

"Dina, can we build a campfire in here?" I asked.

"No," she said.

A few pointed questions made it clear that the only way Justin knew how to cook *anything* was with a campfire. We let him go back to study hall.

Then on Thursday Michelle Piker from third-period study hall agreed to work with us. She was a willing and semicapable helper, but her allergies to disinfectants meant that she sneezed constantly in the kitchen. She wouldn't do.

On Friday we interviewed five people. But no one wanted to be involved in the production of food that was so universally bad. So the first four kids we talked to just plain didn't want to help. The fifth kid, though, a freshman named Jerry Pisney, was gung ho. He sat there with his sideways baseball cap and pleaded his case.

"I love to cook," he said. "I'm all about cooking and food and working hard."

"Super," I said. "Man of my dreams."

"I can grill, broil, braise, bake, fry, sear, steam, and boil. All of it."

"I don't even know what some of those things mean," said Cassie.

"Oh, but there's just one problem," said Jerry.

"What's that?" I asked.

He stood up, cleared his throat, and starting singing:

"For lunch I had a lovely tray,
it had a pile beans, a pile of meat, a pile of slaw,
and it was served up by a queen."

"Stop," I said.

"Molly O., you pretend be detached,
but me I'm hoping you can be catched—"

"Stop it!"

He didn't stop but sang the whole song. When he was done, he said, " 'The Three Pile Song.' Love it! I'm all about *that*!"

"You're a turd," I said.

"Does this mean you don't want to work in the kitchen?" Cassie asked.

"No way I want to work in a kitchen! I just came down here because my peeps dared me to sing 'The Three Pile Song' to you."

"Well, go tell them you did," said Cassie.

"And tell them," I said, "that I'm going to put estrogen in their lunches."

See: wrongness creating more wrongness. How was I supposed to react to something so dumb as Jerry Pisney singing "The Three Pile Song" to my face?

We did a poor job in the kitchen that day, distracted by the five interviews and mired in our own ineptitude. We made tacos, because Cassie thought that it would be easy because the instructions on the taco seasoning packet were so simple they were printed as pictures with no words. How could we mess that up? But we ended up burning the taco shells, adding too much taco seasoning to the ground beef, shredding the lettuce too early so that by lunchtime it was all brown and metallic-tasting, finding that the salsa we'd ordered was actually extra-hot instead of mild, and discovering that we didn't have enough prechopped tomatoes from the food distributor to go around. Also, they tasted like wet cork. To top it off, Clyde ruined a chocolate cake by forgetting to put in the sugar.

So we loaded each lunch tray with a pile of extra-spicy taco meat, some cheese that was chopped instead of grated (the kitchen didn't have a cheese grater because Mrs. Zetz had ordered all her cheese pregrated), a condiment cup of dangerously hot salsa, approximately three pea-size pieces of flavorless tomato, and pineapple tidbits (we'd served these three days in a row).

Also, we'd made an error ordering the milk for the week, and therefore there was no milk.

"This lunch looks weird," Brad Berrington told me as I served him. "Hey is this another pile lunch? A pile of meat, a pile of—"

"No!" I said. "No piles! This is a pile-free lunchroom!"

At the end of lunch, we sat down. Cassie sat across the counter sighing, looking out the window. I gnawed on my fingernails.

"Stop that," Cassie said. "I can actually hear you chewing your fingernails."

"But I'm fed up and . . . and . . . chewing my fingernails helps me think."

"Think about what?"

Something clicked. I had an idea.

"I've got it," I said.

"Got what?"

"Our ticket out of the kitchen."

"How?"

"Look, it's kinda clear that we can't cook our way out of here, right?"

She nodded.

"So we have to find another way."

"Is it something illegal? I'm not going to do anything illegal."

"No, it's not illegal," I said. "It's just slightly unethical."

"How slightly?" she asked.

"Lookit," I said, "we need to get Mrs. Zetz back. That's all. We need to convince her to come back."

"I don't see that happening."

"But what if we played all nicey-nicey and baked her a cake and went to her house and apologized and pretended we all wanted her back and the cake could have a message on it like 'We love you, Mrs. Z!' and it would solve everything!"

"We can't bake."

"So we'll buy a cake, okay? And just pretend we made it."

"No," she said, shouldering her backpack. "That plan is just a big wad of lies."

"But what if it worked?"

"Lies!" she barked and she left.

The bell rang.

"I like lies!" I called after her. Then I muttered, "They're the best."

I rummaged in my messenger bag, found a Tootsie Roll, and unwrapped it. It was my lunch.

On my way to my locker, I walked by the old volunteer sign-up sheet outside Dr. John's office and couldn't help but notice that people had been having a field day with it. It had this list of volunteers:

Clyde Percival Brewell
Mr. Potato Head
Aunt Jemima
Uncle Ben
The Hamburglar

The Ghost of Davy Crockett
MY DAD
COLONEL SANDERS
Captain Crunch
FOFO THE WONDERDOG
an assortment of sticks and acorns
several handbags

I tore it down.

My afternoon class schedule was all the classes that ended in Y—history, geometry, and biology. In biology, my last class of the day, Mr. Craig had us clear the floor by arranging our desks in a circle, then we each were assigned a role in a living representation of a plant cell. I, for example, was a mitochondrion, as was Cassie. Some of the kids formed the cell wall by forming a circle and holding hands. Devin Harper was the nucleus, of course—the starring role. Other people were ribosomes, chloroplasts, and so forth. Cassie got to hand a Nerf ball to Devin—representing some protein or something?—but I just had to float around doing nothing.

When the cell role-playing was over, we all sat down and Mr. Craig went up to the front lab table and opened the black box.

"All right, kiddos," he said, "it's open topic Friday time."

Mr. Craig, who was about six and a half feet tall but had strangely tiny ears, had been doing open topic Fridays since the school was founded. Basically, it just meant that during the last part of class on Fridays we got to discuss any scientific topic. Students put topic suggestions in a locked black metal box with a slot in the top, and he drew a new topic out every week. There were six metal boxes, one for each of his classes, lined up on a table by the classroom door.

"Mr. Craig? Should we put our desks back into rows?" Brad Berrington asked.

"Nah, it's cool, Bradley," Mr. Craig said, fumbling around with his hand in the black box. "Hey, are there *any* topic suggestions this week? Or am I just a man with his hand in an empty box?"

Just then he found a piece of paper.

"Aha!" He unfolded the paper and read it silently.

I looked at Devin Harper, sitting across the circle from me. Sure, I was just a mitochondrion and he was a nucleus, but didn't the nucleus *need* the mitochondrion?

"This one's not so good . . . ," Mr. Craig said.

"Why not?" asked Seth Lawson. His T-shirt today had a big bar code on it and said GLOBALISM PUTS US ALL BEHIND BARS.

"It's just not nice," Mr. Craig said.

"But I thought the rule of open topic Friday was that any question would be game, no matter how controversial," said Seth.

Mr. Craig glanced at me. Why?

"Okay, I'll read it," he said, "in the spirit of an open community and scientific frankness. It says 'From a biological standpoint, how is it possible to make worse food than Mrs. Zetz?' "

The room was silent. Then there was a little bit of snickering. Who snickered? And who wrote that? Cassie and I looked at each other. I felt myself blushing.

"See, I said it wasn't an appropriate question," Mr. Craig said. "I shouldn't have read it." His hand was already back in the black box, searching for another question. "That question was hurtful, and I don't think it was in the spirit of scientific—"

He had pulled out another piece of paper and was reading it now.

"What?" Seth said.

Mr. Craig sighed. "Okay. I guess it'll have to do. It says, 'Could a person subsist on a diet consisting only of today's taco lunch?' Interesting. Molly and Cassie, do you mind if we tackle this one?"

Cassie said no. I shrugged. But I could feel my face blushing again. Why'd he have to draw even *more* attention to us by asking us if it was okay? Of course it wasn't okay! It was horribly not okay! But what was I going to do, protest and therefore let everyone know how embarrassed I was? I looked down at my notebook, doodling with all my might, as if I wasn't even listening to the discussion.

"Okay, people," Mr. Craig said, turning on the projector so that we could see his computer screen, "a little bit of nutrition science. First, what we need to do is break the meal down into its components. Luckily we have the cooks among us, so they can help. Then, we'll look at the nutritional contents of each item, and calculate how these contents would compare to both the ideal and the subsistence-level nutritional requirements of the average adult.

"So first, let's talk about salsa."

Fifteen minutes later, it was over. I left Mr. Craig's room and went down the hallway. I felt my shoulder bump against another student, then another, but I didn't care. I wasn't even watching where I was walking—I was looking at my feet, just going to my locker, just trying to get out of there.

"Hey, Molly!" someone called. It was Johnny Harris. He'd been in bio. with me. "I'm dying . . . eating too many taco lunches . . . can't survive." He slowly sank to the floor like he was dying. "Tacos!"

I just kept walking. My throat felt like it was swollen shut. I threw my books in my locker, then headed to the front door.

Outside, in the October wind, I stood on the steps of the school. I felt hollowed out, like someone had scooped out the parts of me that made me Molly. I stood there as other students passed around me like a river going around a big rock.

"Hey," someone said. "Molly."

It was Cassie.

"You okay?" she asked.

"No."

"But . . . what's wrong?"

"You were there, too, right? When he had to explain the ingredients in our lunch? When Mr. Craig concluded that our lunch would kill the average person in six months? When everybody laughed? I didn't dream that, did I? You were there."

"I was there," she said. "But it's over. Go home."

She started down the steps.

I looked at her.

"You can't live on the school steps," she said.

I shrugged.

"How about . . . how about I walk home with you?" she said.

"Okay."

So I followed her.

As we walked through town, the sun came out and I could tell it was suddenly a beautiful afternoon, but I didn't care, and didn't look up. It took all my energy just to follow, just to plod along. I just stared at the sidewalk in front of me, watching Cassie's feet, trying not to cry. Finally, after a while, I realized we were in front of my house. I turned toward my front door, and Cassie looked at her watch as I passed.

"Okay?" she said.

I shrugged as I walked away from her.

"I gotta go," she said. "Might miss my bus."

I got to the door and fumbled in my bag for my keys. My vision was blurry because my eyes were filling with tears.

I found the right key, unlocked the door, went inside, and sat on the floor and cried. After a while, I went into the bathroom, blew my nose, washed my face with warm water, and dried my face. I looked at myself in the mirror. My eyes were puffy from crying. I blew my nose again. I went into the kitchen and got a drink of water. I looked out the window at the backyard. "Okay," I said. "Okay." I went upstairs, opened the door to my room. I looked at my room. There was nothing I wanted more than to just go in there, shut the door, and not come out.

But for some reason, I couldn't do it. I couldn't go into my room. I was thinking about Cassie. Without her, I wasn't sure I would have made it home. Without her, I wouldn't have anyone who understood what had happened today in biology.

So I got my keys, went into the garage, got into Mom's Prius—she almost always walked to work—backed out, and drove down the street. I went straight downtown, and there, at the bus stop, sat Cassie. I pulled over and rolled down the passenger window and honked.

She looked over.

"Wanna ride?"

A few minutes later, we were rolling down Crosstown Street. We went over the river, passed through the park. The sun was still out.

"This car's neat," Cassie said. "It makes me feel like I'm driving in the future."

We drove on for a little bit.

"When did you turn sixteen?" Cassie asked.

"September seventh." It seemed a long time ago. My sweet sixteen party had consisted of me, Mom, Dad, Grampa, and a DVD my brother had made of himself wearing a birthday hat and playing "Happy Birthday to You" on a kazoo. We hadn't even had cake because I had told Mom that birthday cakes were the epitome of dumbness.

"What about you?" I asked Cassie. "When's your birthday?"

"January first."

"New Year's Day?"

"Everyone's always awake when it becomes my birthday," she said. "A couple of times we had my birthday party at midnight, but then I would have to go to bed like an hour later, so who wants to open their presents and then immediately go to bed?"

"Good point."

"One time," Cassie said, "I woke up on my birthday and my mom had piled all my presents on my bed with me. I was surrounded by presents. That was a good birthday."

Cassie started telling me which turns to take, and soon we were up at the top of the hill above the new golf course, and we pulled into Cassie's driveway. Her house was big and new. The trees in the yard were only about as tall as me. I put the car in park.

"Thanks for the ride," Cassie said.

"Yeah," I said. "Well, thanks for walking me home. So . . . yeah . . . thanks."

"You're welcome."

She reached for the door handle. Then she paused and looked back at me. "Can I ask you something?" she asked.

"Okay," I said.

"That time you put all those bandages in the cottage cheese, how'd you do it without anyone noticing?"

"Oh, I snuck the full tray into the stockroom and did it. I made sure none of the bandages were visible on top. Then I snuck it back into the kitchen."

"Wow," Cassie said. "That was brave."

"I guess," I said.

"No, I mean it, I think you're brave. And not just with cottage cheese."

I shrugged. "Thanks." Then I said, "In the spirit of equal information exchange, can I ask you where you got one of my hairs to put on the cottage cheese?" I asked.

"That was easy," Cassie said. "You know how you stash your messenger bag and headphones under the side counter? I just looked on your headphones and bingo, blue hair."

I nodded. "Cool."

"Yeah, well . . . and I happened to notice something when I did that, and I . . . I . . ."

"What?" I asked.

"Well, I picked up your headphones, you know, and the plug end of the cord came out of your vest pocket . . . and I reached in there to put the plug back so you wouldn't know I'd been messing with your stuff and, uh, there was nothing in there. No iPod I mean. But when you'd come into the kitchen that morning, you had your headphones on, and the cord went into that pocket, and you fiddled with that pocket like you were turning off your iPod—like I'd seen you do before . . . but there wasn't one there."

"I don't have an iPod," I said.

"Do you have a CD player or something? Was it in another pocket?"

"No."

"I don't understand . . ."

"I just wear the headphones."

"You just what?"

"When I wear the headphones, no one bothers me. That's all."

I could tell she was surprised. Why the heck had I told her the truth? This tiny glimpse of my internal weirdness would be too much for her.

But to my surprise, she smiled. "I like it," she said. "That's a good trick." She laughed. "How long have you been doing that?" she asked.

I shrugged. "A year. Since I started at Sunshine Day."

"Hey," she said, "wanna come inside?"

Cassie gave me the tour. The house felt like a cross between a modern-art museum and an airplane hangar. The ceilings were high and angular, and some of the rooms were trapezoidal. The house was so new it still smelled like paint. Finally we ended up in the kitchen and got sodas. The kitchen was huge, with a polished marble island so big you could probably play tennis on it. Above the six-burner stove was a whole shelf of cookbooks. I couldn't help but ask about them.

"We don't really use those," Cassie admitted.

"Does your dad cook?" I asked.

"No. Those cookbooks were Mom's."

"Are your parents divorced?"

"My mom died when I was eleven."

This shocked me. To think I'd been working with Cassie for more than two weeks and I didn't even know such a simple fact that her mother was dead.

"I didn't know," I said. "I'm sorry."

"It's okay," said Cassie.

"Was she a good cook?"

"Yeah. She liked to bake."

"Cakes and stuff?"

"Yeah. I'd come home from school each day and usually there'd be something fresh out of the oven."

"Jeez," I said. "Sounds good."

Cassie nodded. "It was."

We sat there. I sipped my soda. I looked at my fingernails.

"You know," I said, "sorry about trying to get you to do that cake plan to get Mrs. Zetz back. It was dumb."

"And mean," she said.

"Yeah. Thanks for saying no."

She smiled.

"But I wouldn't mind some cake right now," I said. "I'm starved."

"I've got an idea," said Cassie. She got off her stool and went to the cookbook shelf and pulled down a notebook. She came back over and opened the notebook. She showed me a page. "Let's make this," she said. It was a chocolate cake. "My mom used to make this a lot," Cassie said. "And you just said you wished you had a cake to eat. So let's bake it right, just to prove we can."

Part of me wanted to go, flee to my room, leave this day behind me, forget about free topic Friday, and cakes, and Jerry Pisney. But there was another part of me—calmer, more fun— that wanted to stay here with Cassie and make a cake. Why couldn't we do something so simple as make a cake together?

"All right," I said.

We worked side by side and checked each other's measurements and followed the recipe carefully. Soon we put the pan in the oven. We pulled up two chairs and watched through the little window in the oven. When it came out it smelled wonderful. We let it cool, then cut big pieces and put them in bowls, put vanilla ice cream on top, and took the bowls down to Cassie's room and ate the cake while watching television.

"This is fantastic," I said, my mouth full. "This is the best cake ever."

"I know!" Cassie said. "Who knew we had it in us?"

"I can't believe how good this tastes. Is fresh cake always this good?"

"It really wasn't that hard."

"I know, I know!" I said. "It wasn't that hard!"

"Is it wrong of me to want a second piece?" Cassie said.

"No! It would be wrong of us *not* to have a second piece."

"I like the way you think."

CASSIE'S MOM'S CHOCOLATE CAKE

1   cup all-purpose flour

$\frac{2}{3}$ cup sugar

3   tablespoons unsweetened cocoa powder

$\frac{3}{4}$ teaspoon baking soda

$\frac{1}{4}$ heaping teaspoon salt

$\frac{2}{3}$ cup cold or lukewarm coffee (instant coffee is okay)

$\frac{1}{4}$ cup vegetable or canola oil

2   teaspoons white vinegar

1   teaspoon vanilla extract

Preheat your oven to 350°.

Sift the flour, sugar, cocoa powder, baking soda, and salt into a mixing bowl, then stir until the ingredients are well combined.

Make a well in the middle of the dry ingredients and add the coffee, oil, vinegar, and vanilla extract. Stir until the mixture is smooth except for a smattering of small lumps.

Pour the batter into an ungreased, nonstick 8-x-8-inch square baking pan or a 9-inch round cake pan. Bake for about 20 minutes, or until a toothpick inserted in the center of the cake comes out clean.

Let the cake cool. You can serve it with ice cream or whipped cream. The cake can also be frosted, if you wish.

Makes one small cake, about 8 servings.

16

Milk Is Weird

Clyde appeared in the kitchen early Monday morning and went to work in his corner, humming a show tune.

"Whatcha makin'?" I asked him later.

"Date and walnut squares," he announced.

"Gross," I said. And didn't think about Clyde's disgusting-sounding cookies until after lunch, when I tasted one on Dina's recommendation. It was good. It was simple. It was satisfying. Well, everybody got lucky sometimes.

I took two extra cookies and put them in my vest pocket.

After school that afternoon I went into the little auditorium. Portia Babbliabali was up on stage on all fours, with a pencil in her mouth.

"Portia?" I said, approaching the stage.

She looked up. She was using a tape to measure the floor.

"I know you," she said. She stood up. She was barefoot and wearing some kind of jumpsuit that would have made me look like a prisoner, but which made her look like a foxy fighter jet pilot. "You're the subject of 'The Three Pile Song,' " she said.

"Yes," I admitted. "Molly O. I am detached."

"Could be worse," she said.

I told her that I was interested in being a scenic artist for *The Bleepity Bleep Bleep Gang*, and asked if she had time to look at my portfolio. The idea to do this had come to me over the weekend. I decided I deserved to go after what I wanted, namely Devin Harper. To that end, I would infiltrate the winter musical.

Portia took my portfolio and spread everything out on the stage floor and then walked back and forth, looking at my work. She rolled up the sleeves of her jumpsuit.

"Yes . . . ," she said. "Yes, yes, yes. This stuff is wild!" She clapped her hands together and looked at me. "The bad news is I don't need any more scenic artists. But how does the title of art director sound to you?"

"Art director? Me?"

"You're perfect. You've got fire in your heart. You know the difference between a bright twilight and a dark noon. Plus you've got enough talent to crush a mountain."

Say what? And what?

"All right," I said. "I'll do it."

She shook my hand and pulled me in for a sort of manly half-hug. "Good. I knew there was a reason I hadn't put someone in charge of art. I just hadn't found you until I found you."

She produced an apple from one of her pockets and took a bite. "Oh, and I've got to tell you, I've voted yes in the Hot Lunch Poll every day. It's not that the food's perfect. It's just that you and that other girl are in there, every day, doing the work, pulling it all together, or at least trying. It's hard work, and it's thankless, and you two are bold. So I vote yes."

Call it the sympathy vote. Call it the feminist vote. I'd take it.

On Tuesday morning, Clyde brought in two ice-cream makers.

"What's with the machinery?" Dina asked.

"I'm makin' ice cream," he said.

"What kind?" I asked.

"Chocolate."

"Just chocolate?" Who ate plain chocolate ice cream? Preschoolers? "More power to you," I said, anticipating another ruined dessert.

We were, after all, a kitchen that excelled in ruining food, despite Dina's guidance. That day, for instance, Cassie ruined a meat loaf. I ruined a casserole. But Clyde, that little dude, didn't ruin the ice cream. He produced it on time, and the students and teachers raved about it, so at the end of the lunch hour I took the last remaining cup of ice cream and ate it. It was smooth, creamy, luscious, and so chocolatey that it made the inside of my brain tingle.

Homemade ice cream . . . When had I ever had homemade ice cream? Who knew it would be this good? Was there a way to lock Clyde in my basement so he could make this ice cream for me every day?

Clyde was whistling merrily in his corner, cleaning up.

"Seriously," I said, "what is up with two days of good desserts in a row?" He didn't seem to hear me. "Clyde!"

"Hm?"

I put the question to him again. He smiled, then sort of laughed silently. "I had a most interesting weekend," he said. "See, I had been rather depressed about the manner in which my desserts were turning out, so I asked my grandmother, my aunt

Dru, and my second cousin once removed Douglas Nance—who was once an assistant pastry chef on a cruise ship—to each spend a few hours with me over the weekend and guide me toward becoming a better dessert-smith."

"Holy moly," said Cassie.

"It was exhausting!" exclaimed Clyde. "But we had a hoot."

"A *hoot*?" I said.

"I learned so much. And the best advice I got was to test a recipe at home before trying it at school. So that's what I've been doing. And look, two good desserts."

Cassie called me that night.

"Clyde's on to something," she said. "I know it's obvious and everything, but if we want to get out of the kitchen, we have to make better food."

"That sounds hard though."

"How about," said Cassie, "we hang up and each brainstorm and in ten minutes I'll call you and we'll each have one specific idea of how to become better cooks?"

"Sure, bossy lady," I said.

Nine minutes later, I was lying on my back, watching my ceiling fan. So far, my best idea had been to try to blackmail Mrs. Zetz into coming back. That was no good, though. Not a solution. So I went downstairs for a refreshing glass of chocolate milk.

The house was quiet, but the light was on in Grampa's room and I heard his television. I went to his door.

"Hi, Grampa," I said.

He looked up from a magazine. "Hello, dolly," he said.

"Can you think of a way to improve the food in the school kitchen?" I asked.

"Hm. More salt usually helps."

The TV was playing the game show *Family Feud*. It looked like an episode from before I was born.

The host of the show said, "Survey says!"

Survey . . .

In my pocket, my phone rang. I answered.

"Here's what I've got," said Cassie. "We eat at different institutional food outlets each night for the rest of the week. To see if we can learn from them."

"Do we get to eat in a prison?"

"No!"

"Darn it."

"What's your idea?" Cassie asked.

"Uh . . ."

"Did you even take this task seriously?" she asked. "What is *wrong* with you?"

"Okay, here's my idea: a survey?"

"A survey?"

"We ask the students how to improve lunch. Since they're the judges anyway, why not ask them what they want?"

"That's not bad . . ."

Clyde's reign of great desserts continued. Wednesday he made fantastic cream puffs—billowy puffs stuffed with a cloudlike vanilla filling. On Thursday he produced an orange and pecan bread pudding that was drizzled with caramel sauce. And Friday it was brownies that perfectly straddled the fine line between cakey and fudgy.

In other words, he pulled off an entire week of perfect desserts. He, Clyde Percival Brewell. By himself.

Wednesday night Cassie and I ate at the hospital. We noticed that the line for the grill—where cheeseburgers were being served up as fast as they could be cooked—was the longest line of all the serving areas.

"Should a hospital even be serving cheeseburgers and fries?" Cassie asked.

"Good for business," I said. "Future heart patients."

In the spirit of investigation, Cassie had a cheeseburger. She claimed it wasn't bad, but it wasn't good. I had a small salad from the salad bar and a cup of "cheesy" broccoli soup. The soup was lumpy.

Thursday night, we dined with Cassie's great-aunt Dorothy at the Placid Oaks Senior Living Village. We paid three dollars apiece, were seated at a table with two other residents, and served a family-style meal of meat loaf (dry), boiled potatoes (wet), gravy (strayed from the potatoes), corn niblets (cold), stewed prunes (not bad), and a piece of chocolate pudding pie (barely sweet).

Great-aunt Dorothy apologized for the food. She was ninety-one, but she had strong feelings on the subject of food. "The food here tastes like it was made by people who actually hate pleasure," she said. "People who've never eaten a fresh tomato, or real butter, or bacon, or garden peas, or blue cheese, or raspberries from the backyard, or homemade bread with honey on it!"

"I knew that's what it tasted like," I said. "I just didn't know how to say it."

Great-aunt Dorothy eyed me suspiciously. "You're a firecracker, aren't you?"

"That's what I hear."

"If you're interested in real cooking, you should have visited me thirty years ago, when I was still on the farm, and before my arthritis was bad," she said.

"Are we talking about time travel?" I asked.

"I want to say a few words in favor of flavor," she said. "I want you to remember that flavor comes from good ingredients, not out of a can, and not out of a laboratory! Making good food is easy: you take fresh ingredients, you prepare them simply, and that's that. The rest comes with practice.

"Use good ingredients and work hard and you kids can be great cooks and bring flavor and wholesome food to the table, and bring pleasure to your families and your friends. That is one of the great joys of life—to come together over a great meal. So that's what I wanted to say. Now take me back to my room so I don't have to look at this disgusting food anymore."

On Friday night, we ate at Olde Tyme Buffay, out at the mall. We got there early but still ended up waiting half an hour to get in. True, Olde Tyme Buffay wasn't technically an institutional food outlet, but it did serve the food cafeteria style. It had a long conveyor belt that was full of entrees and side dishes and desserts that marched along like some kind of parade of food.

We ate, and it was decent. When we were done we went back over and just stared at the conveyor belt.

"If we could put that in the school lunchroom, we would rock," said Cassie.

Full of Olde Tyme Buffay's bland macaroni and cheese and soggy Tater Tots, we went to Cassie's house and opened up the survey box that had been in the lunchroom since Wednesday.

The survey had only three questions. The first question was: characterize and rate the various aspects of Mrs. Zetz's cooking.

Some responses were:

Quotidian, but not offensive. Worth the $2.50 we pay.

Dude! The dirty dozen was rank! Where did that stuff come from? How could hamburgers be so bad? Did she find that food on the street or something? Only high point was some desserts.

On the one hand: her food was never burned, late, strange, or unidentifiable. On the other hand: sometimes it smelled like the freezer, sometimes it tasted like a can.

The second question was: characterize and rate the various aspects of Cassie Birchmeyer and Molly Ollinger's cooking. A few responses:

Are we allowed to use expletives?

You go, girls!

I try to like the food. Sometimes I try so hard I end up not noticing what it actually tastes like. That's actually a small blessing. Sorry, but it's the truth.

It is taste-bud abuse.

I tried it once.

The final question was: do you have any suggestions about how the hot lunch menu and experience could be improved or expanded?

Oh, I don't know, how about, for example, more food that is actually edible?

Cream puffs every day.

What's needed here is a careful examination of society's relationship to the land via food production, in combination with a new discussion about the viability and ethics of inflicting pain and suffering on animals in exchange for nutrients and flavor that can just as easily be had from plant sources that are: (a) more sustainable, (b) healthier, (c) cheaper, (d) less ethically complicated, (e) more environmentally friendly, (f) just better.

I really wish there was sushi on the menu.

Why must we be forced to drink milk? Milk is weird. Adults wouldn't think of drinking <u>human</u> milk, so why, therefore, do we drink milk from cows?

Simple solution: learn to cook.

CLYDE'S CREAM PUFFS

FLUFFY VANILLA FILLING

- 1 cup whipping cream
- $\frac{3}{4}$ cup sugar
- 1 teaspoon vanilla extract
- 1 cup melted vanilla ice cream, no warmer than room temperature

PUFFS

- 1 cup water
- 1 stick (8 tablespoons) unsalted butter
- $\frac{1}{4}$ teaspoon salt
- 1 cup all-purpose flour
- 4 large eggs

Preheat your oven to 425°.

To make the filling, whip the cream while slowly adding the sugar. When the whipped cream is fairly stiff, whisk in the vanilla extract and melted ice cream. Keep the mixture cold until needed.

To make the puffs, bring the water, butter, and salt to a boil in a medium saucepan, stirring to help melt the butter. Add the flour and stir until the mixture comes away from the sides of the pan and forms a semicohesive mass. Take the pan off the heat and let it cool for 5 minutes. Stir in the eggs one at a time until the mixture is smooth.

Spoon the dough onto an ungreased baking sheet,

making 12 round puffs. Put the sheet in the oven and immediately lower the oven temperature to 375°. Bake the puffs until they're golden and dry, about 30 minutes. Let them cool on a rack.

When the puffs are cool, slice off their tops, remove excess dough from their insides (if desired), and fill them with the fluffy vanilla filling. These taste best the day they're made.

Makes 12 cream puffs.

17

I Made Bad Goo

If anything, Clyde's supremely fantastic desserts became even supremelier and fantasticer during the next week. Monday—which was Halloween, I will note, but I will refrain from commenting upon the idiots, including the teachers, who came to school dressed in costumes—Clyde made molasses cookies that were chewy and had sugary tops that were cracked and glittery.

On Tuesday, we noticed that the line of people waiting to pay for lunch was longer than usual.

"Why the traffic jam?" I asked Cassie, who stood beside me at the serving table.

"Look," said Cassie. Our Boy Scout friend Justin Porter had paid for his lunch, but then went straight to the dessert table, picked up a cupcake, and left. He didn't take any other food—just the cupcake. Then another kid—some freshman with red hair—did the same thing.

"Hey, you!" I said to him.

"Huh?"

"What's your name?"

"Denny."

"You paid for lunch?"

"Yeah?"

"But you're just taking the dessert."

"Yeah. It's the only good part. Sorry."

We served about thirty lunches that day, but forty-five desserts. Good thing Clyde had made extra.

That day after school was the first meeting for the *The Bleepity Bleep Bleep Gang* cast and crew. I sat near the back of the auditorium. Devin Harper and a couple of the school's other drama superstars—Tessy Houghton and Vanessa Tithanwit, aka "Tit and Wit" or just "Tit and Tit"—were up onstage, horsing around. Devin was giving Vanessa a piggyback ride.

Portia wandered in a few minutes late. She had on torn jeans, a too-small boy's T-shirt, and was barefoot again. "Okay, people, this is just a what's-what sort of meeting, so don't get your briefs in a bundle. We're not here to discuss. We're not here to debate the script's subtexts or Jungian precepts. It's a meta-meeting. Wanda, can you hand out these schedules? Also, if any of you still don't have a script, get one from Will here, my second assistant director. Everyone see Will? Stand up, Will." Will stood up. "Sit down, Will." Will sat down.

"I know there's been a delay with casting the lead roles," Portia said, "so I'm going to make some final announcements right now. The problem was that I'd been considering some script changes that would have impacted casting. But that black cloud has passed, and so let me introduce the leads. First, in the role of Cyrus Flickenganger, we have Devin Harper."

I clapped. Wahoo! Devin got the lead! He deserved it! He was awesome!

I kept clapping, and then I realized a few people were turning to look at me. What the . . . Then I noticed that no one else was clapping. I stopped.

"At least you've got one fan," Portia said to Devin. I slumped down in my seat.

Portia went through more cast announcements, a couple of scheduling points, then she asked the key crew members to introduce themselves. The assistant directors, the stage manager, costume designer, and the production designer all stood up one by one and said hello.

"Next is our art director. I'm very excited about her work. Molly, could you stand up?"

I got up. Most of the people in the auditorium couldn't see me. It was pretty dark back where I was sitting.

"I'm Molly Ollinger," I said, "and I—"

"You're detached!" someone yelled.

Some laughter rolled through the auditorium.

I sat down.

Portia introduced a couple more people.

"Oh, and finally," said Portia, "this year I've taken the liberty of hiring Clyde Brewell to supply fresh cookies for each practice. Clyde, as some of you may know, is the person who has been responsible for the super desserts in the lunchroom!"

For the first time in the meeting, the whole room burst into cheers and applause.

"Clyde couldn't be here today," Portia said, "but he sent this box of macaroons."

She reached down and opened a big box at her feet.

Clyde was baking for other people on the side? I felt a little bit betrayed.

"So you each get one cookie as you leave! Only one! Meeting adjourned!"

The rush for the cookie box commenced. I lingered until the riot was over, then wandered toward the box. It was empty.

I went over to Portia. She was talking to her assistant director, but when I got a chance, I asked her where I was on the rehearsal schedule. I'd read the schedule several times, but I couldn't find myself on it.

"Oh, you're down here," she said. She pointed at the very bottom of the page. It said: Tech/Art meeting #1. I'd been looking up at the top of the page where all the actors were listed with which rehearsals they needed to attend. I'd been looking for my name near Devin Harper's.

"After the first meeting," Portia added, "you guys will set your own schedule. Becky will be in charge of all of that. And don't forget that the first meeting is in the art room."

"We're not meeting here?"

"We'll be rehearsing here. Can't have art and tech people running around."

"Oh."

Portia saw someone behind me. "Pete!" she called. "Come here. Good timing."

Did this mean I wouldn't be working shoulder to shoulder with Devin Harper?

"Molly," Portia said, "this is Pete Stamponivich, your assistant art director."

Why had I been so dumb to think that somehow the art director and the lead actor would have any contact with each other whatsoever? Why did I imagine me and Devin painting backdrops together, playfully dabbing each other's noses with tempera paint, and quibbling like a married couple over different wallpapers for the set? Why'd I been so dumb?

Blarg.

"Molly!" Portia said. "Hello?"

"Yeah?"

A guy in overalls stood before me. He had cropped dark hair and was not short and not tall. I was pretty sure he was a junior.

"Pete," said Portia, "this is Molly. Molly, Pete."

"Howdy," he said. "I'm good at lifting, cleaning up, fetching supplies, and juggling, but I'm not much of an artist. But I'll do whatever I can to help you."

"I . . . ," I said. I wanted to quit. I had a better chance of rubbing elbows with Clyde on this dumb play than Devin. But I didn't want or need to rub elbows with Clyde. I wanted Devin's elbows. I needed his elbows.

"Portia, darling," said someone nearby. "Can I get another script?"

It was Devin. It was him. Mere feet away.

"What happened to the last *three* I gave you?" Portia asked.

He shrugged. He noticed me. "Hey, Molly," he said.

"Hi."

"All right," Portia said, "I've got another one in my locker, but I swear if you lose this one, too, I'll haunt your dreams. Come on."

He turned to follow Portia, but as he did so, he looked at me and rolled his eyes at Portia's antics. Then he was gone.

Okay: I would stay. I would art direct the crap out of this retarded musical.

"By the way," said Pete, still in front of me, "tell Clyde awesome cupcakes."

On Wednesday, we served twenty-nine lunches, but sold out all forty-seven portions of Clyde's peach cobbler. And when Dr. John came into the kitchen near the end of the lunch period, he was grinning.

"Commendable effort, all," he said. He counted the Hot Lunch Poll ballots right in front of us, and for the first time ever, the poll numbers broke 50 percent—51 percent, to be exact.

"The desserts!" I said. "The desserts did it! Clyde, you're the man."

He smiled modestly.

"That peach cobbler *was* revolutionary, Clyde," said Dr. John.

Maybe we weren't that far from ending our time in the kitchen. Maybe the desserts would do it. Clyde would do it. Cassie and I wouldn't have to do anything more than we were already doing. That sounded good. That sounded all right.

But early on Thursday morning, wrapped in an extremely long scarf, Clyde appeared in the kitchen and announced that he'd come to a decision about his desserts.

"This is going to change everything," he said.

"I don't like the sound of this," I said.

"I've decided my desserts aren't good enough," he said.

"That's crazy," Cassie said. "They're better than good enough."

He started unwrapping his long scarf. "I just had this brainstorm while I was in the shower, like, twenty minutes ago."

"No!" I said. "You're not allowed to make us picture you in the shower!"

"Okay," Clyde said, still unwrapping his scarf, "here it is. Are you ready?"

"Yes!" we both said.

"The first phase of my desserts was when I didn't know what I was doing and I ruined everything with alarming regularity. The second phase was when I took tutelage under my grandmother and aunt and cousin and tested the recipes at home and improved the satisfaction of my clientele considerably.

"Now," he said, "for the third phase! The best one yet! For this phase, I'm going to stop using other people's recipes!" He said this and spread his arms like he was delivering great news.

"What do you mean?" Cassie said.

"Yeah, I don't get it," I said. "Whose recipes are you going to use?"

"Mine! My own. I'm going to start making up my own recipes. Developing my own recipes. My desserts will be original!"

"You say 'original,' " I said, "and I hear 'horrible.' "

"But this is how the real pastry chefs work! They don't rely on cookbooks. They're inspired by good ingredients. They come up with original recipes all the time."

"But you're not really a pastry chef," said Cassie.

"You're a freshman," I said.

"But I'm going to be a pastry chef!" said Clyde. "And this is where it begins!"

"Or ends," I said.

"Clyde," said Cassie, walking over to him and holding him by the shoulders, "you're the only person in this kitchen who can cook good things. You're the foundation upon which we can build a better kitchen. We *need* you to keep turning out your great desserts."

"But don't you see," he said, his eyes all starry, "that when I develop my own recipes, they'll be even better!"

"You say 'better,' " I said, "and I hear 'icky.' "

"I've got to get to work!" he exclaimed. He walked around the kitchen, whistling louder than usual. He was glowing. He was obviously delusional. He browsed a cookbook and a couple of magazines in his pastry chef corner, then he went into the stockroom and came back with some dark chocolate and oranges. And he announced, "I give you: orange and chocolate soufflés!"

"You give me: nausea," I said.

He laughed silently and went right on with his work. All our nay-saying didn't seem to affect him. It was like he was in his own little universe. We even had to remind him to go to his classes. When he came for his third-period hour, he worked in a frenzy, fussing with eggs and chocolate over in his corner of the kitchen. While his back was turned, Cassie crossed the fingers on both her hands and looked at me.

"We're crossing our fingers over here for you, Clydey boy," I said.

"Thanks!" he chirped, not to be distracted from his work.

In the waning moments of the hour, he came over and sat by me. I was making bread crumbs in the food processor. He was grinning. He wiped his brow with a handkerchief. He put the handkerchief back in his pocket. Who carried a hanky?

"Whew . . . ," he said. "Hard work today."

"Speaking of which, shouldn't you be in your corner?" I asked.

"Everything's prepped and ready to go," he said. "I can relax for a bit."

"Suit yourself."

He watched me. He smiled. "You know the thing that's great about you?"

"My insouciance?"

"No, that you're a total expression of yourself. You are Molly. You are yourself."

I thought about this. On the one hand, Clyde was annoying, on the other hand, there was a possibility that what he'd just said was actually somewhat charming.

"Even when I'm making bread crumbs?" I asked.

"Even then. Especially then."

"So what you're saying is that I'm Molly," I said.

"Yes."

"I've got to write that down. *I'm* Molly. Thank you for clueing me in."

"That's sarcasm!" Clyde said. But it didn't seem to bother him.

The bell rang and he ran off to P.E.

Clyde rushed down from P.E. to put the soufflés in about ten minutes before lunch. We were bustling around, busy at the last moment, and I didn't even think of the soufflés until the lunch bell rang and the students started lining up. I looked back and saw Clyde pulling the trays of soufflés out of the oven.

"They disappeared," he said, surprised.

I went over. There was just a thin black film in the bottom of each custard cup.

"What happened?" asked Cassie, coming over.

"Don't know," Clyde said. "I made goo."

"How does it taste?" asked Cassie.

Clyde dipped a finger in. "I made bad goo," he said.

"Great," I said, going back over to the serving table. "No dessert!" I announced to the line of students. An audible wave of disappointment passed through them. More than half of the people waiting in line just walked away. Cassie and Dina and I took our positions behind the serving table.

After serving the first few students, I heard a thump, and I looked back and saw that Clyde had plopped down on the floor in front of the ovens. He put his face in his hands. I nudged Cassie, motioned toward Clyde.

"Uh-oh," she said quietly. "He's broken."

But later, I glanced back again. Clyde was back in his corner, his little pastry chef corner, and he had three cookbooks propped up around him, and he was writing furiously in a notebook.

18

Everyone Loves Popcorn

We have to do better," Cassie said. It was after school, and I'd been in my room, wasting time on cuteoverload.com when she'd called. "We've lost our dessert man, and we've proven we can't cook Mrs. Zetz's food," she continued, "so we might as well serve the kind of food we want to serve. Or at least aim higher."

"And mess that up, too?" I asked.

"I know we've been avoiding talking about the survey, but it was pretty clear that we have to become better cooks, bottom line. If Clyde can learn to bake in one weekend, we can at least *start* to learn."

"All right," I said, "let's turn the hot lunch into a bistro."

"A what? What's a bistro?"

"It's just a small restaurant with good, unpretentious food. It's cozy. It's not expensive. It's warm on a cold night. It's got a chalkboard instead of a menu. It's like a restaurant in a good dream, and you always eat there with friends."

"You're loony. Is there even a bistro in Minerva?"

"No, not technically," I admitted. The ones I was thinking of were places I'd eaten at in Minneapolis and St. Paul with my parents.

"Ha!" said Cassie.

"Well, what's your idea about what kind of food to cook?"

"Applebee's."

"That's not good food. They don't have cooks there, they have heat lamps and microwaves!"

"Have you ever been to an Applebee's?" she asked.

"No."

"And can I point out that there are not just one but *two* Applebee's in town, as opposed to *zero* bistros. In other words, the entire town has already voted, and Applebee's is more popular than a bistro."

"Look, let's just flip a coin," I suggested.

"How exactly are we going to flip a coin over a phone?"

"You'll just have to trust me," I said.

"Ha!" said Cassie.

"Stop saying 'Ha!'"

"When you suggest flipping over the telephone, I have a right to say 'Ha!'"

"Okay, rock paper scissors."

"Ha!" Cassie said.

"Fine, why don't you suggest an alternative?"

"I'm thinking of a number," said Cassie.

"Nope. I don't trust you either. Ha!"

I heard Cassie sigh. Then we were both silent. I wasn't exactly sure what a bistro was, or how we could cook good food when we weren't even able to cook average food.

"I've got an idea," I said. "How about we hang up, and in exactly one minute we each text each other a message with one number in it—any number—and then we add those two numbers together, and if the result is an even number, it means Applebee's, if it's odd, it's bistro."

Cassie thought about this. I heard her blow her nose. Then she said, "Okay."

A minute later, Cassie sent this text message to me: 2.

At the same moment, I texted this to Cassie: 29,342,828, 588,995,254,310,962,011.

The sum being odd.

Meaning bistro.

We did all the right things. We researched recipes, got the ingredients lists to Edmund, so he could get everything in stock. We spent Saturday morning in Cassie's kitchen, doing a run-through of Monday's menu. We thought we'd be done by noon, but I was there until four, and things hadn't gone well. We didn't even make enough food to feed ourselves and ended up ordering out.

At least, we figured, we'd do better in the kitchen on Monday, though, knowing what the trouble spots were.

But Monday was bad. First of all, some of the ingredients hadn't arrived, thanks to our food distributor. "I tell you, man," explained Edmund, "our distributor has clients fifty times our size, and they just don't care if they get our orders right." Lack of ingredients meant our roasted vegetable minipizzas were downgraded to roasted pepper minipizzas. Then we discovered that the feta cheese we'd ordered was two days past its expiration date, and Dina wouldn't let us use it. So roasted pepper minipizzas became roasted pepper flatbread. But when the flatbread dough rose too high and then collapsed, we just stared at it in horror. We had forty minutes until lunch.

Dina raised her hands and backed away from the bubbling, sunken mess of dough. "Nothing you can do about that. It's ruined."

"What happens if we bake it like this?" Cassie asked.

"It will be dense and taste funky. The yeast is exhausted," offered Clyde.

"We've got roasted peppers," Cassie said.

Yes, those we had. The one thing we hadn't messed up.

"So if we brown some onions," she said, everyone listening, "add some dried herbs, some milk, then we puree it all—roasted pepper soup."

I looked at her. "Where in hell's green acre did you get that idea from?"

"What? What's wrong with it?"

"There's nothing wrong with it. It sounds good. But I'm just asking, how did you come up with that?"

"There was a recipe like that in that cookbook I read, *Pepper's Revenge.*"

"It sounds yumlicious," Clyde said.

We snapped into action, followed Cassie's plan, made the soup. We were very proud of it, but there wasn't quite enough to go around, so we only served bowls filled about one-third full, and then we started getting complaints.

Seth Lawson came up, eyes welling with tears. "That soup hurt my canker sore!" he said. "It's like acid!"

We also heard that Ethan Joskow had thrown up after eating three bowls of the soup on a dare.

Tuesday, we'd planned baked ziti with ricotta and herbs. But the ziti didn't come, so we had to use broken-up lasagna noodles instead. But Cassie overcooked these and they stuck together—a big, gummy mass of pasta. So we put everything in the food processor and called it ricotta soup. Unfortunately, the ricotta floated to the top, the pasta sank to the bottom, and in the middle was a pale, milky, and undersalted broth. Our poll numbers that day were 8 percent—the lowest ever.

Wednesday, we actually *planned* to make soup, a lentil soup. Things were going fine—we'd had all the ingredients for once, and we'd put everything in the pot, but the burner wouldn't light, so we had to move the pot to the other stove.

"I'll do it," said Cassie.

I should have just said okay, seeing as she was the athlete. But the huge pot probably weighed forty pounds, and in the spirit of cooperation I wanted to offer an easier solution than making Cassie carry it.

"Let's put it on a kitchen cart and roll it over," I suggested.

"It's only about six feet from stove to stove," she said. "Plus, we'd still have to move it on and off the cart."

We compromised by deciding to carry the pot together. We each grabbed a handle and hobbled toward the other stove. It was extraordinarily heavy, and I could feel my fingers slipping on the thin handle, and then Cassie wobbled a little bit, and suddenly I was bearing more of the weight than before. The pot slipped and fell.

We had less than half an hour until lunch. Cassie cooked some corn and instant mashed potatoes, and I ran to my house— literally ran—and drove Mom's car to KFC and picked up three buckets of fried chicken. It was the best meal we'd served ever, but it had cost us fifty bucks of our own money. Plus, even though our poll numbers were great, Dr. John voided the results.

Meanwhile, Clyde hadn't turned out a good dessert since last week. He came into the kitchen every morning excited and ready to go—full of fantastic descriptions of what he was going to make—but in the end, everything he worked on came out so totally wrong it was unservable. That wasn't helping our poll numbers. ONE TRAY, ZERO DESSERT was becoming the norm. The students were already used to it and had even stopped asking about dessert.

This isn't to say that Clyde didn't have his fans.

"I remember it all," said Pete Stamponivich, my assistant art director, after school Thursday, as we were doing a bunch of conceptual sketches. We were up in the art room, and somehow we'd wandered onto the topic of Clyde's second dessert phase, the one that lasted for about a week and a half.

"I remember the peach cobbler," Pete said. "I remember the coconut cupcakes! Oh man, do I remember those. And, and, and . . . the brownies! Dude! The brownies were like the brownies they serve in heaven."

"Uh-huh," I said, concentrating on my work. We were sketching ideas for the scenery in the so-called dream forest scene. So far, Pete and I had only worked together a few hours over the past two weeks, but he had proven to be surprisingly not annoying. He was helpful at fetching things and relaying messages, but this was the first time I'd asked him to do actual art.

"And now, for your listening pleasure," said Pete, scribbling away, "I'm going to speak at length about why I believe that the cream puffs Clyde served last Wednesday may in fact be the best cream puffs ever served on the face of the planet."

"Go for it," I said. He did tend to blabber, but amusingly so.

So as Pete was waxing poetic about the cream puffs, I put down my pencil and shook my wrist to relax it. I glanced over at Pete's work. I expected it to be bad, or at least really basic, but it was good. His lines were fluid and expressive. And his vision of the forest—with drapey vines, curving tree trunks, and slanting moonlight—was immediately compelling. Wow. My assistant art director was actually an artist.

"That's really good," I said, interrupting his cream puff reverie. "And that one. That one's perfect. Portia will love it."

"Aw, thanks," he said. "I do good work because I have a good boss."

"Yeah, Portia is kinda fun to work for."

"No, I mean you."

Pete wasn't alone in his admiration of Clyde's so-called Phase Two desserts. On Friday morning, copies of *When It's Noon Here, It's Midnight Somewhere Else*—the sporadic and always ridiculous underground paper—appeared. It was a special edition devoted entirely to Clyde's Phase Two desserts, each of which was treated in depth by a different writer. A couple of the headlines were "Can the World Handle This Kind of Chocolate Ice Cream?" and "I Have Seen the Face of the Eternal Sunrise, and It Is Clyde Brewell's Bread Pudding with Caramel Sauce." At the end of the issue was an editorial by the pseudonymous Blythe Babcock:

I Say: Bring Back the Good Ones

Let's get this straight. I'm not even a dessert person. In grade school I routinely sold the homemade cookies in my lunch box for a dime apiece. A dime!

But then this thing happened the other day where my pal came to me and said I just had to taste the hot lunch chocolate ice cream. I said no. She said yes. I said I don't think so. She said I was being stubborn. I said no I'm not, and to prove it I tried the ice cream. Very mature, I know.

Since that day, until a week ago, I have bought a hot lunch ticket and skipped the first stuff in favor of the dessert. Now, I am not going to go into the details of the delectable desserts of Clyde Brewell's so-called Phase Two. Our writers have filled this issue with thoughtful pieces doing just that. But what I am going to say is this:

Clyde Brewell, I do not know you. You do not know me. But let me speak to you as one soul to another. The holy in me salutes the holy in you. Listen carefully, please, because this is an urgent message: I need you to return to the desserts of Phase Two.

Dear Mr. Brewell, you cannot, in good conscience, supply us with manna from heaven and then take it away as if it were commonplace. That will not do. It is as if you have taken a portion of my soul away. Will I ever taste the majesty of your peach cobbler again? Will I feel myself made whole once more by the aroma of your lovely brownies?

I need these things, Clyde. And I am not alone.

Bring back the good ones.

Cassie and I were in the kitchen, reading the issue when Clyde came in later than usual. He didn't say good morning.

"You seen this?" I asked, pointing to the paper.

"I have," he said, arranging his work space in his corner.

"And?" I asked.

"I said I've read it," he said abruptly.

"So what are you going to do about it?" I asked.

He turned and faced us. "I know what you're asking. And I'm *not* going to return to the land of Phase Two. I can only go forward."

"But your desserts were the only thing we had going for us," I said.

"I have a plan," he said.

"He has a plan," said Cassie. "Let him be."

"If his plan is to be a dumbass," I said, "he's succeeded."

"All I ask for is patience," Clyde said.

"We support you," Cassie said.

"*Not*," I said.

Four hours later, his pound cake an utter failure, his tropical fruit compote burned, he slumped off to P.E. without so much as a good-bye.

It had been an easy morning for us because we were baking a huge pot of cowboy beans in the oven—slow cooking them meant more flavor. This gave us time to read magazines and do homework.

It was after eleven-thirty, when Dina went to check on the beans, that we discovered something was wrong.

"Who turned this stove on?" she asked.

"I did," I said.

"This one?" Dina asked, opening the stove door and pointing to the pot of beans.

"No . . . ," I said. "That one." I pointed to the other stove. The empty stove.

"You turned on the wrong stove?" Cassie asked me.

"No, you put the beans in the wrong stove."

We just stared at each other for a moment. Either way, the beans were a loss. No lunch, no dessert. Cassie sighed, went over to her coat, got her wallet, and checked how much cash she had. "I'll pay for another KFC run," she said.

"No way," I said. "My mom's car reeks of fried chicken from Wednesday."

Edmund walked in. He looked at us.

"What?" he asked. "Who died?"

"The beans," I said.

Edmund raised his hands. "Not my problem," he said. "I'm just the janitor."

"I happen to know that your official title is 'kitchen technician,'" I said. "At least you could *try* to help every once in a while."

"Possibly," he said. He left.

"Jerkbait!" I yelled after him.

"I just wish I went to a normal school," said Cassie, "and had normal friends, and was a normal student, and not running a kitchen."

"We don't have anything we can cook in thirty minutes," I pointed out.

Edmund came back in, carrying three huge cans of diced tomatoes.

"What are you doing?" I asked.

"Just watch, okay?" he said. "Cream of tomato soup."

He melted two sticks of butter in a big pot. When the butter was bubbling, he stirred in some flour, salt, and pepper. It made a thin paste that bubbled and foamed. "This thickens the soup," he said. He added the big cans of tomatoes, then let everything cook for a few minutes. He added milk and water and let the soup come to a simmer.

Meanwhile, he'd instructed Dina and Cassie to pop as much popcorn as they could in two saucepans.

When the bell for lunch rang, we were still popping popcorn.

"We're not ready!" I said.

"Sure we are," said Edmund calmly, tasting the soup, then adding more salt. "All we have to do is puree this."

Edmund and I pureed the soup in small batches while Cassie and Dina served the lunch. Each tray got a bowl of the soup, a mound of popcorn, some carrot sticks—which had been prepared earlier in the morning—and pineapple tidbits.

The students were confused. "I thought we were having beans," said Seth Lawson.

"This is better," said Cassie.

"Why popcorn?" said Seth.

"Everyone loves popcorn," said Cassie.

Seth shrugged. "I guess."

But when the trays came back, everyone had eaten the soup, everyone had eaten the popcorn, and almost everyone told us that it was really darn good. The popcorn and the cream of tomato soup had gone well together. Dr. John said we should add this meal to our regular lineup. Plus dessert, of course.

In the last minutes of the lunch hour, Cassie and I tasted the soup. It was really good.

"How can something so simple be so good?" I asked Cassie.

"Don't know," she said. "Doesn't add up. We work our butts off on complicated recipes and can't make something half this good."

"Where is that Edmund character?" I said.

We found him in the stockroom, checking inventory. We thanked him and asked him where he'd gotten the recipe.

"It's just something I make at home sometimes," he said.

"Can you write down the recipe for us?" I asked.

"Yeah, okay," he said.

"You majorly saved our glutes today," Cassie said.

"Do you cook a lot?" I asked.

"Not really," he said.

"Do you want to help us with the cooking more often?" Cassie asked.

"Definitely not."

Our poll number that day: 79 percent.

EDMUND'S TOMATO SOUP

2   tablespoons butter

$1\frac{1}{2}$ tablespoons all-purpose flour

$\frac{1}{2}$ teaspoon salt, plus more to taste

$\frac{1}{8}$ teaspoon black pepper, or to taste

14.5-ounce can of diced tomatoes

1   cup milk

1   cup water

In a saucepan over medium heat, melt the butter, then stir in the flour, salt, and pepper. Let this mixture bubble for a minute or two. It's okay if the flour browns slightly, but if it shows signs of burning, remove it from the heat immediately.

Stir in the diced tomatoes and their juice and cook over medium heat for 5 minutes, stirring occasionally.

Remove the mixture from the burner and add the milk and water. Then heat the soup just until small bubbles rise. (Don't boil it.)

Puree the soup in a blender or food processor. (You may have to do this in two batches. Also, be very careful, since the soup is hot.) Return the soup to the pan and taste. Add more salt, if desired.

Serve the soup with popcorn, corn bread, or breadsticks. The soup is especially good with grated Parmesan cheese sprinkled on top.

Makes 3 servings (you can double or triple the recipe).

19

Frozen Sour Patch Kids

Later that afternoon, as Cassie and I came out of our last class, Dr. John was waiting for us in the hallway.

"Yo, teach, what'd we do wrong this time?" I asked.

"How about: what have you done *right*?" he said.

We shrugged.

"I come bearing exciting news," he said. "Big news. Get-out-your-drums-and-flutes-and-party-hats kind of news."

We waited.

He said, "Hillary Greenbaum is coming to the school on Monday."

We waited for more.

"What?" I said. "Who?"

"Hillary Greenbaum, the president of our board of trustees. She's coming to look around, take a couple of meetings, and also—ta-da!—to eat lunch with us."

"Uh-oh," said Cassie.

"Did she get the memo about bringing sack lunches?" I asked.

Dr. John laughed heartily at this. "No such thing. Hey, she's heard about what you guys are doing and she thinks it's a wonderful idea, having students involved with the kitchen, and I've told her about how you're changing things and learning and how good the desserts are—"

"Were," I said.

"—and so forth, and the result is that she's looking forward to a great lunch."

"But what if we disappoint her?" said Cassie.

"I'd prefer if we don't reach that eventuality," said Dr. John.

"Say what now?" I asked.

"Look," he said, lowering his voice, "if I request that you are extrasure that Monday's lunch is great, could you do it?"

"Not-burned great or actually edible great?" I asked.

"Perhaps I can even provide an incentive. This is very important to me."

"What kind of incentive?" Cassie asked.

"Let's just say that one great lunch served on Monday would go a *long* way toward fulfilling the terms of your kitchen service."

This sank in. "A bribe?"

"Shh!" Dr. John shushed me. He looked around to see if anyone had heard me. "An *incentive*," he whispered. "But," he said, returning to his normal voice, "above all be true, be yourselves, be diligent, and shine! This is your moment to shine!"

A few minutes later, Cassie and I were heading to the kitchen to strategize about Monday. Cassie said, "I'm not sure I want to shine."

"Personally, I want to do whatever the opposite of shining is."

"Being a black hole?"

"There you go," I said. "But if shining on Monday will get us out of the kitchen, then so be it."

We entered the kitchen, and there was Edmund, mopping the floor.

"Hi, Edmund!" Cassie chirped.

"*Olé*," said Edmund.

"Mr. Tomato Soup!" Cassie said.

"Don't you mean *hola*?" I asked.

"Do I?" he said, wringing out his mop.

"Don't mind us," Cassie said, "we're just here to get a couple of cookbooks. Turns out some bigwig is going to eat here on Monday, and we've got to figure out what we're doing."

"Probably going to replan the menu," I clarified. "Something foolproof."

"Who's coming on Monday?" he asked.

"Her name's Hillary Greenbaum," Cassie said.

"Oh, I know her," Edmund said.

"You do?" I asked. I couldn't quite imagine Edmund—who I pictured living in a trailer behind an out-of-business car wash—rubbing elbows with the president of the board of trustees, ex-hippie or not.

"Or my aunt knows her, at least," he said. "She's coming here? She's eating here? Oh boy."

"What? Why 'oh boy'?" asked Cassie.

"*I* wouldn't want to cook for her. She's picky. She's a lawyer with Schmerta, Schmerta, Ballentine, and Kranz. She hates all the restaurants in town, so she has a condo in St. Paul and goes there every weekend to eat out. She spent six years living in Paris, too, and still goes there twice a year. This is a lady who knows about food."

"As opposed to us . . . ," I said.

"What the frazzle are we supposed to do?" Cassie asked.

"Yeah," I said, "what the frazzle are we supposed to do when we don't know frazzle about anyfrazzle that has to do with frazzling food."

Cassie glared at me. She knew I was mocking her.

Edmund shrugged. "I recommend prayer," he said.

We stood there, watching him swab the floor.

"But, Edmund!" Cassie exclaimed. "You can help us! That soup was so good!"

"I'm tapped out," he said. "That soup is all I've got."

"Crud," said Cassie.

"If you want my opinion," he said, "I'd say take no chances. Make sure everything is perfect."

"But every meal we cook entails massive risk," I said.

"Well," said Edmund, "find a way around that."

"Like how?" asked Cassie.

"Fake it. Like maybe *buy* something and make it look like you cooked it."

"That's cheating," said Cassie.

He shrugged.

"Cheating, yes. But why should a little cheating stop us?" I said. I nudged Cassie in the ribs. "Remember how *important* this is to Dr. John?"

"But it's cheating!" she said. "Plus, if we do that for her, we'd also have to buy thirty servings of the exact same thing to serve everyone else. We can't afford that."

Edmund leaned on his mop. "Ever heard of Splendid Gourmet frozen dinners?"

"No," I said.

"They're really good!" said Cassie. "Me and my dad eat them, like, five days a week."

"Ew," I said.

"Actually, they are pretty good," said Edmund. "They were developed by Klaus Hoffenblau, the chef."

"I'm telling you, Molly, they're not just some soggy microwave dinner," explained Cassie. "You actually bake them in the oven, and they come out perfect."

"And they're only four bucks a pop," said Edmund.

"So we should make a frozen dinner for Hillary Greenbaum?" I asked.

"They're really, really good!" said Cassie. "Really!"

"But how would we make it look like we'd cooked the food ourselves?"

"That's easy," Edmund said. "You can fit thirty Splendid Gourmet meals in the ovens here. Then you dish everything up in serving trays like you made it yourselves."

"But Dina would know," I said.

"Dina can keep a secret," Edmund said. "She doesn't mind anything, as long as it doesn't get her fired. She's only five months away from retirement, you know, which is why she stuck around here when everyone else went for the bigger wages elsewhere."

"Let's do it!" said Cassie.

"I'm not sure. Besides, how can we get thirty of the same dinner?"

"Shop-o-Day! has piles of them in the warehouse freezer," said Cassie.

"Lookit," said Edmund, mopping the floor again, "go home, try a couple of these Splendid Gourmet dinners, and see for yourself. If they're not good enough, or you're scared or whatever, then come up with your own menu and cook your own lunch on Monday. But if you like them, and think it would work, then think how easy it will be.

"And since my aunt sorta knows Hillary Greenbaum," he continued, "I'll tell you what: I'll ask my aunt about what kind of food Hillary likes, and on Monday morning I'll tell you exactly which of the Splendid Gourmet dinners would probably please her most, and then I'll go out in the custodial truck and I'll even buy them for you while you're in lit. class. I'll even chip in. We'll split it three ways. You can't beat that."

"Yeah, you can't beat that!" said Cassie. "You can't! There's no way to beat it!"

So I drove over to Cassie's house that night. Daylight saving time had ended, so even though it was only five-thirty, it was dark. I didn't like that. The grip of a Minnesota winter was closing in fast.

When I pulled into Cassie's driveway, she rushed out. I climbed out of the car.

"Yay! We get to eat Splendid Gourmet!" Cassie cheered. She hugged me. It surprised me.

"Is it like a party every time you eat these frozen dinners?" I asked.

"Well, yes, but also this time they represent our freedom from the kitchen, thanks to Dr. John's bribe."

"Incentive," I corrected.

We went down into the basement, where there was a big standing freezer. She opened the freezer, and inside were all kinds of frozen dinners, frozen pies, frozen lasagna, ice cream, gelato, frozen burritos, frozen pizzas, frozen egg rolls, frozen fish sticks, frozen hamburgers, frozen cakes, and several bags of frozen Sour Patch Kids.

"Sour Patch Kids?" I said.

"My dad loves 'em frozen. Don't know why."

We selected two Splendid Gourmet dinners and took them upstairs and heated them up in the oven and then ate them in Cassie's room. Cassie had a salmon dinner and I had manicotti, the only vegetarian option.

"See, aren't they good?" Cassie said.

I had to agree. Mine was pretty good. It was on the verge of great.

Then we had some frozen Sour Patch Kids. Those were pretty good, too.

When we were done, and had agreed to go ahead with cooking the frozen dinners for lunch on Monday, we sat there in the beanbag chairs in front of the long wall of windows and watched the lights of Minerva twinkle across the river.

"I'm sorry that I got bent out of shape about the whole Devin Harper thing," Cassie said.

"Oh. That. Who cares about that."

"Yeah."

"I'm sorry, too," I said.

"Do you get to spend time with him while you're working on this play?"

"Not really. But yesterday in the hall he dropped his pen and no one else saw it and I was like, 'Devin, you dropped your pen!' and he was like, 'Thanks, that's my favorite pen,' and I was like, 'Cool!'"

"Wow. What kind of pen was it?"

"You know. Bic."

"Neat."

"For the play, mainly I work with this guy Pete," I said. "He's pretty funny."

"Don't think I know him."

"He's a good artist, too."

"So . . . ," Cassie said. "We'll be out of the kitchen pretty soon it sounds like."

"Finally."

"Does that mean . . . Does that mean . . ."

Her tone of voice was odd. Was she about to cry?

"What?"

"I just wonder," she said, "whether we're actually friends, or whether we're just two people who work together."

My mind went blank. She was asking about us. Where had this come from?

"I guess I don't know," I admitted.

"Yeah," she said. "Well." She sniffled. A tear slid down her cheek.

"I think maybe we're somewhere in between."

"I suppose." She sniffled again. "I've been in this stupid town for six months now and I still . . ."

She didn't have friends. Neither did I. And who was I to have been so mean to her in the first place? Why did I specialize in creating a thorny hedge that surrounded me and kept people away?

"Maybe," I said, "we won't know where we're going until we get there. And maybe what matters, anyway, is not the destination, but that we're on the same journey together."

"I see what you're saying. It's just that I get so . . . I put my . . . I . . ."

"Me, too," I said.

"Sorry about the crying and everything."

"It's okay."

I drove home with the radio off. I wasn't sure how I felt about Cassie. *Was* she my friend? If so, why didn't I know for sure? And if she was my friend, then how in the heck did I end up with someone like Cassie Birchmeyer, of all people, as a friend?

I hadn't had a real friend since Patty Cable and I stopped talking to each other a year ago. Being with Patty had made me happy. Maybe it was that simple. You're friends with someone when you're happy to be with them, and also happy to be yourself.

20

Go with Our Blessings, Little Dinners

On Monday, we arrived at the kitchen before school, as usual. We had a conference with Dina and Edmund and Clyde about what we were about to do.

"Fine with me," said Dina, then went back to reading the paper.

"But I just wonder about the ethics of this course of action," Clyde said.

"Understood," I said. "We did, too. But we can overrule you, so when you're done wondering about the ethics, the real question is whether you're a team player."

Clyde's brow furrowed. "I resent the manipulation inherent in the suggestion that my personal examination of the ethical appropriateness of the situation is contrary to my desire for us to succeed."

"Don't be prissy," I said.

"I'm just being honest. That said, I'll do whatever you need me to do."

When we got back to the kitchen from lit. class, Edmund took us to the freezer and showed us the stack of frozen dinners that he'd just bought at Shop-o-Day! Each box contained a pesto-crusted chicken breast, sauteed green beans with sesame seeds and shallots, wild herb rice, and a poached pear half. This was the meal that Edmund had chosen for us, based on his aunt's knowledge of Hillary Greenbaum.

"There's something beautiful about that stack of frozen dinners," Cassie said, looking at the pile. I was about to mock her, but then I realized she was right. For one thing, Edmund could sure make a tidy pile. For another, I felt sort of like I was looking at a big stack of fake gold bullion that would later be switched with the real thing, or a forged art masterpiece that we were about to sell at auction, or some other item of fakery that was about to be part of a daring switcheroo in a heist movie. The frozen dinners were bad, but oh so good. Harmless, but oh so dangerous.

"It's an incredible stack," I said.

"And edible," said Edmund.

He took off his baseball cap and put his hand on the frozen dinners and said, reverently, "Go with our blessings, little dinners."

"Ditto, frozen dudes," I said.

We kept the serving window partition closed all morning, and we also kept the kitchen doors locked, both the outside door and the lunchroom door. Not that anyone ever barged in unexpectedly, really, but it was a necessary precaution. (We also had a plan—involving fake blood—for how to distract anyone who happened to knock on the door.) Then we sat around for most of the morning, drinking coffee, reading magazines, doing homework, and waiting nervously. Clyde did some yo-yo tricks he had invented. One was called Chattanooga Chop-Chop and another was called Sashay That Thang. Dina showed us pictures of her granddaughters. I showed Cassie some of my sketches for *The Bleepity Bleep Bleep Gang.*

After eleven, we went into the freezer and took the dinners out of their boxes—so they'd be ready to go at precisely the right time. We watched as Edmund wrapped the empty boxes in three trash bags and then literally climbed into the Dumpster and buried them beneath other trash.

We preheated the ovens a half hour in advance. We double- and triple- and quadruple-checked the oven temps.

We paced.

Then we waited some more.

There were no banners proclaiming WELCOME, HILLARY GREEN-BAUM!, no organized welcome party, no concert put on by the school band on her behalf. She wasn't the pope or the governor, after all, and her visit had not been announced to the whole school. We didn't even see her until she entered the lunchroom with Dr. John and got in the lunch line. The kids in the lunch-room looked at her. They didn't seem to know who she was, but it was obvious that she was an outsider. Brad Berrington was over in the corner doing his weekly Noontime Expression gig, and he just kept on singing "Slow Bus to Hillsdale Mall." Opposite Brad was Seth Lawson and his fellow Students for Study Hall Interest Group protesters, who today were walking in a small circle wearing huge, crudely fashioned papier-mâché heads with dunce caps on them, in front of a banner that said LESS STUDY HALL = MORE IDIOTS.

Hillary Greenbaum was barely five feet tall. She was shorter than most of the students. But she did have on a very nice tailored suit, and her hair was immaculately styled, and she carried herself with a kind of poise and professional confidence that one never saw in Sunshine Day—where even the teachers wore ratty sweaters and snow boots half the year.

"She was a hippie?" Cassie said quietly to me.

"So they say. A tiny hippie."

She and Dr. John were having what appeared to be a jovial and relaxed conversation as they waited in the lunch line.

Cassie and Dina and I dished out the Splendid Gourmet food. After we'd cooked the frozen dinners, we'd taken great care transferring the food into the kitchen's institutional-size warming trays so that it looked like we'd cooked it ourselves. (We'd even dirtied a few pots and pans and left them in a pile in the sink, to suggest we'd been cooking all morning.) Still, despite our precautions, as I served the food I was nervous, and I stood there over the steaming, faked lunch expecting one of my schoolmates to recognize the food and exclaim, "Hey! That's Splendid Gourmet! You didn't cook that! You guys are frauds!"

If that happened, I decided, I would simply rip off my hairnet, run out the back door, head downtown, take the first bus out of town, and not stop until I reached an ocean, settle there, invent a new name for myself, get a new hair color, enroll in chiropracty school, and never speak of Minerva-Hillsdale again.

But it didn't happen.

True, the students and faculty who were eating lunch today all looked with mild surprise at what they were being served. It didn't look like the usual bungled, improperly prepared

Cassie-and-Molly fare. That said, it didn't look all that fantastic either—no frozen food ever looks nearly as good as the picture on the box, after all. But it smelled great. And it was a *complete* meal, no three-pile mess or missing-dessert fiasco.

"Ah, the queens of the kitchen," Dr. John said when he and Hillary Greenbaum had reached the head of the line. "Hillary, this is Molly Ollinger and Cassie Birchmeyer, the sophomores I told you about. Molly and Cassie, this is Hillary Greenbaum."

We said hello and dished up their trays of food.

"This looks excellent," Hillary Greenbaum said. "And it smells sublime."

"We specialize in smells," I said.

Hillary Greenbaum, to her credit, laughed immediately. Then she said that after lunch she hoped she would have time to pop into the kitchen and chat with us.

And that was that.

Soon the serving was done, and we moved to the tray-return window, and witnessed tray after tray coming back completely bare.

"It worked!" Cassie hissed in my ear.

"Ixnay on the emeschay."

"What?" Cassie said.

"No talky yet . . ."

After a while, Dr. John popped into view with his tray and Hillary Greenbaum's.

"Girls," he said, "that was fantastic. You must have worked on it this weekend, and it paid off, big time. Hillary says the meal was superlative. She's impressed. The bad news is that she got a call and needs to get back to her office, so she won't be able to chat with you, but maybe another time." He started to go, then turned back. "Oh, and I don't even see the point of counting the Hot Lunch Poll today. Uh, let's talk after school."

Then he winked.

We finished cleaning up, then ate some lunch ourselves. The lunchroom started to get quieter as the students began heading back upstairs.

When Dina headed to the main office to hand in some paperwork, Cassie and I were alone in the kitchen for the first time today. We looked at each other, beaming. I put up my hand, and she gave me a high five.

"Did you see him wink?" Cassie asked.

"Yes."

"I think that's it. I think that's the sign!"

"It was so easy," I said.

"Let's go thank Edmund."

We found him in the dark broom closet past the stockroom.

"We just wanted to say thank you," Cassie said.

"Oh . . . ," said Edmund. He seemed a bit glum.

"We owe you one," I said.

"Don't worry about it," he said. "No problem."

"We couldn't have done it without you," said Cassie.

He nodded. Far away, the bell rang. "Okay," he said, "run along, children."

We left. As we were gathering our bags from the kitchen, Cassie looked through the tray-return window.

"That's weird," she said.

"What?" I went over and looked out into the lunchroom. Hillary Greenbaum and Dr. John were engaged in a conversation on the far side of the lunchroom.

"If her schedule is so tight, why are they just standing there?" Cassie asked.

We couldn't hear the conversation, but it looked like Hillary Greenbaum was concerned about something, maybe even upset, and Dr. John was listening, nodding.

"They've got a whole school to worry about," I pointed out. "Probably arguing about whether the school needs even more touchy-feely."

We were running a bit late—the second bell was close—but we took a minute to talk with Dina about tomorrow's menu, and then we rushed to the door that led into the lunch-room. When we opened it, Dr. John was right there, poised to knock.

"Eeep!" I yelped, startled.

"Franklin's mint, you scared me!" Dr. John said.

"You scared *me*," I said.

He put his hand to his chest, like he was trying to catch his breath.

I moved to get by, but Dr. John stopped me. "I'd like a word with both of you."

"But we've got class," said Cassie.

Then I realized he didn't seem to be in a good mood. Where had it gone? Minutes ago he was complimenting our lunch and telling us that we wouldn't have to work in the kitchen much longer. And then we'd seen him having that intense conversation with Hillary Greenbaum, and now . . .

We followed him to his office, through the hallways.

We sat down in Dr. John's office. He shut the door. He sat. He looked right at us and said, "Is there anything you want to tell me?"

"I like your tie?" said Cassie. It was the first time I'd ever seen Dr. John wear a tie. He'd obviously dressed up for Hillary Greenbaum.

"Thanks. Anything else?"

We shook our heads.

"Really?" he asked. "Nothing? Is that how this is going to go? Look, I can try to be the defense attorney and the prosecuting attorney and the judge all at once, but really it just doesn't work. So I recommend your cooperation. You can paddle upstream all you want, but eventually you'll wear out and have to go with the current."

He knew. He knew about the frozen dinners.

"Okay," he said. "Let me tell you about my lunch today. It's an interesting story.

"So I'm enjoying lunch with Hillary Greenbaum, my boss. It was a rather nice lunch. Chicken with pesto. I love pesto. Nice rice pilaf-type thing. Poached pear. All good. An impressive lunch. And I'm eating this food, thinking you two have outdone yourselves, imagining all the planning and practicing that went into this meal, and I'm going on and on to Hillary about how you two have come a long way and how your cooking and cooperation are improving, and I'm *bragging* on you two, talking about how I think maybe we should make the kitchen more student-inclusive *permanently*, make food education part of our curriculum, blah, blah, blah."

Blah, blah, blah? That wasn't like Dr. John.

"And she's listening," he continued, "and nodding a lot, and then after lunch—okay, ready?—after lunch when everybody's gone, she pulls me aside, and do you have any idea what she told me?"

We shook our heads.

"She informs me that she'd been too shocked to say anything at first, and too embarrassed to say it in front of anyone else, but that the meal we'd just enjoyed was in fact a certain brand of frozen dinner that she was familiar with, and *in fact* it was the exact same meal she had eaten this weekend. *Exactly.* And at first I couldn't believe it. It sounded made up. It sounded like a joke, and so I asked her how certain was she that it was a frozen dinner, and she said she was one hundred percent certain. That's pretty certain, isn't it?"

We nodded.

"So, tell me. Was she right? Were they frozen dinners?"

"Yes," I said.

21

I Needed a Lollipop Right Now

Later, after history class, I dragged myself upstairs to my locker. Suddenly, Clyde was beside me.

"Molly! I heard you got called to the office!"

"He found out," I said.

"About the . . . about . . ." It dawned on him.

"Look," I said, "I know you objected to the plan, so please just skip the part where you make me feel worse than I already do."

"How'd he find out?"

"Hillary Greenbaum ate the exact same dinner this weekend."

"She eats frozen dinners?" he said. "Someone like her eats frozen dinners?"

"Apparently they're very popular," I said.

"But what's going to happen?"

"Don't worry, we told him you had nothing to do with it."

"But . . . that's not what I mean. I mean what's going to happen to you guys?"

"Our parents are coming in after school. I wouldn't be surprised if we get kicked out this time."

"Has Dr. John talked to Edmund or Dina yet?"

"Don't know. Probably not. Dina went home already. Edmund—he's just the kitchen technician. I doubt Dr. John suspects he had a part in it."

"Molly," he said, putting his hand on my shoulder, "I'm really sorry this happened."

I looked at him. Pip-squeak do-gooder or not, he meant well, poor tyke.

"Thanks," I said.

I trudged my way through the next two hours. I avoided eye contact with Cassie. I didn't want to be reminded of the kitchen, or the mess we were in, or the fast-approaching conference with my parents, or the prospect of going to Minerva-Hillsdale High. Maybe what was most annoying was that we'd been defeated simply by coincidence: Hillary Greenbaum had recognized the meal as the same one she'd eaten that weekend. How unlikely was that? The odds were staggering. If the plan had failed because we'd messed up, that would be one thing. But we'd done everything right. It was the universe that was against us. How can you fight the universe?

Our failure was just another reminder of our lameness. We couldn't cook, we couldn't learn to cook, we couldn't get along, and we couldn't even scheme our way out of the kitchen. We were just as bad at scheming as we were at cooking. And what was the point of trying to be devious if it didn't work?

After the day's final bell rang, I waited for the upstairs hallway to clear out, then I went and sat on the floor beside my locker. It would be an hour until my parents came, but that wasn't enough time to make it worthwhile to trek home and then back to school, so I'd just wait here. I sat there, headphones on, and did sketches of my toes. But after only fifteen minutes I got so uncomfortable on the floor I had to move. I went down to the study hall room, but the Sudoku Club was meeting in there. Pete Stamponivich was in that club and he nodded and smiled when he saw me across the room. I returned his nod—I didn't even want to think about how much work I would have to do between now and when the musical debuted in late January— sighed and headed to the cafeteria. But there I found the weekly meeting of the Crafternoon Club. So I headed to the kitchen. At least it would be quiet in there. I could do some homework. But when I opened the kitchen door, I found that Cassie was sitting at the central work counter, underneath the buzzing fluorescent lights.

"Oh," I said. "Hey."

"Hey."

Now I didn't want to be here. But I couldn't just leave. So I sat down at the other end of the counter. I got out my sketch-book. Cassie was surrounded by homework. I put my head-phones on.

"Remember," said Cassie, "I know about the headphones."

I'd forgotten she knew.

"Fine," I said, "but can I please just wear them anyway? Do you *mind*? Is it such an *imposition*?"

"No," she said. She went back to her homework.

I sat there, steaming. I looked in my bag and found a lollipop. Thank goodness. I needed a lollipop right now. I unwrapped it and put it in my mouth. I looked at Cassie, scribbling away on her homework. She erased something, blew the little eraser filaments away, wrote again. It irritated me—her earnest home-working, her erasing, her blowing, her writing. *She* irritated me.

"We wouldn't be in this mess if I hadn't listened to you," I said.

She looked up. "Listened to me?" she asked.

"You were the one enthusiastic about how great Splendid Gourmet dinners are."

"I was just saying what I thought was true."

"I can't believe I listened to you. I should have known better. Now look at us."

She pointed her pencil at me. "Actually," she said, "you're the one that talked *me* into it. I didn't like the plan because it was cheating, and you said, 'Why should a little cheating stop us?' and then you nudged me and reminded me about Dr. John's bribe! So you talked *me* into it!"

I shrugged. "Whatever," I said. "Believe what you want."

"Okay, I had a part in it, sure. You're right. I was there. I remember. But you're not blameless. Open your eyes, Molly. Not only did you help talk me into this plan, but you also came up with that stupid cake plan to get Mrs. Zetz back, you schemed to work on the musical just to get close to Devin Harper, you pretended you weren't home when I came to your house that time, you had a saber-toothed *tiger* eat me in your essay just so you could be mean to me without having to do it to my face, and you treat Clyde like a preschooler, and you haven't been working as hard as I have to learn to cook and to get out of this kitchen, and you pretend you're listening to music all the time just so you don't have to talk to people, as if you're so much better than the rest of us, as if you're a saint or something—Saint Molly—when actually you're just sad and scared and mean, and I can see now why I was worried about whether we were friends or not because I *should* have been worried because it's not healthy to be friends with someone like you, because all you know how to do is mope and lie and push people away, and I don't know why I ever tried to get close to you. So . . . *blarg!*"

She started to gather up her books. I sat there, feeling numb, feeling like I'd been hit in the back of the head with a baseball bat, but also feeling like I had to react. I had to fight back.

"Screw you," I said.

"Very helpful," said Cassie, putting her books in her backpack.

"No wonder you don't have friends," I said.

"No wonder *you* don't," she said.

"I hope I do get kicked out so I can go to Minerva-Hillsdale and don't have to see you again."

"Sounds good to me," she said, putting her backpack on.

There was a loud knocking on the lunchroom door. We both looked at it. No one ever knocked on the lunchroom door.

Dr. John poked his head in. "I've looked all over for you two," he said, coming in. We just sort of stared at him. "Mind if I sit?" he asked. He pulled up a stool. He motioned for Cassie to sit, too. She did.

My mind was still caught up with the fight that Cassie and I'd been having, and now Dr. John was here, and I was trying to focus on him. He seemed oblivious to the fact that he'd wandered into a sour situation.

"I understand and respect your decision to protect your friends and coworkers," he said. "That's cool with me. But do you realize that the consequences could have been severe?"

What was he talking about? Protect our coworkers?

"Well, I'm sure you do. Anyway, I had an illuminating conversation with your coworker just after the final bell. I don't really need to name names, I guess. He told me how the whole plan for these frozen dinners wasn't your idea, and how you both resisted it but were swayed by his argument, and how you were willing to take the fall for it. I saw the truth in his story, and so you know what? I'm going to give you both a free pass on this thing. I'm not saying that it's not troubling and I'm not saying that it's contrary to the spirit of community-building, but I'm going to let you off. I honestly don't know what kind of punishment would be appropriate anyway, and I feel that this was just an isolated incident that didn't originate with you two. So that's all. I've already called your parents and explained the mix-up, so they won't be coming in for the meeting."

Hold on a cotton-picking minute. We were off the hook? We were free? We'd been saved by . . . Edmund? *Edmund?*

"But what . . . what about this . . . this guy?" said Cassie. "What's going to happen with him?"

"He and I will work something out."

Maybe there was more to Edmund than I'd thought. He'd come forward to save Cassie and me. It was surprising, but he was, after all, the person who had put the whole thing into motion, so really he was just owning up to his actions.

"You're not going to fire him, are you?" I asked.

Dr. John laughed. I wasn't sure why it was so funny. "No, I'm certainly not going to do that."

"We didn't mean any harm, you know," said Cassie.

Dr. John nodded. "I know. That's why this is a complicated situation. But it's also a useful lesson in the fact that a lot of the harm that arises in this world is not intended. That's why we have to parse our thoughts and actions carefully.

"Can I also point out that though I know you two probably feel like you're working like crazy every day and not making much headway, that in fact you *are* making headway? I mean, a few weeks ago you couldn't even make the basic Marta Zetz lunches, but now you're working on more ambitious menus and you're getting better. And you got a bang-up pastry chef who'll eventually come around to being a steady performer again. And I'd also like to point out that the reason that you're getting closer to running this kitchen like pros is that you two aren't fighting anymore. You're friends. It's really rather simple and amazing, isn't it? When you get along, you can achieve great things."

22

This Car Smells Like KFC

fter Dr. John left the kitchen, Cassie looked at me and then just walked out the back door. Sure, it seemed we were off the hook—miraculously—but we'd also just had a huge fight.

I slumped there at the kitchen counter. I didn't want to go home. I didn't want to go anywhere. I would just stay here under the buzzing fluorescent lights and sketch and fume and maybe do some homework. The kitchen was the only place I figured I could just be alone.

I woke up. There was a rattling noise. I'd fallen alseep in the school kitchen, and it was dark outside and my cheek was wet from the pool of drool it had been lying in.

There was a rattling noise again. I looked around.

"Molly," said a voice from far away.

"Is someone stuck in the refrigerator?" I said.

"Over here. The window."

I looked at the dark window over the sink, and there was Edmund's face. I went over and opened the window.

"Edmund? What are you doing here?"

"Passing by," he said. "Saw the light on."

"What time is it?"

"I don't know. Six."

Suddenly I remembered the whole day, and how Edmund had taken the blame for the frozen dinner fiasco.

"I heard you guys took some heat from the good doctor today," Edmund said.

"Not for long," I said.

"So it worked out? You two aren't suspended or anything?"

"He let us off, thanks to . . . well, he let us off."

"Good. That's good. I'm relieved to hear that."

We were still talking through the window. Cold air was pouring in.

"Hold on. I'll come out," I said.

I put on my vest and went out the back door. Edmund came over and sat on the stoop. I sat down, too.

"Look, I don't really know what to say," I said, "but, I mean, I guess I should point out the obvious: first it's not your fault we went with the plan—we all had a hand in that—and second, it wasn't your fault that what we served was the exact same meal Hillary Greenbaum had eaten a couple of days ago. I mean, there wasn't any way to know that. So I just don't want you to be too hard on yourself."

"Yeah," he said. "Well . . . But look, no reason to hash over the details."

"And obviously, actually, both Cassie and I owe you a big thank-you."

"Sure," he said. "I just wanted to make sure you guys were okay. But I also want to help."

"You already have."

"But I mean I want to really start helping you in the kitchen," he said. "If you'll let me. I haven't been helping at all. I've been in the back, screwing up your orders and pretending it was the distributor's fault. That's why you've been having problems getting ingredients on time."

"You sabotaged our orders?"

"I've been doing that all along," he said. "Plus, remember that chili that tasted like oranges?"

"Yeah."

"I did that. I put orange juice concentrate in it."

"Oh . . . but . . . but anyway, that was a mean thing to do."

"I know. That's why I'm here. That's what I'm saying. I was being a deluxe jackass. Remember that salsa that was supposed to be mild but was actually extra hot? I did that, too."

"What else did you do?"

"Oh, I swapped high-protein flour for the low-protein flour, and that's one of the reasons—and I stress the word *one*—that your biscuits turned out so tough, and a couple of Clyde's cakes were so bad. Also, I put honey in the barbecue pork. Plus, I messed with the thermostat in the ovens, which is why you've been burning a lot of the things you've baked. And I burned those cookies on purpose. And I guess I have to mention my general sour mood and my work slowdowns."

"If I were actually your boss, I think I'd have to fire you."

"Yeah, I know. And if Dr. John knew the whole truth, he'd fire me. So really the power is in your hands, if you want to tell him. I'll go if you want. But I'm here now because I can really help you two. Like that tomato soup, you know? I've got more like that. I can cook. Nothin' fancy, but I can turn out a meal. My aunt's a chef, I've got a few buddies who are line cooks and grill cooks at different restaurants. I know a thing or two. I can really help you guys if you'll let me."

"If you like to cook, why don't you work in a restaurant instead of sweeping up in a school kitchen?"

"I don't have any training as a chef. Besides, I hate working at night. Plus, I tend to get into arguments with chefs. In the school kitchen, no one yells at me."

"Not even Mrs. Zetz."

"Not once. We got along fine."

"Until we came along."

"And my life got a lot harder. I had to do more work. I had to take orders from teenage girls."

"That's why you've been so bent out of shape? I just assumed you were always like that."

"Sort of. But think about it. You were a pill from the start. Even that first day you two had the food fight, do you remember who stopped you guys? I did. Dr. John was trying, but it just wasn't happening, so I jumped in there and stopped you guys. If it hadn't been for me you two probably would have ended up killing each other with hams. And *then*, after the food fight was over, who had to clean up the whole mess? Me. I did. It took five hours. I had to clean the *ceiling*, for frick's sake.

"And then on the day Mrs. Zetz quit, she told Dr. John about catching me smoking, and I almost got fired over that one. So that was your fault. And for the record I was pretty fond of Mrs. Zetz, even if she did tend to be dictatorial and serve prefab food from hell. And you up and made her quit.

"Look, I work at the school because I don't want a complicated job. I like to do my job right and keep to myself. Do you know how hard it is to find a decent, low-stress job that has full benefits? I'm telling you, you won't find it at the mall or in a convenience store or Wal-Mart or even at most restaurants. I like where I am.

"So I guess that's all. That's what my whole deal is."

I nodded. I thought about it. It had been an alarming and tiring day, first with the stress of the frozen dinner scheme, then the surprise of getting found out, then Edmund's confessing to Dr. John, then the fight with Cassie, and now Edmund talking to me civilly, telling me he's a decent cook, saying he'd been working against us but now wanted to help. I believed him. He was for real, for the first time.

"Okay," I said. "I get it. Or I get most of it. So let's start over."

I put out my hand. He shook it.

"Deal," he said. "But don't we have to bring Cassie into this before it's official?"

"Guess so," I said.

"Should we call her, or . . . ?"

"It's a little complicated," I said.

"Why?"

"We had a bit of a fight."

"But you guys specialize in fighting," he said, "so what's the big deal?"

"But I guess that before, when we fought, we were enemies. But now when we fight, we're sort of friends, and so that makes it different."

"Makes it hurt more, but also makes reconciliation more important."

"If I recall, our parting words to each other were that we never wanted to see each other again."

"Okay, but is that true?"

I thought about it. "No."

"Then all you have to do is let her know that."

He was right. I got out my phone and called her. Her voice mail picked up.

"Okay," I said, "I know you're not picking up because you see that it's me calling. That's okay. But I just ask that you listen to my message.

"I apologize for picking a fight with you today. I was in a funk because it seemed like we were back to square one, like we were going to be stuck in the kitchen for eternity. I'm sorry I blamed you for our troubles. That was small-minded of me. I see the part that I played. And I didn't mean it when I said I don't want to see you again, because I do.

"So . . . yeah. So I hope you want to talk to me. If you do, call me. It would mean a lot to me."

"You're cooler than I thought you were," Edmund said.

"I don't think she'll want to talk to me."

"Don't fret about something that hasn't happened yet. Let the universe work."

My phone rang.

"See?" Edmund said.

I looked at the phone. It was her.

Ten minutes later, Edmund and I were in Mom's Prius, heading across town. I'd told Grampa I was going to Cassie's house to apologize for the fight, but I didn't mention Edmund, who was waiting outside, to him. I didn't think Grampa or my parents, who would probably be home in an hour or so, would be that keen on me driving around with a twentysomething slacker with a tattoo on his arm of Pikachu smoking what most certainly was not a cigarette.

"This car smells like KFC," commented Edmund.

The three of us drove to a grocery store. Cassie and I waited in the car while Edmund shopped. Then we drove to the school and went into the kitchen. There, Cassie and I watched Edmund cook a quick dinner. He explained what he was doing as he went along. He made white bean crostini and angel hair pasta with garlic and olive oil. He cooked without recipes, and the food was tasty—better than anything we'd turned out in the school kitchen *ever*—and he'd hardly broken a sweat.

"Why'd you keep your cooking a secret for so long?" Cassie asked him.

He shrugged. "Gotta keep some kind of private life."

"So what do you say?" I asked. "Should we let him help us?"

"Yes," she said. "Let's do it."

I smiled and clapped my hands together and said something like "Hwee!"

"Hwee?" Cassie said, looking at me, amused.

"You heard me," I said.

"Okay," said Edmund, "but we've got to figure out how to run the kitchen. I'm not going to be a dictator. That's just not the way I want to work."

"Then how about a democracy?" said Cassie.

"Or maybe a socialist democracy," I added. "No one is in charge, and we each get one vote."

"What about Clyde and Dina?" Edmund asked.

"They get votes, too," said Cassie.

"All right. Five people, five votes," said Edmund. "Sounds workable."

"But maybe we need defined roles, too," I suggested.

"Like what?" said Cassie.

"Well," I said, "like Clyde's role is desserts. You could be in charge of meat. I do side dishes and fruit. Dina remains responsible for food safety. And Edmund's the overall coordinator and menu planner. Plus, we all just help out when needed, as needed. We have roles, but we're flexible."

"I like it," Cassie agreed. "But I think we still need to keep learning how to cook," said Cassie. "Even with your help in the kitchen, Edmund, we need to know what we're doing, because you can't cook the lunches by yourself."

"What you should do is you learn from the people you know. All you have to do is learn one dish from everybody you know, and pretty soon you'll have a whole repertoire of dishes. That's how I started."

"We could do that!" said Cassie.

"All you need is a string of good poll numbers," Edmund pointed out. "It's not like you have to run a five-star kitchen by yourselves. With a little work, you'll be able to pull it off in no time."

"What about the Thanksgiving lunch?" I asked.

Every year, on the day before Thanksgiving, Sunshine Day hosted all the parents for a big noon meal. Marta Zetz had always prepared all the traditional Thanksgiving dishes, which was just a little bit odd, seeing as most everyone would be gorging on almost the exact same food the next day, but nobody seemed to mind, and the Sunshine Day Thanksgiving meal was always popular and always packed to capacity.

"Can we cancel it?" Cassie asked.

"Can't cancel it. It's a big fund-raiser for the school," said Edmund. "Plus, we've already got the ingredients in stock, including eight frozen turkeys."

"Cooking lunch for thirty people is one thing," said Cassie, "but doing Thanksgiving for over a hundred people . . ."

"Almost two hundred," said Edmund.

"We can't do that," I said.

"If we get five days of good poll numbers," said Edmund, "you'll be out of the kitchen before Thanksgiving anyway."

"What's that mean, though?" asked Cassie. "Will Dr. John produce a new kitchen staff on a moment's notice, to swoop in and cook Thanksgiving?"

"I don't know," said Edmund.

"I think we have to plan on cooking the Thanksgiving meal ourselves," I said. "We have to prepare as if it's going to go ahead, and we're going to cook it. We should practice this weekend. And if we end up getting out of kitchen duty before Wednesday, fine. Maybe that means we won't cook it; but I think we should be ready to *offer* to cook it."

"You may need good poll numbers for Thanksgiving, too," said Edmund. "We don't know. So I think you're right that we have to prepare as if we're going to do it."

"Thanksgiving, schmanksgiving," I said. "We'll cook the crap out of it."

23

Apples Suddenly Exploding

There are enough peas down here to kill a horse!" Cassie said, digging in the back corner of the walk-in freezer.

"How would peas kill a horse?" I asked.

"And here's a whole box of hash browns," she said.

It was early—still dark outside—and we were rummaging for menu ideas for lunch. This was the day we had planned on starting our imitation of Applebee's—because our attempt at a bistro had failed—but that was impossible, because Edmund had deliberately flubbed the ingredients order, and seeing as we were starting a whole new era in the kitchen—the Five Amigos of the Social Democracy of the Hot Lunch Kitchen—we didn't really want to cook Applebee's today anyway, and so now we were just trying to figure out *something* to cook. Anything.

Twenty minutes ago, Clyde and Dina had both responded positively to the new kitchen arrangement.

"Does this mean I get to keep making desserts like always?" Clyde had asked.

"Yes," I said.

"Totally radical!" he said.

Dr. John had also approved of our plan, without hesitation, which I thought was slightly odd, considering that we had suddenly put Edmund into a role of great responsibility—the same Edmund who yesterday had confessed to Dr. John that he was culpable for the Splendid Gourmet plan. Wouldn't this concern Dr. John a wee bit?

I heard a loud thump from where Cassie was down in the corner of the freezer.

"Ow!" she said. "That was my head."

"Sounded like a coconut," I noted.

The door of the freezer popped open. Edmund was there.

"I've got it," he said. "Peppers stuffed with rice and chicken. Simple. Classic."

We were behind schedule, though, and discombobulated, and not used to having Edmund among us, and so it was a hectic morning, and we were all so busy that it was approaching lunchtime before we finally thought to ask what Clyde was busy working on over in his little corner.

"Apple-cinnamon mousse," he said, whisking a huge bowl of something.

"What?" said Edmund. "No such a thing exists."

"Not *yet*," said Clyde. He shuffled over to me. "Here, taste this."

He was holding up a cutting board with pieces of cut apple on it.

"I'm not really a fruit person," I said.

He picked up a piece of apple and moved it toward my mouth. "Fine," I said, and tasted it. It was boring and a little mealy. "Blah."

"Exactly!" exclaimed Clyde. That was a Red Delicious apple from Shop-o-Day! Totally horrible. But now taste this one." He gave me another slice of apple.

The second apple was crisp and spicy and fantastic.

"What the eff, man?" I asked. "That one's awesome."

"My dad picked these at Bobbey Orchard last month. Been in our fridge ever since, but still great, eh?"

"Better ingredients make better food," said Edmund.

Though the rice in the stuffed peppers was slightly under-done—for which Edmund accepted responsibility—otherwise they were good and satisfying, and the lunch was a success. But Clyde's apple mousse came out great. While we stood at the tray-return window, people kept yelling into the kitchen at Clyde.

"That apple mousse rocks, Clyde!" Bill Philly yelled.

"Thank you!" said Clyde.

"Clyde!" called Dr. John. "That was a commendable mousse!"

It went on and on. After all the trays came back, Cassie and Edmund and I sat down and finally had a chance to taste the mousse. It wasn't much to look at. Each little paper cup held a plain-looking bit of foam, but when I tasted it, it was like a whole cosmos of apples suddenly exploding in my mouth.

"This is amazing," said Edmund.

"Wow," said Cassie.

I took a second bite. Then a third. Then I looked over to where Clyde was sitting in his corner, writing in his notebook. "Clyde!" I said. "Come over here."

Clyde came over and sat with us.

"How did you do this?" I asked.

"Well, it starts with a simple syrup. Then I—"

"I don't want the recipe. I just mean after a week of failed recipes, how'd you get this one spot on?"

"First, I got the best apples I could. Second, I planned carefully."

"I like this kid," said Edmund. "He planned carefully."

"But you worked hard on all your other horrible recipes," said Cassie, "and none of them turned out right."

"Yeah," I said. "So what's different?"

"Oh, well, for one thing, I started taking cooking classes this weekend."

"Where?" asked Cassie.

"At the community college. It's a basic dessert course conducted three nights a week. One of the things we started with was mousses."

"You get the award for today," said Edmund. His cup of mousse was empty.

"What award?" asked Clyde.

"I don't know. Just the award," said Edmund. "It's not a real award. It's a verbal award. And you got it. Great apples, great recipe, great mousse."

Dr. John came in and told us the poll numbers: 62 percent.

A few minutes later, I was walking upstairs alongside Clyde.

"Can I ask you something?" said Clyde.

"Sure."

"I mean, I know that we've sort of been through this before, and if your answer is still the same, then I respect that."

"My answer to what, Clyde? I need a question. Give me a question."

"I wondered if you'd go to the Holiday Hop with me."

"Oh."

"I take that as a no."

I stopped walking. Clyde stopped, too. I looked at him. He wasn't such a miserable little squirt. He was just Clyde.

"I'm not sure I want to go to that kind of thing," I said. "It's significantly stupid."

"Oh, I agree with you there," said Clyde. "We're on the same page."

"I think it's best to just leave it at that," I said. "We're on the same page."

Clyde nodded. "All right. On the same page. Not a bad place to be."

I smiled.

Clyde said, "I gotta go to algebra. But I just want to tell you . . . well, remember that time you told me you were mean?"

"Sort of."

"I don't think you're mean. I just think that you pretend to be mean sometimes because it's a shield against hurt. Everybody has their own shield," Clyde explained. "But we're better off when we're aware of them.

"I'll see you later," he said. He walked away.

Clyde was totally wrong, of course.

But then between geometry and biology Seth Lawson came up to me with a way-too-earnest look on his face.

"Hi, Molly! I know you're a super artist and wondered if you would like to help me paint some pro–hemp toilet paper banners after school. The cause could really use your talent!"

"Maybe I don't want hemp toilet paper," I said.

"You don't?"

"But the larger issue here is that you have confused me with someone who doesn't think you're insufferable and painful to listen to."

He shuffled away.

It felt good, as usual, to repel Seth by way of a nicely modulated insult. But then I remembered what Clyde had said. And then I felt bad. So I *did* use my meanness to keep myself separate. But what was I supposed to do with that? What was Clyde, a therapist? It was all very tiring to think about, so when school was over, I was happy to be done with the day, happy to be going home. I was at the bottom of the front steps when Pete Stamponivich came running after me.

"Molly!" he called.

I turned. "Yeah?"

"O exalted leader, please desert me not." He bowed before me.

"What are you talking about?"

"We're supposed to work on the backdrop right now, remember?"

Oh, piddle. I'd forgotten.

"I just spaced out," I explained, turning back toward the school. "I just wanted to go home and watch the *Gilmore Girls* rerun at four."

"Yeah, I totally hear that," said Pete. "I TiVo it every day, so if you want I can burn a DVD for you." He held open the school door for me. Suddenly, Devin Harper was standing in front of me, and then he walked out the door and right past me.

"See ya, Petey," he said to Pete.

"Later," said Pete.

He'd walked right past me . . .

"I'll tell you what my favorite way to watch *Gilmore Girls* is," Pete said to me. "While eating Pop Rocks and drinking chocolate milk."

"Uh-huh," I said.

He noticed Pete, but not me . . .

"Also, I know what you're thinking. You're thinking that I must be gay if I enjoy watching *Gilmore Girls*."

"Uh-huh."

Right past me without even so much as a nod . . .

"But there are a few of us enlightened hetero men who love the CW."

In the art room, Pete kept blabbering as we painted. We'd rolled the huge canvas out on the floor and were busy painting a bunch of psychedelic shapes and colors. There were also some giant insects to paint, per Portia's request. I painted by sitting cross-legged and moving every once in a while. Pete preferred to paint while squatting. When he needed to move, he remained squatting and did a waddling sort of duck walk. He talked about his computer programming class and how he'd written a program that could predict your favorite color; he talked about how for Halloween in sixth grade he and his buddy Clive Chaudry had made dice costumes out of big boxes, but that their arms barely poked out and that made it extremely difficult to ring doorbells and carry candy buckets; he talked about why he preferred white erasers to pink erasers; he explained how he had trained his dog to walk up to strangers and cough dramatically and then flop over like it had died; he told the story of how last year he had walked in on Devin Harper and Francesca Eagleton making out in the props closet behind the stage, and how Francesca had been wearing a prop tutu over her jeans and Devin had been wearing a huge puffy prop hat.

Devin . . . It was like Pete had picked up on my brain waves. Sure, the story was annoying—picturing Devin making out with anyone other than myself was unpleasant—but it was no secret that Devin had dated Francesca last year, even though she was two years older than him. But he was, after all, the boy-genius star and additional material writer of *Ever Since Next Year*. Plus, the hunkiness.

"You worked on the spring play last year, didn't you?" I asked Pete.

"I was just an assistant production assistant."

"Assistant assistant?"

"I swear that was my title. I just did whatever Portia told me to do. She was the assistant director."

Hey . . . now . . . wait a sec. Maybe Pete could be a source of information about Devin. If I couldn't work shoulder to shoulder with Devin, at least I could press Pete for some useful information. I needed all the help I could get. When Devin had walked right past me forty minutes ago without even glancing at me, it had stung. After all, last week he'd said "Hey" to me. How did I go from "Hey" to nothing in one week? That was not progress. That was embarrassing. I needed to renew my quest for Devin. I needed to keep my eyes on the prize. Pete could help. Pete was my boy in the know.

"So," I ventured, "do you know if Devin's doing any writing for *The Bleepity Bleep Bleep Gang*?"

"Any what?"

"Writing."

Pete stopped painting and looked at me like I'd asked if there was one elf or two standing on my head.

"Portia did the writing," he said.

He thought I was asking about this year's musical.

"But remember how last year Devin added all those lines to *Ever Since Next Year*? All that new material?"

"Portia wrote that."

"No, I know she wrote *The Bleepity Bleep Bleep Gang*, but I'm talking about all the additional lines from *Ever Since Next Year*."

"So am I," Pete said.

"So are you what?"

"I'm saying Devin didn't write that new stuff in the play last year. Portia did. I know because I helped her. She would get all hopped up by mixing espresso with Coke and then she would write for like six hours while listening to Gregorian chants."

"Devin didn't . . ."

"You thought Devin wrote that stuff? Devin *Harper*? The boy couldn't write his way out of a wet paper sack, much less write dialogue of the caliber that Portia can write. Where'd you hear that Devin wrote that stuff?"

"Oh, someone told me. Can't remember."

I felt myself blushing.

Of course, no one had told me. I'd made the mistaken assumption that the actor who had delivered the lines so eloquently and with such emotion must surely have been the creator of the lines. I'd never even tried to verify that. I'd just taken it for truth, and on the basis of that I'd worshipped Devin Harper for seven months.

"Well," said Pete, "Devin Harper has about as much creativity as a dead owl. He's a decent guy, sort of, for an actor. But he's not a creative guy."

And wait a second. When Devin had worked in the kitchen that one day, hadn't I complimented his writing, and he'd said thanks? In other words, he'd lied to reinforce my mistaken assumption that he was a writer.

Fine. Fine. Fine. I had been worshipping a faker. An actor. Not a writer. Not a genius. A faker. A liar. An actor.

Fine.

Why shouldn't I use meanness as a shield?

24

What's the Name of Purple Cabbage?

Okay," Dad said. "Hm. Um." He was standing in the kitchen of our house, wearing his NOT RESPONSIBLE FOR SALMONELLA apron. Cassie and I were sitting on stools on the other side of the kitchen island, and I was taking notes, and Cassie was videotaping Dad. It was the first night of learning to cook one dish from everybody we knew. I'd been home from school only half an hour and still had paint under my fingernails from painting the backdrop with Pete.

"I'm just a little nervous," Dad said. "Cooking on camera and everything."

"It's just *us*, Dad," I said. "Calm down."

He took a deep breath, then started talking. "All right. It's true that when I was in college and library school I basically survived because I could cook one thing . . ." He spread his arms above the counter.

"Stir-fry," I said.

"Now, the first thing I like to do when I make a stir-fry is to assemble all my ingredients. I mean actually measuring everything that needs to be measured, chopping everything that needs to be chopped, et cetera, and then I put each ingredient in an appropriately sized bowl, from tiny—such as this little bowl of diced ginger—to big—such as this huge bowl of shredded purple cabbage."

"What's the name of that?" I prompted.

"What's the name of purple cabbage?" Dad said.

"No, what's the name of it when you put all your ingredients out in bowls? I remember you calling it something."

"The French call it *mis en place*," said Dad. It sounded like *meezon plaahs*. "It's just a fancy way of saying getting your shit ready."

"No need for profanity," I said.

"I can edit that out," said Cassie.

Dad looked at her, suddenly terrified. "You mean you're going to show this tape to other people or something?"

"She's kidding, Dad. The tape's just for us."

He walked us through the recipe. First, he fried the tofu in the skillet. Then he set the tofu aside and started cooking the onions in a stir-fry sauce he'd already made from soy sauce, garlic, honey, and so forth. Then he added the cabbage, ginger, and peanuts, and at the very end he threw in some sprouts and then stirred in the fried tofu. That was it, and he served it over brown rice, and it was great.

Grampa muttered about the tofu, though. "This tofu would be better if it were meat," he said. We were all four sitting around the dining room table—Mom was still at work.

"I think it's totally great!" said Cassie. "Mr. Ollinger, if you cook stir-fry this good, you must know at least one other dish we can learn from you."

"He doesn't," said Grampa.

"I don't," said Dad.

"What about you, Mr. Ollinger senior?" Cassie said, addressing Grampa.

"Call me Pappy," Grampa said.

"Don't call him Pappy," I said.

"You know who you could learn from? Your Aunt Polly," said Dad.

"Does that mean you'll buy me a ticket to Seattle to visit her?"

"Or how about learning that great mac and cheese from Patty Cable? That was a great dish."

"Yeah, I don't really know Patty anymore," I said.

"Too bad," said Dad. "'Because I'm tellin' ya, that mac and cheese was fo' rizzle."

After Cassie and I helped clean up, we went to my room and watched the stir-fry videotape, took some notes, conferred with Edmund on the phone, and drew up a shopping list and a plan for tomorrow. We would be making the stir-fry at school.

"Who's that?" Cassie asked, pointing to a picture on my corkboard.

"That's Patty Cable."

"Wait—the Patty who makes the mac and cheese?"

"Yeah. She was my best friend. Obviously in that picture we'd just finished spending an entire afternoon painting each other's faces. And arms."

"She doesn't go to Sunshine Day, does she?"

"No. She's in Minerva-Hillsdale. I haven't talked to her in a whole year."

"Why not?"

"We had a fight over a boy. Sort of. Then right after that we started going to different schools. Now I hear she's a cheerleader, so that means she's not the same Patty Cable anymore."

"How do you know?" Cassie asked.

"I just do."

"But maybe she's a nice cheerleader."

I shrugged. "Hard to imagine."

I couldn't sleep that night. I pulled my laptop under the sheet and wrote an e-mail to Les.

Bro:

So Cassie came over tonight, and I realized that no one but Mom and Dad had been in my room in a long time. It was weird having Cassie looking at my pictures, touching my stuff, asking why Patty Cable and me aren't friends anymore.

Meanwhile, I've discovered that Devin Harper is a liar and not nearly as interesting as I thought he was. Why'd I waste my energy on him? And because of him I'm now doing the artwork for a huge and disturbing winter musical about an orphaned chimney sweep who decides to build a rope bridge to a land called "Elanestra" with the help of a band of street dancers who wear flowerpots as hats. Said artwork being behind schedule. The director, Portia, is constantly asking for "more clarity of confusion" in the backdrops. What? Me and my assistant Pete—he's a good kid—sometimes aren't sure if she asked for more "clarity of confusion" or more "confusion of clarity."

And now I'm thinking of Patty Cable. How can a friendship like that just go poof and disappear?

Meanwhile, Cassie and I are actually learning how to cook, and the big Sunshine Day Thanksgiving lunch is looming, and there's schoolwork to worry about, and Dad slipping college brochures under my door three times in the last week—did he do that for you?—and how early the sun sets these days, and how late it rises, and I have four hangnails that I've turned into scabs, and I feel a sore throat coming on, and my stomach is growling, and the neighbor's dog is barking, and it's too hot under the sheets.

I just want to sleep. It's that simple. Then why is it not simple to do?

/Moe

25

Ah, My Old Friend Tofu

In the waning minutes of the next day's lunch hour, Cassie and I sat at the counter. I put my head down and closed my eyes. We were waiting for the poll numbers for our stir-fry. I was sure they wouldn't be above fifty.

"You feel okay?" Cassie asked.

"I didn't sleep much last night."

Dr. John came in. "Tofu!" he belted. "Ah, my old friend tofu." He counted the ballots right in front of us, then did the math on a piece of paper. He smiled knowingly.

"What?" I said. "What's the number?"

"Fifty-two percent," he said.

"Close one!" said Cassie.

"All right, that's two days in a row," Dr. John noted, getting up. "See you tomorrow." He went back into the lunchroom.

I put my head back down on the counter.

"That was too close," I said. I could hear Cassie leafing through the ballot cards.

"This one says, 'Less garlic, more heat,' but this other one says, 'Too hot, but not enough garlic.' "

"They're messing with us."

"We should thank Clyde for his dessert," Cassie said. "Without it, there's no way we would have made fifty percent." Clyde had already left the kitchen. "Let's go look for him upstairs."

"You can thank him for me," I said.

She left and I had the kitchen to myself. So I had a bit of silence, a bit of solitude.

When I *had* finally slept last night, I'd dreamed about Patty Cable. In the dream, Patty and I were playing a game we'd invented called High/Low. In that game Patty started on one trampoline, and I started on another, and then one of us would say either "high" or "low," and then on the count of three we would propel ourselves toward the other trampoline, and whoever was "high" jumped high toward the other trampoline, and whoever was "low" jumped low, and in this way we switched trampolines and passed each other in midair without colliding. We'd played this game pretty often for about two years in Patty's leafy backyard. While playing, we'd lose all track of time, and play until it either got dark or Patty's mom called us in for dinner.

And that's exactly the way it happened in the dream. We played and played—bouncing through the afternoon—until Patty's mom called us in for dinner. And then suddenly Patty was gone and it was just me out there by myself.

I had awoken from the dream crying.

After school, Ivy Franklin came to the school kitchen and showed Cassie and me how to cook her fiesta pie, which was sort of a Tex-Mex casserole. Basically, she browned some ground beef with peppers, onions, and spices, put all that in the bottom of a casserole dish, and covered it with a corn bread batter and baked it. We would make it for lunch tomorrow.

I walked home. There were snow flurries, and it was dark already. The snowflakes streaked through the cones of orange light beneath the streetlights.

At home, I went to my room and closed my door. I turned off my phone and kicked my shoes to the other side of the room and got under the comforter and closed my eyes. I tried to sleep. But my eyes were twitching, and I had the beginnings of a headache. So I went downstairs and sat by the window in the den, looking at the snow falling in the street. No one else was home. I turned on a few lights around the house and then I went back upstairs and sat on the floor and picked up my phone. I sat there, holding my phone, watching Harley the goldfish putter around his bowl for I don't know how long, and finally I opened my phone and dialed a number from memory.

"Hello?" It was Patty Cable's mom.

"Is Patty home?" I asked.

"She's at one of her cheerleader meetings."

What more depressing response could I get?

"I can give her a message," said Patty's mom. "Who's calling?"

"It's okay, I'll call—" I said.

"Oh, wait a second. Patty just walked in the back door."

I heard footsteps, and muffled voices. I could still just hang up. I didn't have to do this. I felt strange. It felt like I was in their house again. I could tell they were in the kitchen, and I could picture it, and I could picture Patty stamping the snow off her feet and taking off her coat, and I could picture Mrs. Cable standing with her hand over the mouthpiece of the phone.

I was about to hang up.

"Hello?" said Patty.

The next day, just after dark, Cassie and I rang Patty Cable's doorbell.

"I feel a little sick," I said.

"You're going to be fine," said Cassie.

There was an eruption of barking inside the house.

"I forgot to tell you that they have dogs," I said.

"Cool. How many?"

"I don't know. They used to have five."

The door swung open and Patty Cable flew out of the house and hugged me. It was like getting hit by a bag of bricks. Soft bricks, but bricks nonetheless.

"Molly-o!" Patty squealed. "Baby! Where have you been?"

"At home," I said. Patty was squeezing me.

Suddenly, two dogs streaked out of the open door and into the yard.

"No! Fugly! Poe! Get back here!"

We chased the dogs for about ten minutes.

Being back in the Cable kitchen made me feel like I was inhabiting a dream. The fridge had dozens of pictures on it of Patty and her little brothers, including a few pictures with me in them. How many batches of brownies had Patty and I made in here over the years? How many times had we made popcorn here late on a Friday night? How many pancake breakfasts had Mr. Cable made for us on that stove?

Patty showed us how to make the mac and cheese. I took notes while Cassie videotaped. First Patty started some pasta cooking. Then she melted some butter and whisked in flour, salt, and pepper. This reminded me of Edmund's tomato soup recipe.

"Flour in a mac-and-cheese recipe?" Cassie asked.

"Yes, we're making a white sauce first. Flour is the thickener and binder. The sauce makes the mac and cheese creamy instead of clotty and dry, like some baked mac and cheeses," said Patty.

She whisked milk into the flour mixture to make a thin sauce, then put shredded cheese in it. She drained the cooked pasta, put it in a casserole dish, poured the cheese sauce over it, and sprinkled more cheese and bread crumbs on top. Then into the oven.

That was it? It was so easy. A few months ago, the recipe would have seemed pretty foreign to me, but now I saw how straightforward it was.

"Okay, enough work," said Patty. "Now we play. How do you two feel about trampolining in the dark?"

Was she serious?

"Ha! Relax!" she said. "Let's go to my room."

In Patty's room, which was exactly as I remembered it—loft bed, lava lamps, deep carpet—we looked at pictures from grade school and junior high.

"Let's see," Patty said, "that's us in the Health Parade in sixth grade."

"Health Parade?" Cassie said. "But it looks like you're having fun."

"Oh, we specialized in fun," said Patty. "No matter the circumstances. For instance, in that parade Molly got to carry a flag that said GOOD HYGIENE MAKES YOUR WHOLE PERSON SHINE and she tripped and the flag got filthy muddy. Oh, the irony."

Cassie laughed.

Cassie asked a lot of questions about the things Patty and I used to do. Here she was, Patty, my once best friend, and yet I felt disconnected. She was a *cheerleader*. Maybe it was that. But she didn't *look* like a cheerleader. She had a boyish bowl cut and was wearing beat-up work boots and brown jeans and an inside-out T-shirt. She looked like the old Patty.

When the mac and cheese was done, we ate. We were alone, the three of us, because Mr. and Mrs. Cable had taken Patty's little brothers to a movie. We ate, with the dogs circling the table, and the mac and cheese was truly great—crusty on top, soft inside.

"What I really want to know," said Patty, "is how you two ended up being in charge of the kitchen. I mean I want the *whole* story."

Cassie and I looked at each other.

"Did you *volunteer*?" Patty asked.

"Oh, hell no," Cassie said.

"We fought our way into the kitchen," I said.

We recounted our original food fight, and Patty started laughing. Then we went into the problems we'd had when Mrs. Zetz was still around.

"How many bandages did you put in the cottage cheese?" Patty asked.

I smiled. "Two boxes. Sixty bandages."

"Sixty!?" Cassie exclaimed. She'd never heard the total.

Patty nearly fell on the floor laughing. "But wait! Wait!" she said. "How long did it take you to, you know, make them look like they'd been on someone's finger, make them into cylinders?"

"At least an hour," I said. "I did it at home the night before."

We were all laughing now.

Patty kept asking questions and we kept telling stories—about dropped meatballs, airborne spaghetti, "The Three Pile Song" (which I sang for Patty), the wrangling over Devin Harper, and so on. And somehow talking about these horrible things, and laughing at them, made them seem not-horrible. Patty was laughing a lot, and when I told her how Clyde's LUNCHROOM ATTENDANT badge was homemade, she laughed so hard she fell out of her chair, which made me laugh so hard I spewed soda through my nose.

"Gross!" Cassie screamed.

"I forgot you did that!" Patty said, getting up from the floor. "You always used to do that if we got you too excited!"

I held my hand over my face, trying to suppress further laughing.

"You're the *same* Molly Ollinger," said Patty. "I wasn't sure at first, but now I know: you're the same. No! You're *better* than ever. I can't believe it. It's so great!"

"I've never seen her spray soda from her nose," said Cassie. "But I look forward to seeing it again."

"It actually hurts a lot," I said.

"One time," said Patty, "I was in the wrong place at just the wrong time and I got nose-sprayed soda all over my face."

"Yick," said Cassie.

"It's true," I said.

"We were on some kind of pretend double date with Bryan Rostran and Howie whatisface," explained Patty, "and the next thing I know I've got Wild Cherry Pepsi on my face, and then Molly informs me that my glitter eye shadow is running."

"I tried to convince you it was a good look," I said.

"That's because you liked Bryan and he was *my* date, but with my damaged makeup, you saw your chance to steal him. Hey, why'd we ever fight over him anyway? He was an idiot. He paid his brother to do his homework for him. He wore the same socks for like a week at a time. And he's the guy who pushed Dana Sudwit's little sister down the stairs at a basketball game and she broke three teeth."

"He did that?" I asked.

"Found that out later," Patty said.

"You two fought over this guy?" Cassie asked.

"Believe it or not," Patty said, "this Molly girl is kind of stubborn. And I'm super-stubborn. So we fought. I don't even know what we were thinking."

We got bowls of ice cream and went into the den and put all five beanbag chairs into one pile and climbed on and ate ice cream.

"So are we still buddies or what?" said Patty.

"Okay," I said.

"Okay, what? Say it!"

"We're still buddies," I said.

"Good. Don't forget it."

"Okay."

"And what about this girl, this Cassie girl," said Patty, pointing her spoon at Cassie. "Is she our buddy, too?"

"Yeah."

"Is that okay with you, Cassie?" asked Patty.

"Yes."

"Good, because we like you. You're okay. You're a good bean."

"I never thought I'd be friends with a cheerleader," I said.

"Cheerleader! How'd you find out about that?" asked Patty.

"My grampa talked to your grandma. And then when I talked to your mom the other night she said you were at cheerleader practice."

"Whoa!" said Patty. She got up, stood there with her bowl of ice cream. "You think I'm a cheerleader?"

"Aren't you?"

"You think I'm a *cheerleader* cheerleader?"

"As opposed to a noncheerleader cheerleader?" I said.

"Well, it's time you found out exactly what kind of cheerleader I am." She sat back down. "I'm a special kind of cheerleader. It's quite marvelous. Okay, see, there's this club at our school where a bunch of dweebs and malcontents get together every once in a while to shoot off model rockets and eat pizza. It's called Rocket Club, and I wanted to join because it's one of the only cool things in the whole school, but I didn't really care about the rockets or anything and so I asked if they wanted a cheerleader and they said okay, but actually I don't have to do any actual cheerleading. I just get invited to all their meetings and I don't have to do any rocket stuff."

"Rocket club?" Cassie said.

"You're a cheerleader for Rocket Club?" I said.

Then we all three looked at one another and broke out laughing.

We had made, on Thursday, Ivy Franklin's fiesta pie, and Clyde had made perfect lemon-ginger cupcakes, and with Edmund's help and our tutorial with Ivy and Clyde's damn good dessert, we managed an 85 percent poll figure, our highest ever.

Each dessert that week was great, and suddenly nearly the whole school was eating dessert each day. Clyde didn't mind the extra work of making sixty desserts instead of thirty. Actually, though he was busier than ever, he was also happier, and sometimes we would have to order him to stop humming merrily. Once, though, on Friday, when we requested that he stop humming merrily, he asked that the issue be put to a vote. Cassie and I voted against the merry humming, Clyde and Dina voted for the merry humming, and Edmund stood there and thought about it for a little bit and then said, "Actually, I like it," and voted for it.

We made Patty Cable's mac and cheese that day, and everything went well, and we served it with peas, toast, an apple from the local orchard, and Clyde's raspberry meringue pie. After lunch, Dr. John came into the lunchroom with the ballot box and he was smiling. He didn't say anything but just rubbed his tummy contentedly and sat down at the counter and started counting the ballots. Usually, he put the yes votes in a pile on the left, and the no votes in a pile on the right, but today ballot after ballot went into the pile on the left. We watched as the pile grew.

Finally he put the last ballot on the yes pile.

"Don't need a calculator for this one," he said. "One hundred percent."

PATTY CABLE'S SKILLET MAC AND CHEESE

8   ounces pasta, such as elbows, ziti, or penne
2   tablespoons butter
2   tablespoons all-purpose flour
    scant 1 teaspoon salt
    freshly ground pepper
$1\frac{1}{3}$ cups milk
$6\frac{1}{2}$ ounces (about $1\frac{1}{2}$ cups) shredded cheese, such as
    Gruyère, Colby jack, cheddar, or a combination of
    two or three cheeses
    bread crumbs
    paprika, optional

Preheat your oven to 350°. Boil the pasta according to
the manufacturer's recommended time.

While the pasta is boiling, make a sauce by melting the
butter in a 10-inch skillet over medium heat, then whisking
in the flour, salt, and pepper until smooth. Let this mixture
bubble for a couple of minutes but be careful not to let it
burn. Slowly whisk in the milk to make a smooth sauce.
Let this sauce cook until it thickens and bubbles, whisking
constantly. Remove the skillet from the heat.

Add the cooked pasta to the sauce in the skillet (see
note below). Add about $\frac{2}{3}$ of the shredded cheese and stir
well. Top with the remaining cheese, some bread crumbs,
and a fine dusting of paprika, if desired.

Bake for about 25 minutes, until bubbly and lightly
browned. (Overbaking will result in a dry mac and cheese.)
Serve hot.

NOTE: This dish is baked in the same skillet you make the sauce in, but if your skillet is not ovenproof (if it has a plastic handle, for example), just bake it in a small casserole dish.

Makes 4 generous servings.

26

A Mean Bird

Before sunrise on Saturday, I drove the Prius across town and into Hillsdale. I picked up Cassie at her house.

"Aren't you early?" she said, yawning.

"Only six minutes," I said.

"Still, technically I'm right."

We drove out past the interstate to the Shop-o-Day! supermarket, which was open twenty-four hours, and filled a cart with the things we needed. When we got to the checkout, there was no one around—no employee to help us.

"Dude!" I said. "We gots to get this turkey in the oven! This delay is unacceptable."

Cassie reached over the checkout counter and picked up the phone next to the register and punched a button on it.

"Little help at checkout," she said, her voice booming out over the store's PA system. "Little help at the checkout."

She hung up the phone. "That should do it."

I was staring at her with my jaw open. "You did *not* just do that."

"I did," she said. "So suck on it."

Back at Cassie's, at about seven o'clock, we sat down and planned what needed to be done. Basically, the point of the day was to practice—by ourselves—for the Thanksgiving meal on Wednesday, and to that end we'd decided to start this early in order to match the schedule we needed to keep on Wednesday.

True, if we got above-fifty poll numbers on Monday, Cassie and I were not required to work any longer in the kitchen—Dr. John had two new kitchen staffers ready to start work any day—but we had volunteered to take charge of the Wednesday Thanksgiving lunch—and crew of volunteer helpers—regardless of whether we'd been released from kitchen duty or not. Hopefully, it would be our last hurrah in the kitchen.

But our Thanksgiving rehearsal was not a resounding success. The bird took longer to cook than we'd planned, so we didn't end up eating until after two. The turkey was okay but dry. The dressing was okay but dry and undersalted. The mashed potatoes were okay but undersalted and cold. And so forth.

Clyde's pumpkin pies—he'd shown up at noon with them—on the other hand, were fantastic.

"I would like to say something to the table," Clyde said as the three of us were stuffing our faces with his pie.

"You want to talk to the furniture?" I asked.

"I know that your guys' time in the kitchen is nearing an end. I honor your successes, and I am grateful you allowed me a chance to hone my craft. I sometimes bumbled, but you let me find my own path. Now I want to tell you both that I have asked Dr. John if I can remain in the kitchen making desserts even after you guys have left. Dr. John has agreed. It has given me great joy to learn the way of the pastry chef, and the prospect of ascending yet higher in the art of my chosen vocation fills me with excitement."

"I like your style," I said.

Cassie raised her dessert plate in a salute and said, "Here's to Clyde, and the wonderful desserts of Phase Four and beyond!"

After pie, Cassie and I decided we would cook the whole dinner over again, starting right then. When everything was finally ready—almost ten o'clock that night—we were pleased that our work had paid off.

It tasted scrumplicious. And we had done it without Edmund or Dina. We had done it ourselves. Just the two of us.

To celebrate, I slept over.

And we cut each other's hair.

Late in the day on Sunday, I swung by the school to drop off a roasting pan Casssie and I had borrowed for the weekend.

I dumped the pan in the kitchen, but as I was locking the kitchen's back door, I looked up and noticed the lights were on in the art room. That was not totally odd—teachers and students often came in on the weekends to work on projects. But it reminded me of the behind-schedule artwork for *The Bleepity Bleep Bleep Gang*. So I decided to go up and check our progress, maybe even work for an hour or two before I went home.

The door to the art room was wide open, and all the lights were on, but there was no one there. At first I couldn't even find any of the projects we'd been working on. True, we'd rolled up and stored two of our backdrops already. But late in the week we'd started making 120 paper lanterns for the "flight of wonder" scene in act two. Pete had figured out how to make the lanterns, but it took about fifteen minutes to make just one, so by Friday afternoon—the last time I'd checked—we'd only finished fourteen.

So where were they? We'd had a whole assembly line spread out on two tables, and it was gone.

Then I saw them. The paper lanterns were stacked carefully in two huge boxes. There were . . . dozens of them. Dozens and dozens . . . Were they all done? *All* of them?

Suddenly, someone yelped behind me.

"Gah!" I blurted. I turned around.

It was Pete. Pete had come into the art room.

"Pete! Why'd you sneak up on me?"

"I didn't sneak up on you!" he said, clutching his chest. "You appeared randomly where I didn't expect you. So in a sense, you snuck up on me."

"Well, either way," I said, "let's not do it again."

"Hey, no argument there."

"Did you finish the Chinese lanterns?"

"Yeah," he said, coming over, "just now."

"But you must have worked a ton . . ."

"I worked yesterday and today."

"That's amazing. You didn't have to do that."

"I knew you were busy, and I knew we were behind schedule, so I did what I needed to do. For you. Besides, I got better at making them, so it only took about ten minutes per lantern."

I was looking at a lantern. It was perfect. "You're the best assistant art director ever," I said.

"Thanks, Molly." He smiled.

"I'm not sure why you're the assistant art director instead of the art director."

"Oh that's easy," he said. "I'm a maker. But you're a creator."

I felt myself blush. "Thanks," I said. I wasn't sure whether I was thanking him for calling me a creator, or for the work he did, or what. Mainly I didn't know what else to say.

"Hey," he said, "what happened to your hair?"

"Oh, my friend Cassie cut it. We got a little crazy last night."

"It looks good. It looks great."

"Thanks."

We walked through the school together, and I asked if he needed a ride home and he said no, and then he pointed to a house just down the street. "That's me, right there," he said.

"Coolio," I said.

Coolio? What was wrong with me?

He walked away across the soccer field.

I arrived home to find Mom staring at a raw chicken and muttering. "I'm going to roast this chicken if it's the last thing I do," she said.

She had three cookbooks open on the counter. Where had they come from?

"I can help," I said. After all, I'd just spent all day yesterday figuring out how to roast a turkey, so I figured roasting a chicken couldn't be so different.

Mom looked at me. "That would be lovely," she said.

So we consulted the cookbooks, and put some garlic cloves under the bird's skin, then coated it with olive oil and salt and pepper and put it in the oven. While the bird roasted, we cooked rice and steamed some broccoli.

A few weeks ago, I wouldn't have even wanted to touch meat, much less have an idea of how to cook it. But it made me happy to help Mom.

"You two roast a mean bird," Grampa announced at dinner. We ate in the dining room.

Dad agreed that it was great. "You know," he said, "you two have inspired me, and after dinner I'm going to go get my old notebook of recipes and I'm going to make us dinner *twice* this week. And not just stir-fry."

"Don't forget Thanksgiving," said Mom.

"Why don't I take charge of Thanksgiving?" I said.

They all looked at me.

"I will," I said. "I can. I need a little help, but I'll be in charge."

While Dad cleaned up, Grampa and I played gin rummy.

Later, in my room, I did some homework, then I tidied up. I found one of my shoes that had been missing since summer. I found a bag of green apple sours and popped two in my mouth, but after a minute I spit them out because they seemed so fake. I took down my angry expressionistic drawings I'd put up in the spring. I threw out a bunch of magazines, and there, behind a small landslide of magazines, were my headphones—the chunky ones I wore at school so no one would talk to me. I remembered I'd worn them on Monday, but I must have left them home the rest of the week. Monday seemed like a long time ago.

27

Food for Children!

onday morning, I walked to school in the predawn, and soaked it in. The stars were twinkling overhead, bright and steady, and the town was quiet. I had come to enjoy my walks to school in the early morning. Things felt less complicated at this hour. And to think that my early morning walks to school were coming to an end, well, it made me a little sad, but in a healthy way. It was time to move on, get on with the business of just being Molly again.

With our four days of above-fifty polls in the kitchen, all we needed was one more—today. We would get it. Because we'd been busy practicing the Thanksgiving dinner all weekend, Edmund had volunteered to take charge of the menu and ingredients for today, so he was planning a meal that played to his strengths. Clyde was making some almond cookies, which would certainly please everybody. As for Cassie and me, we just had to work hard, work carefully, and not screw up anything.

• • •

It was quiet in the kitchen. Dina had called in saying she would be late. Clyde wasn't there because on Friday afternoon he'd made the cookie dough and put it in the fridge. So he didn't need to do any work until his study hall. And at the moment, Edmund was in the freezer, gathering ingredients. Cassie and I sat at the central work counter.

"It's going to be a little weird, isn't it? Not working in the kitchen anymore," I said, looking around—at the pots hanging on the wall, at the stoves, and the big sinks.

"Yeah," agreed Cassie. "You know, though," Cassie added, "the thing about it is that if we hadn't gotten into the fight and then been put in the kitchen and then gotten into more fights and then forced to find our way out of this place, then . . . well . . ."

"We wouldn't have become friends," I finished for her.

She nodded.

"Did I ever tell you what I wrote in my response?" she asked.

"Your what?"

"The dumb assignment where we were stuck on opposite sides of the river. Did anyone ever tell you what I wrote about you?"

"No," I said.

"I wrote that we both put as many supplies in our pockets as we could and then both swam into the river and met on a rock halfway and you said to me, 'Hi, I'm Molly, and together we're going to be a-okay.' And then we both swam back to my side of the river and managed to survive."

"I said that?" I asked.

"Yep."

"That was neat of me," I said.

"Yep."

"And we survived?"

"We did," she said. "We had a good time."

We sat there smiling at each other. I could see a gleam of tears in Cassie's eyes.

The back door slammed shut.

"Here comes Edmund," said Cassie. She wiped her eyes with her cuff.

"Hey," I yelled toward the hallway, "what the eff took you so long?"

Cassie laughed.

Then, in the hallway, when Edmund appeared around the corner ... it was not Edmund. It was someone else ... My mind was off balance. My mind seemed unreliable all of a sudden. I couldn't make sense of it. It was not Edmund.

It was Mrs. Zetz.

"Hmph," said Mrs. Zetz.

I stopped breathing.

It wasn't real. It couldn't be. But it *looked* like her. She was scowling. She was wearing a long coat. She put her hands on her hips.

"You," she said.

We stared.

"You two," she said.

I swallowed.

"You two *girrells*," said Mrs. Zetz.

She was real. It was her.

I heard the back door open and close again, and soon Edmund came around the corner, his arms full of frozen packages of pork chops. He was reading one of the package's labels as he walked, so he hadn't seen Mrs. Zetz yet.

"Okay," he said, "maybe while I pan sear these you can—"

He saw Mrs. Zetz and dropped the meat.

Mrs. Zetz pivoted to look at Edmund. I thought there was a chance she was going to start shooting death rays from her eyes.

"Oh," said Edmund.

He looked down at the packages of meat. He looked back at his old boss.

"Pick up," said Mrs. Zetz.

"Yeah," he said. "Yeah."

"Where Dina?" said Mrs. Zetz.

"She . . . she'll be here soon," said Edmund, gathering the packages from the floor. "She had to take her granddaughter to school this morning."

"Mm," said Mrs. Zetz. "Late Dina," she said. Then she thought. She looked at Edmund. "Clumsy dropper," she said. Then she looked at Cassie and me. "Lying *girrells.*"

But but but! I wanted to scream. This wasn't fair! She didn't belong here! We didn't need her. We didn't want her. She'd quit. *We* were in charge. This kitchen was *ours.* Then why'd I feel powerless?

Edmund put the packages of meat on the counter. Mrs. Zetz took off her coat, put it on a hook. She walked across to the phone. She picked it up, dialed.

After a moment, she said, "Dr. John dis Marta Zetz. I am here. Come down to kitchen now." She hung up.

She looked at Edmund, who was just standing there, staring like we were. "Where the clean aprons?" she asked. "You move them."

Edmund got a clean apron from the stockroom. Mrs. Zetz put it on.

"Dare," she said. "Clean apron. Ready for work."

"For work . . . for work . . . ?" said Edmund. "Mrs. Zetz, are you back for work?"

"I am here!" she yelled. "I am back! For work!" She slapped the countertop for emphasis.

I felt like I had failed at something large. I felt inconsequential. The only thing I wanted to do was leave. I glanced at Cassie. She seemed stunned.

Mrs. Zetz wagged a finger at Cassie. "Get me hairnet!"

That made me mad. "You don't have to yell at her," I said.

"I don't yell," said Mrs. Zetz. "I speak with power. Get me hairnet!"

"I . . . I . . . ," I stammered, "I think that's yelling."

Mrs. Zetz stepped closer to me. "When I yell, little *girrell*, world knows it."

Cassie got up to fetch a hairnet.

I heard footsteps in the cafeteria—someone running toward the kitchen—and soon there was a bang as this person ran into the kitchen door.

"Ow!" said this person on the other side of the door. "Son of a fruitfly!"

Edmund went and unlocked the door, then opened it.

Dr. John was standing there in the dark cafeteria, rubbing his nose. He was out of breath. He looked at Edmund, then at Cassie and me, then at Mrs. Zetz.

"Marta. . . ," he said.

"Dr. John," she said. "Good mor-a-ning. I am here to work. I am back to be cook. I think about dis. I think about it. I not like it, thinking about dese lying *girrells* running my kitchen, cooking, touching food, feeding children food. Lying girls not make healthy food. Food for children! To nourish! Food. Lying *girrells* not know nothing. And I think, who will make the Thanksgiving? Who will do dis? It is holy meal, this meal. It is community meal. And I say, *I* have to cook dis Thanksgiving meal. I cook it right. Not lying girls. So I decide: I come back. I come back for good."

"Okay," said Dr. John, nodding. "Let's talk about this."

"Yes," said Mrs. Zetz. "Talk. But not in front of lying *girrells*. I see enough of them already. They hurt my eyes."

We waited in Dr. John's office. It was quiet in there. It was still long before the other students would arrive. Even Ivy Franklin wasn't there yet. So we sat in Dr. John's office, not talking, listening to the clock tick, watching the dawn come. I chewed my fingernails. I felt tired. I felt like it was the end of a long day. I also felt like we were in trouble again, like we were waiting for Dr. John to punish us.

"You know," said Cassie, after a long time, "it's what we wanted anyway. We didn't want to work in the kitchen. And now she's back, so . . ."

She started crying. I got a box of tissues for her, and pulled my chair over next to hers and put my arm around her.

When Dr. John finally came in, he looked a bit shell-shocked

He sat behind his desk. "I don't know what to say. Are you two all right?"

"We're okay," I said.

"So she's back for good?" Cassie asked.

"Yes," Dr. John said. "She's back. She wants control of the kitchen again, she wants her old menus, she wants things to be just like they were."

"We would have been done anyway, after today," I said.

"That's true," said Dr. John. He took a tissue and blew his nose. "Excuse me," he said. "The long and short of it is that the promises I made to Mrs. Zetz after she quit mean that she can come back anytime and start work again. So that's that, really. And I hereby release you two from any further obligations to the hot lunch program. You can be proud of what you have done. I'm sorry it didn't end more gracefully.

"Also, Mrs. Zetz has asked for a couple of conditions to be met in order for her to work again."

"Like what?" I asked.

"I'm warning you that it's petty," said Dr. John. "I tried to talk her out of it . . ."

"What is it?" I said.

"You two aren't allowed in the kitchen."

"Fine," I said.

"Yeah, that's fine by me," added Cassie, her eyes red.

"Or in the cafeteria, actually."

"What?" said Cassie. "Where are we supposed to eat?"

"Ah, well, actually, she's asked that you not be allowed to eat her food."

We sat quietly. Then I said, "We don't want to."

Dr. John nodded. "Look, I can ask her to reconsider these conditions. Later, when she's cooled down."

"No," I said. "We're okay with them. A-okay."

For lunch that day, we ate in the art room. It had banks of windows along two walls, and a good view out across the river. Not that the view was that beautiful today, having turned into a misty, gray day. Ivy Franklin had gone to the sandwich shop down the street and brought us back soup and sandwiches, seeing as we weren't allowed to eat Mrs. Zetz's lunch, and hadn't brought food of our own.

We'd just started eating when there was a knock at the doorway. Pete stood there.

"Mind if I join you?" he asked.

"As long as you don't mind joining the ranks of the banished," I said.

"I would consider it an honor," he said.

"Did you already eat?" Cassie asked.

"No," he said. "After eating the lunches you two prepared, I'm not going to go back to Mrs. Zetz's food. I'll just go hungry."

"You're my hero," said Cassie.

I was glad Pete was there, because I really didn't feel like talking, and I don't think Cassie did either, but Pete kept us entertained with stories about working for Portia Babbliagali on *Ever Since Next Year*.

After lunch, we wandered together toward the lockers. The students were still milling around after lunch. Seth Lawson came toward us.

"What the hey!" he exclaimed. "You guys were robbed! *We* were robbed. Your lunches were better than Mrs. Z's. You guys were *thinking*, you know. You were going somewhere. Mrs. Z is going nowhere. She's going backward."

"We were going to be out of the kitchen as of today anyway," I pointed out.

"I'm just saying, no justice, you know?" Seth said. "Where's the student voice in this decision? Where's the community? This is the whole school's hot lunch program, not just Mrs. Zetz's."

Suddenly I saw Clyde at the other end of the hall. He was in a hurry.

"Hey, it's Clyde," I said.

"We forgot about him," said Cassie.

Seth looked. "I saw him crying in the hallway a couple of hours ago."

"We gotta go talk to him," I said.

"All right," said Seth. "Power to the people!"

We left Seth and intercepted Clyde. He didn't make eye contact.

"Clyde?" Cassie said.

He kept walking.

"Clyde!" I said. "What happened?"

"Nothing," he murmured. He kept walking.

I grabbed his arm. "Hold on! Tell us what happened."

"Let me go!" he said, and he yanked himself away and ran down the hall.

"See this is *backward*," said Seth. He'd followed us and was just behind us. "This is no good. This is not progress."

"We've got to find Dr. John," I said.

"And tell it to him straight, man!" said Seth. "Let him hear the truth, from the mouths of the people!"

We didn't see Dr. John in the upstairs hallways, so we headed downstairs. He was outside his office, watching the students, looking a bit preoccupied.

"We forgot to ask about Clyde," I said. "What happened to Clyde?"

"Yeah, I forgot, too, at first," said Dr. John. "Then apparently Clyde walked into the kitchen during his study hall, and Mrs. Zetz promptly banned him."

"That bites," I said.

"But she said he could still be lunchroom attendant," said Dr. John.

"At least he'll have that," Cassie pointed out.

"Well . . . ," said Dr. John, and he pulled something out of his pocket. It was Clyde's LUNCHROOM ATTENDANT badge. "He just gave this to me."

28

The Less Meaty Team

In the morning, I woke up sick. My throat hurt, I felt like I had lead in my veins, and my eyes were puffy. I got up anyway. I stood in the shower, hoping it would make me feel better, but it just made me feel sick *and* wet. As I dried off, I started to feel dizzy and I had to go lie down. I looked at the clock and realized I had gotten up at my normal going-to-the-kitchen time.

I stayed home from school. I ventured downstairs once to have lunch with Grampa, and once to look at the mail. But most of the day I spent lying on my bed in the fetal position with the blanket drawn over my head. There was no thought going on in my brain, just little fizzles and pops of activity that were related to basic body functions and occasional flashbacks to yesterday—the image of Mrs. Zetz glaring at us, hands on her hips, or the moment when Dr. John had pulled Clyde's crumpled LUNCHROOM ATTENDANT badge out of his pocket.

Mom and Dad both checked on me after they got home from work. They brought me soup and I ate it in bed. I put a whole saltine cracker on my tongue and let it get soggy before I chewed and swallowed. After dark I watched four episodes of *Freaks and Geeks* on DVD, then went to sleep without brushing my teeth.

The next morning I felt a little better, and so I went downstairs to eat breakfast. But Mom took my temperature and it was 101°, so she made me stay home again.

Midmorning, I checked my e-mail. I had three.

The first one was from Seth Lawson. It just said:

Power to the students, yo!

The second one was from Cassie:

Hey there. Wondering what's up, why you weren't at school yesterday. Hope you're okay. Let me know if you need anything. C.B.

The final e-mail was from an address I didn't recognize:

Howdy, Molly. Pete your trusty assistant art director here. Are you sick? Get well soon. Get well!

I don't think anyone at Sunshine Day had ever missed me when I was sick, much less checked up on me. I wrote Cassie and Pete back, reassured them I was just a tiny bit sick. After I sent the second message, I heard a car door slam in the driveway. I rolled out of bed and crawled to the window. There was a taxi in the driveway, and Les was getting out. He was home for Thanksgiving. I went downstairs to greet him.

"Poor sick Moe," he said, and hugged me softly.

"I'm sorry I'm so pitiful," I said.

I kind of collapsed into his arms. It had been three months since I'd seen him, and that was too long.

"I can hold you up for about ten more seconds," he said.

"Ten, nine, eight . . ." I counted it down, letting him hold me up for the full ten seconds. Then I stood up and looked at him. He brushed my bangs off of my face.

"Molly, Molly, Molly," he said. "You didn't tell me about the blue hair."

"I didn't dye it, I swear. It came out that way on its own."

"Are things really that bad?" he asked.

"Yes. Blue-hair-inducing bad."

Despite the fact that he'd been traveling since about 4 A.M., Les happily spent the next few hours playing board games with me, like Habitat Challenge and Cribblebix. I ate a banana and a tin of shortbread cookies that Les had brought.

As we finished off the cookies, I told him about Mrs. Zetz's return.

"Sounds complicated," he said.

"I guess," I said. "Is life always so complicated?"

He thought about this. "Mostly," he said. He bit into a cookie.

"I just wish it were simpler, you know," I said. "I feel like it used to be simpler."

"Yeah, and you used to be five years old."

I nodded.

"Isn't it weird," he said, "how sometimes you don't know how you feel about something until it's taken away from you?"

"What do you mean?"

"Getting kicked out of the kitchen has been a big blow for you. A couple of weeks ago you were sending me e-mails complaining about the kitchen. It sounds like you've learned a lot and come to appreciate food in a new way."

Yes, why exactly had I been so down—and literally sick—since Mrs. Zetz's return? I couldn't put my finger on it.

"The kitchen was *someplace*," I said.

"Someplace?" asked Les. "Please explain."

"It was . . . it was . . . I don't know. It was the center of something . . ."

Grampa and his friend Dennis came in just then, and regaled us with a loudly told tale of how Dennis had just hustled a couple of guys out of two dollars playing pool at the senior center and now they were debating whether to catch the shuttle bus to the Ruby Fandango Riverboat Casino and test their luck on the nickel slots.

I trudged upstairs for a nap.

I woke up because Les was poking my shoulder. "Wakey, wakey," he said.

"Not a chance," I said.

"Cassie's here," Les said.

I sat up. "Cassie?"

He pointed to a bouquet of flowers on the shelves by my bed. "She brought those. She's downstairs. She wasn't sure you'd feel like being bothered."

I looked around on the floor. "Where's my phone?"

Les found it and handed it to me. I called Cassie's cell.

"Where are you?" I asked.

"Um, Pappy is showing me his golf trophies."

"Come up here."

"I wasn't sure whether—"

"Come up!"

"All right."

Soon, she was at the door. "Hi," she said.

"Sorry about my hair," I apologized. "And my sweatpants. And my brother."

"I'll leave," Les said. He stepped out.

"Look," Cassie said, sitting on the floor in front of me, "I wrote down our assignments from today and yesterday."

I took the sheet of paper. "Thanks. And thanks for the flowers."

"Are you feeling better?" she asked.

"Hard to know. Opinions differ. Did I miss anything good at school?"

"Actually . . ."

"How was the Thanksgiving lunch?"

"I didn't get to taste it, of course."

"Oh, I forgot."

"But I saw it. I watched from the doorway."

"Why?"

"Brad Berrington told me I should come."

"What? Why?"

"This." She pulled a CD out of her jacket.

"If he wrote another song about me . . ."

She looked a little embarrassed.

"He did?" I said.

"Let me explain," she said. "During the meal, there was a showcase of our school's talent, you know, and Brad was the final singer, and he got up onstage and he sung a couple of his usual songs, and then—"

"Tell me this is not going to be 'The Three Pile Song.' "

"No. Well, I'll just play it."

She put the CD in my stereo. The track started and I could hear a crowd in the background—the cafeteria, people eating. Then Brad said, "This song is for Molly Ollinger and Cassie Birchmeyer, and a guy called Clyde. It's called 'Hot Lunch.' "

"No way," I said.

"Just listen," she said.

Brad started playing guitar—fast, steady, strong. Then he sang:

> *I never knew it until they went away, went so*
> *far away . . .*
> *I couldn't chew it, this new regime—well, I*
> *missed the queens . . .*
> *So now I wonder why we let them go without*
> *a cry,*
> *Why no one asked us about the change . . .*
> *Why we simply took it, why we showed no*
> *rage . . .*
> *Hot lunch! Got lunch?*
>
> *I miss the stir-fry and the veggie theme, the less*
> *meaty team . . .*
> *I miss the tomato soup and the mac and*
> *cheese—yeah, I'd like more please . . .*
> *And don't forget dessert, the sweetest food,*
> *made by Clyde the dude . . .*
> *He baked cookies that made me cry, he baked*
> *cupcakes as soft as the sky . . .*

*Hot lunch! Made by Molly O., Molly O. with
    the bluest hair!
Got lunch? Made by Cassie B., Cassie B. with
    the athletic air!
Hot lunch! Got lunch?
So now I wonder why we let them go without
    a cry,
Why no one asked us about the change . . .
Why we simply took it, why we showed no
    rage . . .
Hot lunch!!! Got lunch!!!*

The guitar and voice had grown stronger and stronger as the song went on, and as they did I felt my heart swelling. The last guitar chord rang in the air, and then there was a strange pause—a bubble of silence. I realized that the sounds of eating and talking had been silenced. The whole lunchroom—students, teachers, parents—must have been transfixed by Brad's performance. And then there was applause—modest applause—and a few hoots and whistles.

"Who's cheering like that?" I asked.

Cassie was smiling. "A few students. Everyone else was simply stunned."

The recording ended.

"And he told you to come watch?"

"Yeah. And at the end of the song he pointed at me."

"And then after the song? What happened after the recording?"

"He left the stage. Nothing happened. People started eating again."

"But what does it mean?" I asked.

"I don't know."

I looked at the stereo. The song had been powerful. The song had made me self-conscious at first—sort of like how "The Three Pile Song" had—but then it had made me feel proud. And capable. And appreciated. And defiant. There was a whole new feeling inside me, a sense of possibility.

"Play it again," I said.

29
Steam Rising

Saturday night, Cassie and I stayed at Patty Cable's. We baked a chocolate torte and it came out fabulously well.

"Sometimes," Patty said as we were all sitting on the floor of her room, eating torte, "I think cooking is magic. Or at least one of the closest things to magic we have in this world. Think about it. You take a bunch of ingredients, most of which are not great on their own, and you combine them in a certain way, and you apply heat in a certain way, and *voilà*—you end up with something that's more than the sum of its parts. And that, my girls, is magic."

"Then why's it so hard to do?" I asked. "'Cause I went through a magic phase in third grade and let me tell you, making a quarter disappear is easier than cooking a decent meal."

"Everything worth learning is hard to learn," Patty said. "Think about it. Hard to learn to read. Hard to learn to write. Hard to learn a musical instrument. Hard to become a doctor.

Hard to become a writer. Hard to be a mother. Hard to play sports. Hard to travel. Hard to cook."

"It's easy to eat, though," Cassie pointed out. "Thank goodness."

"Now I will make this torte disappear," I said.

"So do you miss cooking at school?" Patty asked.

Cassie and I glanced at each other.

"I don't know," I said.

"Sure you do," said Patty. "Somewhere, you know. That Brad guy who sang that song, he misses your cooking at the school. If you could wave a magic wand and solve problems like lack of experience and the stresses of schoolwork and time constraints, would you want to work in the school kitchen again?"

"Tell me more about this 'magic wand' of which you speak," I said.

"I'm serious," said Patty.

"I'll tell you what I miss," said Cassie. "I miss that feeling of being in control, you know. And not just in a power trip sort of way, but in the sense that we were the ones responsible for how good or how bad the food was. It was up to us. I miss that."

I nodded. "And how we could tell how successful we were by how clean the lunch trays were when they came back through the tray-return window."

"Instant feedback," said Cassie.

"All right," said Patty, "so I say fire this crazy head cook that won't let you in her kitchen, and then build something new. If you want that, then fight for it."

"Fire Mrs. Zetz?" said Cassie. "We don't exactly have the authority."

"Well someone does," said Patty.

On Monday, it was a bit odd being back in school. It had been an entire week since I'd been here, and I felt different than I had a week ago when Cassie and I had been about to end our time in the kitchen. I felt more conspicuous. Lots of people said hi to me—people who I'd never really talked to before—and everyone was looking at me. Did I look different? Had someone put a I'M A DUMBASS sign on my back?

Even in class, people kept looking at me.

And in study hall, Seth Lawson snuck over, crouched down, and smiled at me.

"What's your malfunction?" I said to him.

"Are you ready for the revolution?" he whispered.

"Do I have to be?" I said.

He winked and left.

For lunch, Cassie and I went to the art room.

"Seriously, I'm getting tired of being stared at," I told Cassie.

"You've had two songs written about you," she said. "You're sorta famous."

It wasn't worth trying to think about too much, though. So instead we started complaining about the big lit. paper due next week—six pages long. After a few minutes, we heard someone running down the empty hall toward us.

"Who's that?" Cassie said.

Suddenly, Pete Stamponivich skidded to a stop in the open door of the room.

"Pete?" I said.

"You guys gotta come downstairs!" he said, out of breath.

"Why?" I asked.

"Just hurry!"

We followed Pete down the hall and then downstairs. He kept urging us to run. "Come on! Come on!"

"Pete, my boy," I said, "you're just going to have to be at peace with the fact that we're not going to go faster than a casual walking pace."

We reached the double doors that went to the lunchroom. It was then that I noticed the strange silence. Where was the usual babble and laughing and Noontime Expression gig of lunchtime?

Pete opened the one door and held it open. Inside the lunchroom, the students were all seated at their usual tables, but they were just . . . just sitting there. They weren't talking. They weren't looking at one another. And they *weren't eating*.

"See," whispered Pete, "it's a silent boycott. No one ate lunch today."

I looked at the serving counter. I could see steam rising from the full trays of food. Mrs. Zetz was standing back in the kitchen, scowling.

There were banners covering the walls. STUDENTS FOR SCHOOL LUNCH CHOICE! read one. BRING BACK MOLLY AND CASSIE! said another. And the biggest one, on the far wall, read ONE TRAY ONE *GOOD* DESSERT!

Suddenly, Seth Lawson stood up. "There they are!" he shouted.

What? There who is?

"It's Molly and Cassie!" he announced, pointing.

Oh, there *we* are.

Everybody turned to face us.

Cassie and I looked at each other.

Seth climbed up onto a table. He started clapping, and soon the whole lunchroom was clapping and whistling.

I felt dizzy.

"Bring them in!" shouted Seth above the applause. "Let them speak!"

"No!" shouted a voice louder than Seth's. "Not the lying *girrells*!"

Mrs. Zetz was standing in the doorway to the kitchen.

The applause stopped.

"Dese girrells," she said, "are not allowed in lunchroom! Dat is rules! Dat is the way it be!"

We stared at Mrs. Zetz. She stared at us.

Dr. John appeared. He came over to Cassie and me. He had his hands in his pockets, like this kind of protest was an everyday event.

"Those are the rules," he said softly.

"We're not coming in," I said. "We just came to see."

Dr. John nodded. "I understand," he said.

30

Same Dumb Log of Premade Cookie Dough

We met with Seth Lawson and six other student activists after school. They talked to us about their ideas for healthier lunch menus, the inclusion of more local food producers, ongoing student involvement in the kitchen, a vegetable garden on the school grounds, and a way to make food education and cooking part of the curriculum.

"You know," Cassie told them, "we never intended to become some sort of model for a student-inclusive kitchen."

"But don't you see that what happens when you do good things," said Seth, "is that the good results spread further than you intend?"

After the meeting, as Cassie and I walked out of the school together, someone whistled to us from across the street. It was Edmund, sitting on the curb. We went over and sat next to him. It was a cold November afternoon, and Edmund was wearing a chunky red stocking cap with a pompom on top.

"That hat rules," I said.

"Thanks," said Edmund. "My cousin knit it for me. She's only ten. Look, there's a little pocket in the back."

"Special."

"She claims to have invented pockets on stocking caps. She wrote a letter to Oprah about it, but she never heard back."

"Damn that Oprah," I said.

"So . . . ," Edmund said, "Mrs. Zetz is furious. She thinks you arranged the boycott."

"You might as well tell her we did," I said. "Not that it matters."

"This is a woman," Edmund continued, "who hates wasting food more than she hates Democrats, and we threw away bucket-loads of food today."

"No one ate at all?" Cassie asked.

"Nope."

"Not even any of the teachers?" I asked.

"Not one," he said.

"Jeepers," said Cassie.

I could see how throwing all that food away would enrage Mrs. Zetz. I didn't like it either. But the boycott was a strong statement from a seemingly unified school.

"So what do you think we should do?" I asked him.

He shrugged. "You tell me. I'm not the inspiration for this student movement. I'm not in a position to make decisions about the future of the kitchen. I'll tell you guys, though: the kitchen's not the same without you."

"Does Mrs. Zetz let you cook?" asked Cassie.

"Nah." He suddenly remembered something. "Oh!" he said, reaching in his jacket pocket. "These are for you." He pulled out a peanut butter cookie, wrapped in napkins. "I stole it from the kitchen, just in case you wanted to break the rule about how you can't eat her food."

"Sweet!" I said. I broke the cookie in half and handed half to Cassie.

"This cookie's no good," Cassie pointed out, chewing.

"Same dumb log of premade cookie dough," Edmund explained.

"All right," I said, "maybe you don't have any power in the kitchen, but tell us, hypothetically, if you're interested in the things the students are talking about."

"Hypothetically? Yes." He looked across at the school for a moment. "But there's something I need to tell you. It's not something I'm proud of, but . . . better late than never."

"What is it?" said Cassie.

"Remember the thing with the frozen dinners and Hillary Greenbaum and all?"

"You think we forgot?" I said.

"No, I know you didn't. I just . . . I sort of engineered the whole thing."

"We know," I said. "We were there when you talked us into it."

"Yeah, but more than that, I mean. The fact is I knew that Hillary Greenbaum liked Splendid Gourmet dinners, and so that's why I suggested them to you."

This sank in.

"You set us up?" said Cassie. "You meant for us to get in trouble?"

"What the hell, bro?" I said. "That's so low."

"I know."

"Why?" asked Cassie.

"It's like I told Molly, you guys were a thorn in my side from the start. I just wanted you gone."

"So did it make you happy when we nearly got kicked out?" Cassie asked.

"No," said Edmund. "If you recall, I started helping you after that. I felt horrible."

"You should have," I said.

"Yeah, and actually there's a little bit more to it. Um, see, I went to Hillary Greenbaum's house the night before she came to the school, and I went through her trash to find out exactly what kind of Splendid Gourmet dinner she'd eaten recently, and then I—"

"You had us buy the exact same one," I said.

"Yep," said Edmund.

"Oh, Edmund," said Cassie. "That's sad."

"I know. I know. I'm sorry."

"Wow," I said. "But just out of curiosity, did you tell Dr. John all of this, too, or did you leave the details out?"

"Do what now?" said Edmund.

"When you told him that you'd put us up to the plan, you did tell him at least part of this, of course," I pointed out.

Edmund looked like he didn't even understand what language I was speaking.

"You think I talked to Dr. John about this?" asked Edmund. "Yeah, as if."

"Wait—what?" I said.

"I never told him anything."

"Yeah, you did," said Cassie. "That afternoon you told him how you'd talked us into the scheme. That's why we didn't get punished."

Edmund raised his hands, as if in surrender. "I mean, I *wish* I had done that, believe me. That would have been the right thing to do, but I didn't."

"This doesn't make sense," said Cassie.

"He said I told him about the plan?" Edmund asked.

"Yeah," I said. "*And* when you talked to me later that day you basically accepted responsibility. You asked if we'd gotten in trouble and whatnot. You basically apologized. You volunteered to help us from then on."

"Yeah, because I felt like crap. I knew I'd done the wrong thing and I knew I wanted to help you guys. And I wanted to know if you'd gotten in trouble because I *needed* to know. But you said it had blown over."

"It had blown over, but only because you fessed up to Dr. John," I said.

"Which I didn't."

"Come to think of it," Cassie said, "he didn't use your name. He said one of our 'coworkers' had confessed. And it was a 'he.'"

The three of us sat there for a few seconds.

"Oh, shit," I said. "Clyde."

Twenty minutes later, I stood on the stoop of Clyde's house. I had come alone.

I rang the doorbell.

Clyde's house was a squarish two-story house painted a nice plum color. There were intricate handmade paper snowflakes hanging in the front windows.

I rang the doorbell again. Maybe he wasn't here. But it was odd. He hadn't been at school today, so presumably he was sick, and so why wouldn't he be at home?

Finally I heard footsteps running toward the door. The door opened, and there stood a girl about eight years old.

"Who are you?" she said, in a way that was not entirely friendly.

"I'm Molly. A friend of Clyde's. Is he home?"

The girl thought about this, looking me up and down. Then she turned and yelled for Clyde. She disappeared into the house, leaving me in front of the open door.

I waited for a little bit, but then stepped inside and closed the door.

Soon I saw Clyde coming down the staircase. He was wearing sweatpants and a floppy sweatshirt, and his hair was messy. It wasn't the same polished and proper-looking Clyde I was used to.

"Hi," I said.

"Hey," he said.

"I'm sorry to surprise you like this."

"That's okay."

He was a bit mopey, like he'd just woken up.

"Are you feeling better?" I asked.

"Yeah. It was just my stomach, that's all."

We sat on a long couch in the living room. His little sister ran through the room and shouted, "I'm not listening!"

"Don't mind her," Clyde said.

"You missed an interesting day at school," I said. I filled him in on the boycott. He seemed to brighten up a little bit as he heard about it. I told him about the banner that read ONE TRAY, ONE GOOD DESSERT. I told him how Cassie and I had met with the protesters, how we were trying to figure out what to do.

"Clyde, I've got something to ask you."

He looked up, expectant.

"Molly and Edmund and me have been talking, and we sort of happened upon the conclusion that after the frozen dinner fiasco, you talked to Dr. John. Is that true?"

It took him a moment.

"Yes."

"And did you tell him that you'd engineered the whole plan?"

"Yeah."

"Why'd you do that?"

"Because I could keep you two from getting into trouble. I knew that you guys were running out of chances with Dr. John. But I wasn't."

I nodded. "Okay. And why didn't you tell us?"

"Didn't need to."

"Did you get into any trouble?"

"Dr. John and I talked for about an hour, but that was it."

"Well, on the one hand, we're all grateful to you for taking the heat off of us. On the other hand, it wasn't your responsibility, and so it was highly stupid."

"I know."

"But for the record, I want to say thank you."

"You're welcome," he said.

I went on. "And I want to thank you for being part of our kitchen. For working hard, and being original, and doing your part. It meant a lot to us. To me."

"You're welcome," he said. "Thanks for telling me that."

"Not that I was always nice or approachable or easy to work with."

"But you're changing," he said. "I've seen you changing."

"Thanks," I said. I felt myself blushing. He really was a nice guy. He was warm, he was honest, he was sincere. Why I put up all kinds of barbs and thorns to keep myself distant from even the nicest of people, I don't know. There was no reason we couldn't just be two normal people who were nice to each other.

"So . . . ," I said. "Wow. What a weird semester."

"Yeah," he said.

"So do you still want to go to the Holiday Hop with me?" I asked. I hadn't planned this. It just sort of came out. I'd never asked anyone to a dance.

Clyde cocked his head and blinked, like he wasn't sure I'd said what I'd just said. "The Holiday Hop? Sure."

"Okay. We'll hop together. It'll be grand."

He nodded. "Absolutely."

"So, do you think you'll be at school tomorrow?"

"Yeah."

"Good, because Cassie and Edmund and I are having a meeting after school in the art room, and we want you to be there."

"Okay. What's the meeting for?"

"Our *futures*, that's what."

31

Nacho-Flavored Buffalo-Wing Pizza Bites

assie and I were on the phone that night several times. We were both trolling the Internet, reading things to each other, bouncing ideas off of each other, brainstorming, debating. We read about childhood obesity, early-onset diabetes, childhood arteriosclerosis. We read about oversize portions, the problems with processed foods, pesticides, and the long distances most foods had to travel before they reached the table. We read about schools that no longer even had hot lunch programs but just leased them out to fast-food chains. And some schools had nothing but vending machines. We read about the profound lack of knowledge in teenagers about food, nutrition, and cooking. We'd been living proof of it a couple of months ago.

But we also read about schools whose kitchens were run by actual chefs, chefs who strived to bring fresh food and great-tasting, evolving, seasonal menus to their kitchens. There were some schools that strove to use as much fresh local food as possible in order to support local farmers and reduce their dependency on long-distance transportation of food—thereby reducing their impact on the environment by using less energy. And there were schools that included students in the kitchen, and made food part of the curriculum. There were schools that offered vegetarian options.

Later, when I was trying to get to sleep, my mind was still working, still full of information and ideas and feelings. What did food mean to *me*? How had I become a "candy vegetarian"? And how much had I changed in the past several weeks? Why hadn't I ever thought about food before, and how it impacted not just me and my health, but the health and well-being of my community and my planet? Not to mention my taste buds. I remembered the cake that Cassie and I had made—the first from-scratch cake I'd ever made—and how good it was. I remembered Edmund's simple but delicious tomato soup. I remembered how that local apple Clyde had let me taste had made the supermarket apple taste like dust. I remembered Great-aunt Dorothy's speech in favor of flavor. And I remembered Patty's suggestion that cooking was like magic.

I had all this stuff swirling in my head, but what was I supposed to do with it? What did it all mean to me right here and now?

It meant, for one thing, that I didn't get to sleep until well after midnight.

No one ate the hot lunch Tuesday either, and peeking through the doorway of the lunchroom, Cassie and I could see Mrs. Zetz in the kitchen, pacing, angry. The protest was silent again. Everyone was eating sack lunches calmly. After just a minute or so, we went back upstairs to the art room.

As we ate in the art room, I found myself talking. All the ideas that had filled my head last night seemed to have developed as I slept.

"If you think about it," I said to Cassie, "everyone eats three times a day, and schools—even such a hippie-centric school like Sunshine Day—put no effort into teaching us about what food is good for us, and how to prepare it, and where it comes from, and the impacts different foods have on the planet. Three times a day we eat! But our schools don't teach us about it! We learn calculus—which, I mean, really, I'll never use anytime in my whole life—and we learn about the French Revolution—which is important, sure, but not knowledge I can use three times a day. And we even watch those horrifying videos every year about fire safety and drunk driving. And at most schools you can take a class in driver's ed. But no one teaches us anything about food! Not one word!"

"You're getting a little angry about this," Cassie pointed out.

"You bet I'm getting a little bit mad about this! Because when you start to think about it, it just doesn't even make sense. Why isn't food education as important as math and reading? They're all things you'll use every day of your whole life."

"It's almost like a conspiracy," Cassie said. "Like they don't want us to know. Like *The Da Vinci Code*, for food!"

"Except that stuff was fake, and this is all very real."

First thing after school, Cassie, Edmund, Clyde, and I met in the art room. Pete was there, too, working on *The Bleepity Bleep Bleep Gang* artwork at the back of the room.

"I call this meeting to order," I said.

We briefed Clyde and Edmund about the topics Cassie and I had been discussing over the past day. Then I started ranting again. I seemed to have a lot of rant in me today. It felt good to let it out. It felt good to be on the right side, to believe in something, to have enough knowledge about something to make a strong argument.

"What can bad food give you?" I asked. "Oh, heart disease, early-onset diabetes, obesity, cancer, stroke, families without bonds, environmental ruin. And what can *good* food bring you? Pleasure, health, strong communities, a healthy environment, family bonding. And yet food's ignored in school, like they don't want us to have those things. They want us to be part of the huge capitalistic machine and eat fast food and crappy frozen food and nacho-flavored buffalo-wing pizza bites coated with artificial flavor and artificial color and artificial *taste*."

"Sing it, sister!" said Cassie.

"And meanwhile," I continued, "no one knows how to cook at home, no one knows how to prepare vegetables so that they actually taste good! And our environment's suffering! Cows contribute a gazillion tons of methane to the atmosphere and thus add to global warming. Most of our crops are sprayed with toxic chemicals. Everything is trucked in from hundreds of miles away—adding to global warming, and destroying taste. And we're just supposed to sit here and take it!? And eat this awful supermarket food, this awful processed food, this awful casual-restaurant food, this awful school-lunch food, this awful vending-machine food?! I think not. I don't think that's going to stand! I don't think I like that! I don't like it at all!"

"Hear! Hear!" exclaimed Edmund.

"So what should we do?" Clyde asked.

"Look," I said, "everything is centered around one place: the kitchen. The kitchen connects the land and the food to the plate and the stomach. The kitchen is the place of power. The kitchen chooses what food to prepare, and how to prepare it. So that's where we need to be. That's where I *want* to be."

"I'm one hundred percent with you," said Clyde, smiling.

"Me, too," said Cassie. "But, Edmund, we can't speak for you, because this isn't just a pet project for you, it's your job."

"That's true. But what you're proposing is worth risking my job, and therefore, I'm on board."

We discussed a few details, knowing that much of this would have to be worked out later. We drew up a list of proposals—Cassie serving as our scribe. Then we decided to go look for Dr. John so we could tell him what we were interested in doing. We headed out of the art room.

"Molly?" Pete said from the back of the room, just as I was about to go through the door. "Can I have a word just for a sec?"

"Sure." I told Cassie I'd be down in thirty seconds. Pete probably just had a quick question about the dimensions of the obelisks we were building for act three.

I walked toward the back of the room. "What is it?" I asked.

Pete came and met me. "It's nothing, really, it's just . . ."

Suddenly, he kissed me. It was just a little kiss on the lips, but it came totally by surprise. But as he drew away, my lips felt like they were buzzing.

"Holy crap," I said.

"I'm sorry," he said.

"Wha . . . why . . . ?" I said. I was stunned.

"I couldn't help myself. I've been wanting to kiss you for weeks, but I kept forcing myself not to, and now I just couldn't stop, and I didn't plan it. I think I totally have a crush on you, like pretty bad, 'cause you're a girl who knows herself, and you've got this energy inside you that comes out in your art, and it comes out in the things you fight for, and it's about the most incredible thing I've ever seen in anyone, and that's all I wanted to say, and sorry about being awkward and everything, I'm not good at this kind of thing, and I didn't plan this, and I don't expect you to think I'm all that or anything, and if you don't want to keep working with me, I understand, but I hope maybe you'll go to the Holiday Hop with me, even if it's just as friends."

This was a lot to take. I had a hard time keeping up with him. And I'd never seen him flustered. Plus, I was flustered.

But my lips were still buzzing. There was that . . .

"But," I said, looking at my feet, "I'm already going to the dance with someone."

He nodded vigorously. "Oh. Okay. That's okay."

"No, but, I mean, but—"

"No, it's okay," he said. "Besides, you need to go now, I know. They're waiting." He started walking back to the corner of the room where our project was set up.

"Yeah," I said.

His back was to me now, and he was already sitting down on the floor to start working on the cardboard obelisk pieces again.

I looked at my feet again. Then I left the room.

The hallway was empty. It felt stuffy suddenly. I walked toward the stairs. I went down the stairs. Sunlight was streaming in the windows in the stairwell, and I felt its warmth on my skin. My mind was blank, and I knew that I should fill it with something, but that seemed beyond me at the moment.

In the hallway on the first floor, Cassie was standing outside Dr. John's office.

"You okay?" she said. "You look spaced-out."

I realized I had my fingertips resting on my lips, like I was trying to hold on to the sensation of the kiss. Had I walked the whole way from the art room like this?

"Seriously, Molly," Cassie said, "say something. You're scaring me."

"I think Pete just kissed me," I said.

"Pete? Arty Pete?"

"Uh-huh."

"What do you mean you *think* he kissed you?"

"Because we were up there in the art room, and he was like, 'Can I talk to you for a sec?' and I was all 'Okay' and then he came over and then he didn't stop at the distance where normal people have normal conversations, he just kept coming, and there was a split second where I was thinking what the hell is happening?, our faces are going to collide, and then he was kissing me, and then it was done, and nothing like that has ever happened in the history of Molly, and so even though it happened, there's still part of me that suspects it didn't happen, simply because it's so improbable."

She looked carefully at me. "Wait a second . . . ," she said. "Hold on a second. You *like* him. I can tell."

She was right. A few minutes ago, I hadn't known this. Even a few seconds ago I hadn't known it. But now that she said it, I connected the dots—the kiss, the buzzing, the sense of disbelief. Pete my assistant. Pete the artist. Pete the hard worker. Funny Pete, cute Pete, normal Pete. Why hadn't I seen it before? Why hadn't it even occurred to me? Pete. Yes. Petey. *Yes.*

"I think I do," I said. "But I don't think he thinks I do."

"That's okay," said Cassie. "That we can work on."

Edmund appeared from Dr. John's office. "Hey, we're ready in here," he said.

"We're coming," Cassie said.

Edmund went back into the office.

"I'm not sure I can focus on school lunch right now . . . ," I said.

"Don't worry," Cassie said. "We'll do the talking."

"I'm unhinged," I said.

"I know, dear," she said, and she dragged me into Dr. John's outer office. "Just try not to touch your lips like that and you'll be fine."

We went into Dr. John's office. Dr. John, Clyde, and Edmund were standing in there, and Dr. John was doing something with a string and a round piece of plastic that seemed to be floating in the air. What the—? Oh, a yo-yo. He was showing Clyde a trick. Was I that out of touch that it took me a few seconds to recognize a yo-yo?

"And that," said Dr. John, "is the Banana Shoeshine Boxcar trick."

Clyde clapped.

We arranged some chairs in a circle of communication, and Cassie started talking.

"It has been a long road, and a surprising one," I heard Cassie saying, "and in the past week our beliefs have been challenged and rechallenged. But we have finally come to a decision about the direction we would like to go."

For the next several minutes, I nodded often, and said "Absolutely" a few times, and answered one or two short questions, but mostly the whole event seemed like it was happening very far away from me. I heard Cassie talking about nutrition and diabetes and overweight teenagers. I heard Edmund talking about chef-run school kitchens and locally grown vegetables. I heard Clyde speaking about student involvement in the kitchen and "curricular inclusion."

Suddenly, I started talking. I hadn't planned it. I hadn't scripted it. It just came out of me.

"I have come to understand," I said, "that the kitchen is the locus of great power. The kitchen is the link that connects the earth to the plate, the farm to the stomach, the farmer to the diner, the sun to the tongue."

They were all looking at me like I was half-crazed. But I wasn't done talking.

"The decisions that are made in the kitchen affect the health of our planet, our community, and our bodies. The food we prepare and the way we prepare it speaks to our deep and abiding bonds to the earth and each other, and that is why we are coming to you today to ask you to let us return to the kitchen."

They were still looking at me, slightly stunned.

Then Edmund spoke. "Well said."

"Indeed," said Dr. John.

"And on that note," said Cassie, "we present you with these proposals."

She got out the list we'd just drawn up minutes ago.

"First," she said, "replace Mrs. Zetz with Edmund.

"Second, groom Edmund to become executive chef by sending him to culinary school on the weekends.

"Third, install Molly and I as the student chefs and Clyde as the pastry chef. Let Dina be the kitchen manager.

"Fourth, let our kitchen emphasize fresh, seasonal, healthy, and flavorful cooking.

"Fifth, let us cultivate a network of local farmers as food suppliers. And let us start a Sunshine Day vegetable and herb garden.

"And sixth, let us take on students as apprentices so they can take over when we leave. And let us involve students in a multitude of other ways, perhaps through internships in restaurants, gardening, research projects, and so forth."

Cassie put the list down.

Dr. John sat there, nodding. When I thought he was about done nodding, he nodded some more. He was like a bobblehead doll on the dashboard of a car. Why was it taking so long for him to respond?

Cassie fidgeted in her seat. Then she said, "We understand that these are sweeping changes that we're asking for, with many details that need to be worked out, and with many risks. So we understand if you can't give us an answer now."

Dr. John smiled, still nodding. "Yes, well," he said, "but I *am* going to give you an answer now."

"You are?" said Cassie.

"Yes. Because I *know* the answer. When you are presented with truths, the correct response is to act on them. But do you mind if I lump all your proposals together and give you one answer to all of them?"

"Sure," said Cassie.

"Okay," said Dr. John authoritatively.

"Okay, go ahead," said Cassie.

"Go ahead with what?" said Dr. John.

"Give us the answer."

"I just did."

"You did?" said Clyde.

"Did I miss something?" said Edmund.

"I said 'okay,'" said Dr. John.

"I know you said 'okay,'" said Cassie, "but what about—"

It dawned on me. "Guys," I said, "he's saying 'okay' as in 'yes.'"

Dr. John touched his nose with the tip of his finger. "Bingo," he said. "I'm saying 'okay' to everything! Or to put it more clearly, to your first proposal, I say 'I will.' To your second proposal I say, 'Okeydoke.' To your third proposal, I say 'Absolutely.' To your fourth proposal, I say, 'Heck, yeah!' For your fifth proposal, I'm with you all the way. And I don't actually know how many proposals you gave me, but I'm saying yes to all of them. Every single one."

Clyde jumped out of his seat and gave a whoop.

Cassie clapped.

"All of this, though," Dr. John said, "is contingent upon two things. First, your ability to carry through with what you have proposed. That is no small task, but one that I believe you are capable of. The second condition is that the only way this can happen is if Mrs. Zetz agrees to quit."

"Why?" asked Cassie.

"Because I don't have the authority to fire her without cause. She'll have to make the decision to leave on her own. But considering all the pressure on her from the boycott, plus being shorthanded in the kitchen, I suspect she'll do it."

32

The Thick Scent
of Hot Sauerkraut

She won't do it," said Dr. John. It was the next day, Wednesday, and Cassie and I were finishing our lonely lunch in the art room. Dr. John had come in and sat on the table. "Mrs. Zetz won't give up her job."

"But that's crazy," I said. "No one's eating her food. It's just making her angry."

"And stubborn," said Dr. John. "I talked to her last night, and I talked to her twice this morning in the kitchen, and she's not interested in leaving."

"But you agree with our ideas about a new direction for the kitchen," Cassie said. "So why don't you just give her notice that we're taking over the lunch program in January, and that therefore her position is ending."

He shook his head. "I can't do that. She's done nothing wrong."

"Dagnabbit," said Cassie.

"Look," Dr. John said, "I'll talk to her again next week. Maybe the boycott will wear her down. Maybe she'll reconsider."

When he left, I looked at Cassie. "This is so not right," I said.

"It makes sense, though," she said, "that he can't just fire her for no reason."

"No, I know. But . . ."

"But what?"

We had managed to drive Mrs. Zetz into retirement once before, so surely we could do it again. I was tired of being the kind of Molly who just let things happen to her, who took what came her way, who wallowed in her own inaction, who stewed in her own juices. That Molly needed to go.

It was like the thing with Pete. Like how there was this wall now between what I wanted to say and do and what I could actually say and do. It was stupid. Profoundly stupid. What was stopping me? Fear? I suppose. Not wanting to stick out? Yeah. But what had that kind of inaction gotten me in the past couple of years?

"Dr. John can't do anything," I said. "But we can."

"How?"

"First, we have to make sure we believe in what we're doing. So do you?"

"Yes," she said.

"Me, too. That's it. That's all that matters. Now come on." I took her hand, and we left the art room and walked down toward the lunchroom.

"Do you have a plan?" Cassie asked.

"Sort of," I said. "It isn't right for us to have come this far only to be denied. Besides, if Mrs. Zetz wants a stubbornness contest, she picked the wrong opponents."

We stopped outside the closed lunchroom doors.

"Now, do you trust me? Because I need you to trust me."

"I do."

"Allrighty," I said. "Let's go."

We went into the lunchroom. It was packed. Everyone was there, silently eating their lunches from home—their brown bags, their old Power Rangers lunch boxes from grade school, their Tupperware.

We marched toward the corner where the Noontime Expression microphone was set up.

"They're here!" came a yell from across the room. It was Seth Lawson.

Some cheers went up.

We reached the microphone. I saw Brad Berrington nearby.

"Brad!" I called. "Turn on this thing."

He jumped up and turned on the amp and microphone.

"That's right," I said, "Molly and Cassie are here. We're in the lunchroom again!"

"Yeah!" yelled Seth, his fist thrust into the air.

"And we have a question for you, the people. Do you want us in the kitchen?"

Everyone was watching now. They answered almost with one voice—"Yeah!"

"Do you want better food, fresher food, and a more sensitive kitchen leadership that seeks ways to involve students in all manner of ways that contribute to the sense of community and self-direction?"

Again they answered: "Yeah!"

I whispered to Cassie, "That sounded better in my head."

"No, it was good," she said. Then she nudged me. Everyone was looking at me, waiting for me to say something else.

I saw Dr. John standing across the room. He was making no move to stop us.

"And do you want one tray, one *good* dessert?" I asked the crowd.

This set them off, yelling, cheering, whistling. They were with us. The cheering dragged on this time. They liked the desserts. Clyde was our ace in the hole.

So I scanned the lunchroom. Where was Clyde? I saw him, sitting at a table with some drama production staff dweebs. I pointed to him.

"Do you want *him* to make your desserts? Stand up, Clyde!"

He stood up, and the crowd cheered wildly. Clyde waved.

I was drawing in my breath, about to ask the crowd another question—what, I didn't yet know—when a door slammed extremely loudly on the opposite wall.

Everyone turned.

It was Mrs. Zetz. She was standing outside the kitchen door. Her hands were on her hips. She was glaring at Cassie and me.

"Watch out!" I said into the microphone. "The dictator stirs!"

She raised her finger and pointed at us.

"No! Dis is not allowed! Dese *girrells* not allowed in lunchroom!"

"Boo! Hiss!" yelled Seth.

But the rest of the crowd was silent.

"Go!" Mrs. Zetz yelled. "Go from my lunchroom!"

"What kind of school is it," I said calmly in the microphone, "where two well-behaved students aren't allowed in the lunchroom?"

"Dis school!" yelled Mrs. Zetz.

Dr. John was moving. He was moving slowly toward Mrs. Zetz.

"What kind of lunch program doesn't allow all of the students to eat?" I asked.

"We want Molly!" yelled someone. I looked into the crowd. It had been Pete. My Pete!

"And Cassie!" yelled someone else.

"And Clyde!" yelled a few people.

"*Molly and Cassie and Clyde*!" yelled Seth. "*Molly and Cassie and Clyde!*" He yelled it like a protest chant. Soon the crowd took up the chant, banging their palms on the tables along with it.

"*Molly and Cassie and Clyde! Molly and Cassie and Clyde! Molly and Cassie and Clyde!*"

Mrs. Zetz was talking to Dr. John. Her face was red. She was waving her arms around, pointing at us occasionally.

"*Molly and Cassie and Clyde! Molly and Cassie and Clyde! Molly and Cassie and Clyde!*"

Suddenly, Clyde came out of the crowd and joined us.

"Hi," he said.

"Hey, buddy," I said.

"This is fun," he said.

Then, from across the lunchroom, Dr. John was beckoning to us.

"Here we go," I said.

We went into the kitchen: me, Cassie, Clyde, Dr. John, and Mrs. Zetz. Inside, were Dina and Edmund. The kitchen reeked with the thick scent of hot sauerkraut.

"Dis not what we agreed to," Mrs. Zetz said to Dr. John. "You said I have job anytime I want. You said okay to no *girrells* in lunchroom or in kitchen. You said so."

"I did," Dr. John said calmly.

The sound of the crowd chanting our names was still thunderously loud, and it almost seemed like it was getting louder. *"Molly and Cassie and Clyde!"*

"But here they are, in lunchroom, in kitchen," Mrs. Zetz continued. "Get children in frenzy, with yelling and not eating food and we throwing away food every day! Piles of food! Dis good food! Dis food wasted!"

"I know," said Dr. John.

"Molly and Cassie and Clyde!"

"But dis break promise!" she yelled.

"Molly and Cassie and Clyde!"

Dr. John looked at us. Then he looked at Mrs. Zetz.

"Marta, you have served our school well for many years, and for that we honor you. We also honor your employment contract, and would never try to alter it. But I also have to honor my commitment to serve all of the students, including Molly and Cassie, and therefore, though I am not altering the terms of your employment with us, I must, in good conscience, retract the restrictions on these two girls. This is their school as much as it is mine or yours, and they have every right to use the lunchroom and to eat your food. And from this moment on, I will allow them to do so."

"Molly and Cassie and Clyde!"

Mrs. Zetz wobbled a little bit. "You do dat," she said, "then I work no more."

"That's your decision to make."

"Molly and Cassie and Clyde!"

"Then I retire," she said. "For good."

She sighed. She untied her apron.

33

I Dropped My Nuts

On December first—just two days after Mrs. Zetz had quit for good—Cassie and Patty and I went to Minerva's winter festival. We grabbed all the candy we could at the parade, got our pictures taken with Santa, harassed some jugglers on stilts, and then walked down to the river and went to the square dance. After the dance, we sat in the big empty tent and ate hot sugared almonds, waiting for the fireworks.

"All right, gals," said Patty, "I've got a bit of news."

"Such as?" I asked.

"Seeing as Minerva-Hillsdale High School is a loathsome institution of secondary education," she said, "peopled by un-couth, unimaginative cretins, and seeing as I have not been served well by the so-called college track course work there, and seeing as my best friend, one Molly Ollinger, attends a certain private high school that sits on a hillside not all that far from here, and that I have met with the administration of this school and found that I qualify for a scholarship and that my parents are agreeable to helping me pay for the rest, I will, as of January, enroll in Sunshine Day High School."

I dropped my nuts.

"What!?" I said. I lunged at her. We were sitting cross-legged on the dance floor, and I lunged at her and knocked her over.

"Ow!" screamed Patty. "That's my hair!"

After I calmed down, we decided that I should go buy more nuts, seeing as I had spilled mine and Patty's when I tackled her. I walked out of the tent, and across the parking lot. There was a short line at the nut cart, and I put up the hood of my jacket and waited. There was a toddler in front of me in line—holding the hand of someone in a huge puffy black parka. The toddler looked around at me. He looked down at my boots. I was wearing red snow boots.

"Red. Toes," the toddler said. His cheeks were pink.

"That's right," I said. "You are correct, tiny person."

"Red. Toes," he repeated.

Then the parka-blob whose hand the toddler was holding turned around. It was Pete. Pete my assistant. Arty Pete. Pete of the kiss.

"Oh," Pete said.

"Pete," I said. "I didn't recognize you in your coat."

"It's something of a blimp," he said. He smiled. Was he blushing?

"Red. Toes."

"This is my little brother. He likes your boots, I think."

I wasn't sure how to feel. Part of me was nervous, scared, and unhappy I'd run into Pete accidentally like this. But another part of me was just fine. That was the Molly that had stormed into the lunchroom two days ago and instigated a kitchen takeover. In fact, I realized that the nervous, scared part of me was mostly controlled, at the moment, by the storm-the-lunchroom part of me.

So we bought nuts together, and I invited Pete to come hang out with Patty and Cassie and me, and he said sure, and took his brother back to his parents, then joined us in the tent.

Later, Pete and I walked up the hill into Minerva together.

"So," I said, "do you think you could come to the Holiday Hop even though I've already got a date? Because I'd really like to see you there, and in the spirit of total disclosure, I should tell you that my date is Clyde Brewell, and that it's a friend-date kind of thing."

"I think I can show up at the dance," Pete said. "That might work just fine."

"Good. Let's shake on it." I don't know why I said this. But he stuck out his mittened hand, and I stuck out my mittened hand, and we shook mittens.

Pete and I parted on Spring Street. I walked home in the dark, looking through windows to see the Christmas trees in houses. I felt good. I felt sure about being Molly. I felt happy that Patty was my friend again, that Patty was coming to Sunshine Day. The stars were shining overhead, and I stopped in the middle of the street and looked up at them.

At home, Les called to tell us that he'd been offered a job in St. Paul after he graduated in May, and that therefore next year he'd practically be in the neighborhood.

34

Fruit Cup

There was a moment, early during my date with Clyde, when I realized I had to force myself not to think the word *dork* or I would be distracted and annoyed all night long. True, Clyde was basically a dork. He showed up at my house—having walked from his house—wearing huge snow boots and a strange pea green suit, and he gave me a large wrist corsage, which I had not expected. He kneeled and put it on me.

"Gee, thanks," I said.

"You are most welcome, milady," he said.

"Listen, no more kneeling, and can the 'milady' crap right here and now or we are not going to set foot outside this house."

It didn't ruffle him. He laughed silently. "Very well, Ms. Ollinger."

"Molly! Call me Molly!"

We then got in the Prius, and I drove to Patty's house and picked her up, then to Pete's house and picked him up, then to the school. We all went into the school and down into the cafeteria, which was decorated—for some odd reason—like a schoolhouse. Even though this was a schoolhouse.

I danced with Clyde. The student jazz band was playing what seemed to be a funk version of "Pop Goes the Weasel," and Clyde proved that even if he wasn't the best dancer, or even a good dancer, he was a fun dancer.

Of course, in heels I was a fair bit taller than him.

Cassie arrived after a while, with her date, Brad Berrington. Brad was looking dapper in a white tux. He'd been trying to grow in his sideburns, though, and the effect was unfortunate. Cassie and Patty and I sat at a table and ate peanut butter and jelly *petit fours.*

"Am I crazy to come with Brad Berrington?" Cassie asked.

"Yes."

"Well, he's nice. And he hasn't sung to me yet. And exactly when did you lose your whole brain," Cassie said, "and agree to come to the Holiday Hop with Clyde? Especially when you had a chance to go with Pete."

"It's all very vague, and yet, here I am, and there's Clyde, standing over there in his pea green suit, and there's Pete, looking nice, eating fruit cup over there."

"He looks like he's enjoying that fruit cup," said Cassie.

"I think that's his third fruit cup," I observed.

"The boy likes fruit!" said Patty. "I love it!"

But the boy, the Pete of my dreams, didn't ask me to dance the whole night. I danced with Clyde, I danced with Seth, I even slow danced with Portia. She had on a drop-dead-gorgeous vintage dress with ruffled cuffs and lots of beadwork. I looked down as we danced, and she was, of course, barefoot.

"I gotta say," she said as we danced, "that you and Cassie are my new role models, with what you pulled off in the kitchen."

We were *her* role models? She was a senior, after all, and some kind of genius.

"Thanks," I said. "That means a lot to me, seeing as you're one of my role models."

"Can role models be each other's role models?" she said. "Interesting question."

"Maybe you could write a play about that."

We bumped into another couple. It was Devin Harper dancing with Vanessa Tithanwit.

"That boy," Portia said, "if he wasn't such a great actor, he honestly would have no redeeming qualities."

"I hear *that*," I said. "But maybe he'll get better with age."

"Let's hope so."

Near the end of the dance, I realized I had three new messages on my cell. They were all from Dad, who said that it was snowing pretty heavily and that I was totally forbidden to drive home. I could either call him and he'd pick us up with the all-wheel-drive car, or we'd have to hoof it.

Patty, Clyde, Pete, and I voted. We all four voted for hoofing it.

Walking up Spring Street, a good twenty or thirty feet in front of Clyde and Pete, I leaned into Patty. "This night has been slightly underwhelming," I said. "I mean, why didn't Pete even talk to me?"

"That's just the way these things go," Patty said. She looked back over her shoulder at Pete and Clyde. "Besides, I think he's just a little shy now, after being so forward with the kiss. After all, why do you think he volunteered to walk with us? His house is right across from the school."

"Maybe he just wants to talk to Clyde about dumb Japanese comic books."

"True, manga does brew a curious and disturbing kind of madness in the brains of teenage boys. But I suspect he's tagging along because he wants to be near you."

We passed Clyde's house first, saying good night. Then we walked to Patty's house. After that, it was just Pete and me. He walked me all the way home, and he talked most of the time about how many different musical instruments he had tried to learn to play.

"Well, I guess my first idea about what the coolest instrument in the world was, was the trombone. Because when I was like five, I thought it was the best because it was one of the shiniest, one of the loudest, one of the funniest, and also definitely the longest instrument. I thought the length was especially important. So I got trombone lessons when I was seven, even though it was difficult for me to hold it because I was too little. I even had a kid-size trombone, but no, too big. I tried though. And I took lessons in the little room over the music store, you know, on the square downtown, and I learned a total of three songs—well, four if you count an improvised version of 'Dixie' that I favored above any of the other things I could play. But my trombone phase ended when I went to a parade that summer and saw the bass drum."

And on he went. He went into great detail, and I realized that he was nervous. He was nervous around me. When had I ever made a boy nervous by my mere presence? I didn't know. But his nervousness made me somehow less nervous, like I was in control.

There was only an inch or two of snow on the ground. There was no wind, and the snowflakes were floating straight down, almost in slow motion.

"Gosh, I love this kind of snow!" said Pete enthusiastically as we walked through the park just a block away from my house.

"You mean the floaty, quiet kind?" I asked.

"No, the surprise kind, the kind you don't expect, it's just suddenly snowing and you're like, 'Cool! Snow! Awesome!' That kind."

I understood him. I felt the same way.

"I'm just happy to be here," said Pete as they got near my house.

"Here as in walking down this street right now?"

"Yes. With you."

He looked at me.

"I can't stand this anymore," I said. I stopped. I stopped right there.

"Stand what?" he asked.

"Waiting!"

"Waiting for wha—"

But he didn't finish, because I kissed him.

Note

If you're interested in learning more about improving school lunches, check out websites like www. healthyschoollunches.org and www.fns.usda.gov/cnd/ lunch/. Or read the book Lunch Lessons: Changing the Way We Feed Our Children, *by Ann Cooper and Lisa Holmes (2006).*

A great book about why fast food is a poor choice for our health is Fast Food Nation, *by Eric Schlosser (2001).*

If you're interested in learning more about cooking, ask your favorite cooks to help you. You can also teach yourself with books and magazines. Everyday Food *is a widely available magazine that presents simple, straightforward food. As for cookbooks, there are thousands to choose from, so ask your librarian or parents for suggestions.*